DEADLY ECHOES

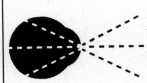

This Large Print Book carries the
Seal of Approval of N.A.V.H.

DEADLY ECHOES

NANCY MEHL

THORNDIKE PRESS

A part of Gale, Cengage Learning

GALE
CENGAGE Learning·

Farmington Hills, Mich • San Francisco • New York • Waterville, Maine
Meriden, Conn • Mason, Ohio • Chicago

GALE
CENGAGE Learning·

LIBRARY OF CONGRESS CATALOGING-IN-PUBLICATION DATA

Mehl, Nancy.
    Deadly echoes / by Nancy Mehl. — Large print edition.
        pages cm. — (Finding sanctuary ; book 2) (Thorndike Press large print Christian mystery)
    ISBN 978-1-4104-7647-0 (hardcover) — ISBN 1-4104-7647-2 (hardcover)
    1. Missing persons—Fiction. 2. Large type books. I. Title.
    PS3613.E4254D43 2015b
    813'.6—dc23   2014048773

Published in 2015 by arrangement with Bethany House Publishers, a division of Baker Publishing Group

Printed in Mexico
1 2 3 4 5 6 7 19 18 17 16 15

To my friend and sister, Jolene,
who taught me that true friends are
friends forever

CHAPTER ONE

The old familiar fear returned with a vengeance, along with the musty smell of neglect and the sweet scent of sweat.

I was back in that small dusty place under the stairs. The one place in the house that escaped Mom's rigorous weekly cleaning. It was used to store things that were only needed on special occasions, like our old luggage and the cane Dad had used when he sprained his ankle.

But this night, the often-ignored storage area was the most important place in the entire world. Hannah's arms tightened around me, and she whispered in my ear that I must be quiet. That I couldn't say a word, couldn't sneeze, even though the dust tickled my nose. The terrible noises from outside had stopped, and now there was nothing except an awful silence. The only sound left was our rapid breathing. Hannah breathed in; I breathed out. Without meaning to, I began to inhale and exhale in harmony with my sister. In and out. In and out. Tears slipped down my face unbidden, but I ignored them and concentrated on our labored breaths. It was the one thing I could control.

Footsteps from the other side of the door stopped only inches from where we sat. Suddenly our breathing seemed too loud. Could he hear us? Something rose inside my throat. Fear turned into an urge to scream that would surely reveal us to the evil that lurked outside our secret spot. Hannah seemed to sense I was losing restraint, and she covered my mouth with her hand.

"Be still," she whispered. "Whatever you do, Sarah, be still."

I tried desperately to hold my breath, not knowing if I could do as she asked. Terror seemed to have wrapped my sister and me in a cocoon of unreality. Surely this could not be happening. Mom and Dad were okay. We would scurry out from beneath the stairs, and they'd laugh at us. Tell us how silly we were to be afraid. Then Mom would make tacos and we'd watch TV. Life would go on as it always had.

All of a sudden, the handle on the door of our safe haven rattled. Hannah gasped and

8

took her hand off my mouth. The small door swung open and light washed over us, blinding me. I screamed and buried my head on Hannah's shoulder.

Then there was blood. So much blood. Flowers began to rain down from the sky, white orchids mixed with crimson. I screamed again and again until I woke myself up. My body trembled uncontrollably from the fear that gripped me, my sheets soaked with sweat. Pushing myself into a sitting position, I could feel my heart pound. Why had the nightmare returned? I'd been free from it for almost two years.

I got out of bed and made my way into the bathroom. The person who looked back at me from the mirror wasn't Sarah Miller, the twenty-four-year-old schoolteacher. She was Sarah Miller, the six-year-old child who hid in a closet the night her parents were murdered.

I splashed cold water on my face and dried it with a towel. Then I went into my small kitchen and checked the time. A little after four in the morning. Although I hadn't experienced this particular dream for a long time, I remembered the routine that accompanied it. There would be no sleeping the rest of the night. I turned on the coffee maker. It would take several minutes to brew, so I opened the door that separated my apartment from the school and stepped into the large classroom. I loved walking through the school when it was empty, before the day began. Desks sat in the dark, waiting for the students who would soon fill them. Since I was still wearing my pajamas, I kept the light off. I walked toward the front window and gazed outside at a bleak winter's day. The streets of Sanctuary were deserted, but an hour from now things would change. Randi Lindquist would arrive to open her restaurant, The Oil Lamp, while across the street, Mary Gessner and her daughter, Rosey, would get ready to greet customers at The Whistle Stop Café, the only other place to eat in town. Of course, Randi and Mary weren't in competition. This was Sanctuary, Missouri. The two restaurant owners were close friends and worked together to serve good quality food to the small town. People in Sanctuary helped one another out whenever it was needed.

A couple of hours later, after the restaurants were already greeting their customers, Rachel Stoltz and her mother would turn on the lights in the quilt shop, while Abner Ingalls got ready to start business at the hardware store. Not long after that, Martha

Kirsch would open the library next door, and Evan Bakker would arrive at the post office on the other side of the school. The three of us shared the large brick building that had once housed a saddle and tack store back when Sanctuary was called New Zion, a town founded in the 1800s by a group of Mennonites who sailed to America from Germany. As the Mennonite population dwindled and others moved here, the name of the town was changed to Sanctuary.

Around eight o'clock, the farmers would begin to ride into town. Some of them in trucks. Some of them in buggies. Sanctuary combined modern culture and the simplicity of its Conservative Mennonite citizens with complete success. This was a special place, and everyone who lived here protected the spirit of Sanctuary with quiet zeal. The town's name was more than a label. It was a way of life for its residents, some of whom had come here because they were looking for a safe refuge from the past. Others because they were just looking for a simpler life.

I turned around and went back to my apartment. Once used as storage space, it had been converted to three rooms about a year ago. The efficiency kitchen took up a corner of the living area. A table in the kitchen held my laptop and printer. I used it as a desk to grade papers and create work sheets and tests. I had a desk in the school-room, but I didn't like working there alone at night. The front of the room had large storefront windows, and I felt too exposed. I also used the table as a place to eat the meals I prepared when I didn't go to my friend Janet's house to eat. A tiny bedroom held my bed and a dresser. Next to that was a bathroom with a toilet and a tub. I had everything I needed, and I found my little home cozy and peaceful.

I ate a quick breakfast and then got dressed, trading my pajamas for a simple dress that was appropriate for a teacher in a conservative Christian school. After a time of prayer and Bible reading, I closed up my apartment and spent the next couple of hours at my school desk grading papers and preparing for another day of teaching bright, inquisitive minds. I loved teaching, and I loved my students. My life was quiet and safe. Exactly what I wanted.

Around seven-thirty, the front door swung open and my very first pupil arrived.

"Good morning, Jeremiah," I said loudly.

"Good morning, Miss Miller." The fourteen-year-old son of Conservative Mennonite parents, Jeremiah Ostrander always came early to help me prepare for the day. After taking off his coat and hanging it up on one of the hooks near the door, he went straight to the large blackboard at the front of the room and began erasing the lesson from yesterday. After that, he would clean the erasers, make sure the chalk was ready, and then sweep the floor. Jeremiah was a quiet boy, but he was fully committed to school. An illness as a baby had caused a profound loss of hearing, so I kept his desk in the front of the room and worked with him after school sometimes to make sure he had everything he needed to complete his lessons. Several months ago I'd started teaching him a little sign language. One sign in particular was extremely useful. When he had trouble hearing me, or when I accidentally turned away from him as I talked, he would make the sign for *help* — his right hand in a fist with his thumb up. Done correctly, the left hand should support the right hand and lift it up slightly, although Jeremiah didn't usually add the second component. Since it embarrassed him to ask for assistance, he would make the sign so only I could see it. It was my signal to go back over what I'd just said without stopping the lesson because he'd missed something.

His lessons were progressing very well. Sign language had made it much easier for him to learn and to feel a part of class instead of standing on the sidelines. I'd approached his parents, offering to show them how to better communicate with their son, but Jeremiah's father, William, wouldn't have anything to do with it. He was a harsh man who acted as if there were nothing wrong with his son. I could tell his mother, Trina, wanted to learn, but she was under her husband's thumb and went along with every edict he proclaimed.

William had made it clear that he expected Jeremiah to stay in Sanctuary and take over the family farm someday, but I suspected his son had other dreams. I doubted that farming would satisfy his obvious passion for learning. It would be interesting to watch him mature and make choices about his life. I couldn't tell Jeremiah what to do, but I could encourage him to follow his heart. I hoped he would.

The front door opened again, and I looked up from my desk, expecting another student. Instead, it was Janet Dowell, the woman who had become like a mother to me.

"What are you doing here?" I asked.

She smiled, her blue eyes twinkling. "I

14

made a large pot of chicken and noodles over the weekend. I'm just dropping some off for your dinner this week."

Janet was a great cook. Even though she'd tried to teach me, I didn't have her knack in the kitchen. I was happy she kept me supplied with plenty of good food.

"Sounds wonderful," I said gratefully. "Can you put it in the refrigerator for me?"

"Sure." She went into my apartment, coming back moments later. "I'm on my way to the clinic, but I'll be home by three. Why don't you come over tonight? I'll make meat loaf."

"I'd love to. I'll be there around four-thirty."

She nodded and waved good-bye. As she walked out, my students began to file in one by one. After a few minutes of greeting one another, we settled down to work. Although the nightmare that had awakened me left me feeling unsettled, as the day progressed, the children helped me push the dark monster back into a place where it lurked quietly, its terrifying power diminished by the joy of challenging young minds.

About twenty minutes before the lunch break, I was surprised to see Janet return, accompanied by Paul Gleason, a Madison County deputy sheriff who had become a friend to Sanctuary residents during a kidnapping case several months earlier. I knew him to speak with, but we weren't close friends. I actually had a small crush on him, but he was so handsome and self-assured, I was certain I wasn't the kind of woman he'd ever notice. As I swung my attention to Janet, the look on her face stopped me in the middle of my sentence. She walked up to me and whispered in my ear.

"Let the children go home, Sarah. We need to talk to you."

The fear that had gripped me in the early morning hours returned in a rush that took my breath away. I tried to speak to my students, but nothing came out of my mouth. Finally Janet addressed them.

"Children, school is over early today. I need you to go home. If any of you need a ride, or if someone needs to call your parents, I want you to go next door to the post office. Mr. Bakker will help you contact your folks. If you can't reach them, he will take you home. Please have your parents check with me about school tomorrow."

The children closed their books and filed out quietly. Jeremiah stood next to his chair, staring at me, his large brown eyes framed by his rather long blond hair. At first I thought he was going to say something, but finally he turned and left, following the others out.

"What . . . what . . . ?" was all I could get out. I felt six again, trying to grasp the idea that I'd never see my parents again. My eyes fastened on Janet's. She asked Paul to lock the front door. As he walked to the front of the room, Janet knelt down next to my chair and took my hands in hers.

"I would do anything to save you this pain," she said softly, her eyes full of tears. "But I can't. I'm here for you, Sarah. We *will* get through this. You've got to trust me. Okay?"

I nodded. Tears dripped down my cheeks and landed on my dress. Even before she said it, I knew what was coming. It was the only thing that could plunge me back into darkness. The dream had come to me for a reason.

"It's Hannah," I whispered, my voice shaking like an old woman's. "What happened?"

"I don't know exactly," Janet said. "We don't have many details yet." She pronounced each word carefully, as if it pained her to speak them. "I got a call this morning from Hannah's next-door neighbor. Cicely and some other girls were at a sleep-

17

over at her house. When Cicely got home this morning, she found her mother . . ." Janet took a deep, shaky breath. "She found Hannah . . ." She gulped and shook her head.

"She's dead."

Janet nodded, tears cascading down her face. "Yes, honey. She's gone. I'm so sorry."

"What happened? Was it her heart? She had some problems. . . ."

"No, Sarah." Paul had come back and stood behind Janet. "It wasn't a medical condition." He looked at Janet for help, but she just shook her head, overcome with emotion.

He took a deep breath and the words tumbled out in a rush. "She was murdered, Sarah. Someone broke in and stabbed her to death."

"Oh no. Not . . . not again." As my mind tried to process the information Janet and Paul had given me, a strange unearthly calm filled my body. Before I could sit down, I felt myself drift away into the shadows that surrounded me. The last thing I remembered was Janet's arms reaching out to catch me.

CHAPTER TWO

I awoke to someone wiping my face with a damp cloth. Janet stared down at me, a worried look on her face. I sat up, even though she encouraged me to stay still. It took me a few seconds to figure out where I was. As I gazed at the empty schoolroom, I remembered. For just a moment I wondered if I'd had another awful nightmare. Maybe this was nothing more than a bad dream. Then reality hit me, cruelly tearing hope away. Hannah was gone. Janet put her arms around me and let me cry. I had no idea how long we sat like that, but slowly my sobs began to decrease in intensity. Little by little my mind cleared until I felt I could think again. When I let go of Janet, I realized Paul was still in the room. The look of compassion on his face chased away my initial embarrassment at breaking down in front of him.

"Let's get you home," Janet said gently.

I nodded and tried to get to my feet, but my body felt limp — almost devoid of strength.

"Here," Paul said, reaching down and helping me up. "Just lean on me."

The three of us left the school, and Paul held on to me while I got into his car. Though Janet's house was only two blocks away, I was too weak to walk. When we reached our destination, Paul's strong arms supported me while we went up the steps and into Janet's house. As I leaned in to him, I could smell his shaving lotion. Masculine but gentle. After helping me up the stairs and into the old room where I'd lived before moving to my apartment at the school, he quietly left the room. Janet got me settled, making me lie down on the bed. Then she went downstairs to get me a glass of water.

"Is Paul still here?" I asked when she came back.

She nodded. "He's downstairs. I told him he could leave, but he didn't want to go until he was certain you were okay."

"That's very kind." A thought suddenly struck me. I felt ashamed that it only occurred to me now. "Cicely. Where is Cicely?"

"That's something we need to talk about, Sarah. You're her closest relative."

I sat up straighter in the bed. "I'm her only relative. Her father isn't part of her life. I've got to get her. She'll have to come here, Janet."

She nodded. "We probably need to contact the police department in Kansas City and let them know that."

"You're right." I tried to get up but immediately felt dizzy and fell back.

"Let me do some checking," Janet said. "I'll find out who you need to talk to."

"And ask where she is now. She's only ten years old. I don't want her to be afraid. I need to speak to her. Let her know I'm coming."

"I'll take care of it, honey." She frowned. "I know Hannah's foster father died several years ago, but didn't you say her foster mother was still alive?"

"She's in a nursing home. In the last stages of Alzheimer's." I shook my head. "She doesn't even remember Hannah. There's no reason to call her."

I pushed the quilt off and swung my legs over the side of the bed. Although I felt another wave of dizziness, it dissipated quickly. My shoes sat on the floor so I slipped my feet into them. "I'd like to talk to Paul."

Janet took my hand. "Are you sure?

21

Shouldn't you lie down a bit longer?"

I grabbed her hand. "I've got to keep myself together for Cicely. I'm so thankful Hannah and I found each other again after all these years. If we hadn't, I probably wouldn't know about her death, and Cicely would be all alone."

Janet hugged me. "She is blessed to have you for an aunt. There isn't anyone else in the world who could take care of her the way you will." She stroked my hair. "I think it would be best if you moved back to my house, Sarah. Right away. Your apartment is too small for two people, and I have an extra room for Cicely. Besides, I can help. Be a support for both of you."

I wiped away tears of gratitude. "I don't know what I would do without you. You're the best friend I've ever had, and I know Cicely will love you too."

"We'll all be okay," she said quietly. "God will walk us through this."

I finally got to my feet. "He'll have to. I know I can't do this under my own power."

Janet slid her arm through mine. "I'll make you something to eat while you talk to Paul."

"I'm not hungry."

"I understand, honey, but you need to keep your strength up. Just trust me. Okay?"

I gave her a small smile. "Whatever you say."

She returned my smile, though her eyes held the pain of the past few hours. "Now, that's what I like to hear."

She helped me downstairs. I found Paul sitting on the couch in the living room. When I came into the room, he stood up.

"How are you feeling?" he asked, his eyes wide with concern.

"Better, thank you. I'm sorry I fainted."

He shook his head. "Please don't apologize. I'm so sorry for your loss."

"Thank you." I sank down into the chair next to the couch.

"If you'll excuse me," Janet said, "I want to make Sarah some lunch. Will you stay and eat with us, Paul?"

"I'd like to, but I've got to get back to the station. They're probably wondering where I am. After you called me, I told them I would help you deliver the news about Sarah's sister and then report right back."

"I called Paul after I talked to Hannah's neighbor," Janet explained. "I wanted to make sure what she told me was true. Paul contacted the police in Kansas City to confirm the details."

"Thank you, Paul," I said. "I appreciate all your help."

"I want to thank you too," Janet said. "Not only for your assistance with the police, but for helping me get Sarah home." She patted my shoulder and left the room.

"I'm so embarrassed," I said to Paul. "I can remember fainting only one other time in my entire life."

"You were told some incredibly shocking news. Fainting is a natural reaction."

"You're very kind."

He nodded and stared down at the floor for a moment. When he looked up again, his expression was somber. "When you got the news about your sister, you said, 'Not again.' I hope you won't think I'm sticking my nose in where it doesn't belong, but I couldn't help but wonder what you meant."

I cleared my throat. Sharing my past was something I didn't often do. Only a few people in Sanctuary knew my history. With Hannah's death, the past had suddenly come roaring back.

"When I was six and my sister was twelve, we lived in Raytown, Missouri, a suburb of Kansas City. One night my parents were murdered. Hannah and I were both in the house when it happened. Hannah hid us in a small storage area under the stairs. If she hadn't, we probably would have been killed as well. Some things were taken from our house, so the police ruled the killings the result of a burglary gone wrong."

Paul looked stunned. "That's terrible. I'm so sorry."

"Paul, did I hear Janet right? Did Cicely find Hannah?"

He nodded.

I covered my face with my hands, trying to compose myself. When I finally brought them down, I took a deep, shaky breath. "When my parents were murdered, our next-door neighbor called the police. I guess he saw the killers leave and thought it looked suspicious. Unfortunately, he couldn't identify them. It was night. Too dark to see anything clearly. Hannah and I stayed in that closet until the police came, but as they removed us from our home, we saw our parents' bodies."

"I can't imagine how traumatic that was."

I nodded. "Hannah saw more than I did. I was so young all I can remember is blood . . . and white orchids. I guess my mother had them in a vase. In the struggle they fell on the floor next to her."

"I'm so sorry, Sarah." He paused for a moment. "I understand you and Hannah only recently reconnected. Did you get separated after you lost your parents?"

I nodded. "It's a rather complicated story."

"I'd like to hear it sometime. If you want to tell me, that is."

I stared at him in surprise. "I'm not sure you'd find it very interesting." I was startled to see him blush.

"Actually, I'm very interested in you." He coughed lightly. "In your story, I mean."

Not knowing what to say, all I could come up with was "Thanks." I shook my head. "I . . . I'm sorry. It's hard for me to think right now."

"I understand. I wish I could do something more to help you."

"You've done enough," I said, trying to smile at him. "I'm very grateful you were here."

He stood up slowly. I sensed his concern for me, and I fought back the tears that threatened to overtake me again. He'd seen me cry enough for one day.

Paul's eyes were locked on mine as he ran his hand through his thick, dark hair. "Someone from Kansas City will contact you soon. Again, please feel free to call me if I can do anything. Anything at all."

"If you learn any details about the investigation, will you share them with me?"

He put his hat on his head. "Certainly. But I'm not really involved with Kansas City. I do have a friend who works for the department there. If you want, I can call him and ask him to keep me updated. I really doubt he'll be able to tell me anything different from what the police will tell you."

"I'd really appreciate it, Paul. Whoever killed our parents was never caught. I really don't want to see that happen again."

"Give the police a chance, Sarah. Don't give up on them before the process even begins. Just because law enforcement let you down once doesn't mean the same thing will happen this time."

I sighed. "I'm sure you're right. It's just that I've lived without closure for all these years. I don't want that for Cicely."

"I understand. I'll give my friend a call. For now, you take care of yourself and your niece."

"Thank you so much. Cicely will need a lot of help. Believe me, I know what it's like to feel all alone in the world."

"I'm sure you do. Cicely is blessed to have you to turn to." He walked over to the front door. "I'm going back to the station. You know how to reach me?"

"I do. Thank you."

He paused with his hand on the doorknob. "Again, I'm really very sorry, Sarah."

"I know you are. Thanks."

I watched him leave, hoping he would follow through on his promise to call his contact in Kansas City. I really wanted the person who killed my sister brought to justice. Not knowing who had killed my parents was like having an open wound in my soul that had never healed. I'd lived my life in the shadow of their murders. How could I be in the same situation again? I struggled to push the thought out of my mind. For now, I needed to concentrate on bringing Cicely home. Even more than seeing Hannah's murderer brought to justice, I was certain my sister would want to know that her daughter was safe and loved. I was determined to do everything in my power to make that happen.

CHAPTER THREE

I spent the rest of the afternoon sitting at the desk in my old bedroom, talking to the police department in Kansas City. Janet had given me some numbers to call, but it still took a while to find the right person. After being transferred more than once, I was finally connected to a very kind woman who worked with the Department of Children and Families. She informed me that Cicely had been placed in emergency foster care. When she said the words *foster care,* a chill ran through me. But the woman assured me this was one of their best homes and that Cicely was doing as well as could be expected. After telling her who I was, she promised they would work with me. Although she couldn't give me Cicely's number, she told me she'd arrange to have someone call me. About an hour later, the phone rang. It was the woman who had provided Cicely emergency shelter. She introduced herself as Cora Anderson.

"She's in shock," Cora said. "I'm doing my best to comfort her. Tomorrow morning she'll see a counselor. He'll assess her emotional condition." She sighed. "She may need some follow-up help after she leaves here. She discovered her mother's body, you know. I can't imagine how that feels."

A picture of blood and orchids flashed through my mind, and my stomach turned over.

"I appreciate everything you're doing to help her," I said. "I'm working with the Department of Children and Families to clear the way for me to bring her home."

"I hope you won't have any trouble," Cora said slowly. "It would help to have something that mentions Hannah's wishes."

"She asked me to be responsible for Cicely if something ever happened to her, but I don't have anything in writing."

"Can you prove you're Cicely's aunt?"

"I suppose our birth certificates would prove Hannah and I are sisters. And Cicely knows me. Shouldn't that count for something?"

"Of course. But you'll have to work through DCF. There's nothing I can do to help you. I'm sorry."

"I just want to get her home so I can take

care of her."

"I know," Cora said. "Hopefully it won't take long. Here she is now."

I heard Cora talking softly, and then Cicely got on the phone.

"Aunt Sarah?"

The pain in her voice made my heart drop. "Yes, honey. I'm here."

"Are you coming to get me?"

"Yes, I am. There are some things I have to do first, but I'll get them taken care of as quickly as I can. The people in Kansas City want to be certain you'll be safe with me."

"Try not to take too long, okay? Cora is very nice, but I don't know these people."

"I understand, sweetheart. You just hold on. I'm sure it won't be long."

"Am I going to live with you?"

"Actually, my friend Janet has asked us to live with her. Do you remember her big house? You'll have your own room. There's lots of space here."

"I like Janet," she said slowly. "And Murphy too. My mom wanted us to have a dog, but we couldn't because she wasn't home enough."

I found myself nodding like an idiot. As if Cicely could see me. "Murphy will be very happy to see you. He's crazy about you." At that moment I wanted to hug Murphy's neck — along with all the other dogs and cats that had the ability to fill a void in a child's life like nothing else could. Animals were one of God's miracles. Unlimited love and understanding all wrapped up in a furry body.

"Someone killed my mother," Cicely said suddenly, as if she'd just realized it.

"I know. I'm so sorry. But you're not alone, Cicely. I'm here, and I'll take care of you. I promise. Okay?"

There was a long silence on the other end before she whispered, "Okay."

I so badly wanted to be with her right at that moment, but all I could do was work through the process the state had set in place to protect children. It was a blessing as well as a curse, but it was necessary.

I told Cicely to give the phone back to Cora. Then I asked Cora to allow Cicely to call me whenever she wanted to.

"Of course," she said. "And I'll phone you after her appointment in the morning. Do you have any idea when you'll get here?"

"Not yet. I want to make sure I have everything I need before I arrive. Shouldn't be too long though. I want to bring Cicely home as soon as possible."

"I understand. Please don't worry. I'll take good care of her."

"Thank you, Cora. Good foster parents are worth their weight in gold. I know that from firsthand experience."

"You were in the system?"

"Yes. Some of it was good, but a lot of it was awful."

She sighed. "I'm sorry. We're working hard to make it better for all the children, but bad parents slip in sometimes because the need is so great."

I thanked her again, and we said good-bye. I breathed a prayer of gratitude to God that He'd sent Cicely to Cora. Now I needed to get all the paper work together that DCF needed, talk to the police, and plan Hannah's funeral. I was trying to figure out how I could possibly get everything done when I heard the doorbell ring downstairs. A couple of minutes later, Janet knocked on the bedroom door and then opened it.

"It's Jonathon," she said. "He's come to check on you."

Jonathon Wiese was the pastor of my church, Agape Fellowship. Although I didn't really feel like seeing anyone right then, I knew talking to Jonathon would probably help me. He seemed to always know what to say in certain situations. Since he'd come to Sanctuary a few years earlier and become our pastor, his ministry had blessed me many times. Next to Janet, he knew me better than anyone else, and he was aware of my history.

"Okay." I stood up but swayed a little. Janet ran over and grabbed my arm.

"You poor thing. You need some rest," she said. "You're so busy worrying about Cicely, you're not getting the time you need to deal with this yourself."

"I'll be fine. To be honest, having Cicely to think about is a big help. It makes me focus on her instead of Hannah."

"I understand that. But you still have to take care of yourself, Sarah. If you won't do it for yourself, then do it for Cicely. She needs you to be strong."

I nodded. "Okay. Thanks."

"Let's get you downstairs. I'll fix you a cup of tea."

"That sounds wonderful."

She followed me down the stairs, probably afraid I was too shaky to make it down alone. I had to admit that I felt a little weak. Grief over Hannah's death had left me numb except for a queasy feeling in the pit of my stomach. I couldn't shake the idea that if I could throw up I'd feel better. It didn't make any sense, but the thought wouldn't go away.

When I walked into the living room, I found Jonathon sitting on the couch. He stood up when he saw me.

"Thank you for coming, Pastor," I said.

He came over and took my hands in his. "Of course," he said. "I'm so sorry, Sarah. What can I do to help?"

Jonathon was in his early thirties and unmarried. Although an unmarried pastor wouldn't be accepted at Sanctuary Mennonite Church, his election as pastor had been unopposed at Agape. He'd been the assistant pastor until our head pastor, Pastor Barker, moved away. Jonathon's sincerity and knowledge of the Bible made him the only logical choice. He was very careful around the single women in our church and avoided dating. That wasn't to say there weren't quite a few young ladies in Sanctuary who were interested. Jonathon was very handsome, with dark hair and intense blue eyes.

"I'm making Sarah a cup of tea, Pastor," Janet said. "Can I get you anything? Tea? Coffee?"

"A cup of coffee would be great. If it's not too much trouble."

She smiled at him. "Not at all. I'll be right back."

I pointed to the couch. "Please, Pastor.

Sit down." I took a seat in a nearby chair. "I don't know that you can do anything except keep us in prayer. Right now I'm trying to make arrangements to bring my niece to Sanctuary."

"I remember meeting Cicely a few months ago when she and her mother were in town," Jonathon said. "I can't imagine what she's going through." He clasped his hands together and leaned forward. "But I guess you can, can't you?"

Tears sprang to my eyes, and I tried unsuccessfully to blink them away. "Some of it, yes. I was younger than Cicely when my parents were killed, so I don't remember much. Cicely is ten. She'll probably have more to deal with than I did. Finding her mother like that . . ." My voice trailed off. I couldn't say anything else. It was too horrific to think about. I dabbed at the tears that fell down my cheeks.

"She'll need a lot of understanding, Sarah. If I can do anything to help her, I'm more than willing. I'm here for both of you. Please call me anytime. Talking things out can make a difference. Many people make the mistake of thinking they can just ignore the pain and 'get over it.' But grief doesn't work like that. You have to acknowledge it."

"I'm afraid there's not much time to

grieve, Pastor. Maybe after I get Cicely home . . ."

Jonathon shook his head. "Sarah, have you ever heard the expression, 'Feelings buried alive never die'?"

"No, I don't think so."

"It means we have to find a way to deal with our feelings, because they don't just go away. Burying them will only cause problems in other areas."

"That makes a lot of sense. I'll work on that."

He smiled at me. "Don't turn it into work, Sarah. Just allow yourself to grieve. And if you need a shoulder to cry on, I'm here."

"Thank you."

He sighed and leaned back. "Forgiving the person who did this will be one of the hardest things you'll ever do."

I could almost feel my heart harden inside my chest. "Right now that's not even on my mind. I'm concentrating on Cicely. Maybe I'll never know who killed my parents, but I want this animal arrested. If not for me, for Cicely. She shouldn't have to spend the rest of her life wondering what happened. Wondering why."

Jonathon was quiet for a moment. Frankly, I was surprised at the sudden rush of emotion I felt. I'd tried so hard to put my parents' murders behind me. Hannah's face suddenly floated into my mind.

"I may have uncovered something about the people who killed Mom and Dad, Sarah," she'd said during her last visit. *"It's possible I'm close to finding out what really happened."*

I'd listened politely to everything she told me, but I couldn't allow myself to go down that road again. I had no desire to revisit the confusion and hurt that had followed me for years. Besides, how could Hannah solve murders that the police in Kansas City couldn't crack? It didn't make sense. Nor did the information she'd collected. A bunch of loose facts that didn't fit together. No solid evidence. Even Hannah admitted she didn't understand it all. Sensing my lack of interest, she'd changed the subject, but I could tell she was hurt that I hadn't been receptive.

"The Bible tells us that God will fight for us," Jonathon said gently, bringing me back to the present. "Let Him take care of whoever did this."

"I don't have much of a choice, Pastor."

At that moment Janet came back into the room with coffee for Jonathon and a cup of hot tea for me. We thanked her, and I quickly picked up my cup. For some reason having something to hold on to made me feel better. After casting a concerned look my way, Janet left the room.

Jonathon took a sip of coffee and put his cup down on the coffee table. "You may have some unresolved feelings about what's happened. If you do, it's perfectly normal. Please don't suppress it. God can handle your anger. He's not upset with you. He wants you to be free, because He loves you."

"I'm trying to stay calm. I keep reminding myself that just because the police didn't catch the man who murdered my parents doesn't mean they won't find the killer this time. In fact, maybe they already have that person in custody." I sighed. "Thinking that way helps me some. I really do want to see the murderer punished, Pastor. I can't help it. Being raised Mennonite, you probably find the idea of retribution offensive."

He smiled. "Mennonites believe in justice, Sarah. They just don't believe in vengeance meted out from the hands of men."

"I wish I could be like that, but I guess I'm just not as perfect as you." My comment sounded rude, but I hadn't meant it that way.

Jonathon raised his eyebrows in surprise. "I'm not perfect." He stared down at the floor for a moment. "I'm going to tell you something I've never told anyone in Sanctu-

39

ary except the elders in our church. I shared it with them because I felt they had the right to know." He took a long, deep breath. "I almost shot a man once. Thankfully, I didn't have to. But I was ready to do it."

To say I was shocked was an understatement. This friendly, quiet, unassuming man had pointed a gun at someone? "But you lived as a Conservative Mennonite before you came here."

"Well, I looked like a Mennonite, and I went to a conservative church, but obviously I wasn't living by all the principles."

"Can I ask why you wanted to shoot that man?"

"Yes, you may. I was afraid he was going to kill the woman I loved. I raised my gun to protect her."

"Did she live?"

"Yes. Someone else took the shot before I did."

"So someone else saved her life?"

He nodded.

"Are you grateful to that person for protecting her?"

"I'm grateful she lived, but I'm also glad her attacker survived. If I'd shot him, I believe I would have killed him." He sighed. "Believe me, when I was caught up in that moment, wounding him was not my intention. I still have to face that every day. Don't get me wrong. I know I'm forgiven. I don't feel guilty anymore, but that incident showed me what I'm capable of. It forced me to take a hard look at myself. In the end, I decided I had to start trusting God to protect me and those I love."

"You said you loved that woman, yet you're still single."

He nodded again. "Yes. She married someone else."

"But . . . but you were willing to kill to protect her. Why isn't she with you?" I suddenly realized how personal my question was. "I'm sorry, Pastor," I said quickly. "That's none of my business."

He smiled. "It's all right, Sarah. I don't mind. She married a man who would have died before going against what he believed. I wasn't as strong as he was . . . then. But I believe I am now."

"What does your story have to do with me?"

"It has to do with making wrong choices for the right reasons. In the next few weeks, you might begin to feel incredible rage toward the person who killed your sister. With your past, there could still be unresolved feelings about your parents. I hope you'll deal with those feelings honestly and not keep them locked inside. You and Cicely will need to heal. Just remember, exposing a wound to the air brings healing faster than covering it up." He stood up. "Look, I've taken enough of your time. But please consider what I've said. Let God bring justice. You work on restoration — and forgiveness. It will be very important in the upcoming days."

"I'll think about it, Pastor," I said softly. "Maybe there is some unresolved anger inside me because I've lost so much."

Jonathon came over and put his hand on my shoulder. "God's in the healing business, Sarah. Just rest your burden on His shoulders. He's willing to carry it."

"I'll try. Thank you."

Jonathon smiled. "I believe some of the women in town will be bringing food by. Both churches are getting together to help."

Fresh tears stung my eyes. "That's so nice."

"People want to let you know you're loved. They truly care about you."

As if someone were listening to our conversation, the doorbell rang.

"I'll walk you to the door," Jonathon said. "I need to get back to the church."

I nodded and we both headed toward the door as the bell rang again. Janet came into the room from the kitchen.

"It's okay," I told her. "I'm already on the way."

I swung the door open and found Jeremiah standing there, his eyes wide. He looked back and forth between Jonathon and me.

"I . . . I'm sorry. I didn't mean to bother you," he said, staring at me. "I . . . I just wanted to tell you . . . I mean, I'm sorry about your sister. My mother is bringing a casserole by later."

Jonathon greeted Jeremiah and then said good-bye to both of us. I waited until he'd walked down the steps before addressing Jeremiah.

"That's so considerate of your mother," I said. "Please tell her how much I appreciate it." I pointed toward the living room. "Would you like to come in?"

He shook his head. "No. Mama said not to keep you. We were over at the post office, and Mr. Bakker said you had mail. He let me bring it to you so you wouldn't have to go over and pick it up."

He handed me the stack of mail in his hand, and I thanked him. Before I could say anything else, he turned and almost ran down the steps.

I closed the door and leaned against it, praying that no one else would visit today. I needed some time to myself. For some reason my legs felt like rubber.

Janet came into the room and saw me. "Sarah, you're exhausted. Come here and sit down on the couch. I'll make you another cup of tea."

"Thank you." I managed a small smile. "You'd better start clearing out space in the refrigerator and freezer. I understand the women of Sanctuary have taken to their stoves."

"Oh, for land's sake," Janet said. "We're going to be drowning in fried chicken and strudel."

As she hurried off to prepare her kitchen for the onslaught, I plopped down on the couch. Immediately Murphy jumped up next to me. I stroked the golden retriever's soft fur and then began to riffle through the mail. When I read the return address on one of the envelopes, disbelief flooded my body like an electric shock, and I cried out for Janet. She came running in from the kitchen, her eyes round with alarm.

"What in the world?" she said when she saw me. "You're as white as a ghost."

I held out the envelope. "It . . . it's a letter. From Hannah."

"What?" Janet took the envelope from me and stared at the postmark. "It was sent

44

Priority Mail yesterday. Oh my goodness." She started to hand it back to me, but I waved it away.

"No. Will you read it? Please? I . . . I can't —" A sob cut off the rest of my sentence.

Janet sat down and slowly opened the envelope. Then she pulled out the folded paper inside. "Honey, are you sure you want me to read this?" she asked.

I could only nod.

She put the envelope down on the coffee table and opened the letter. Then she took a deep breath and began to read:

"Dearest Sarah,

This past year has been the best year of my life. Finding you again was the fulfillment of a long-held dream. Reuniting with my sister is one of the greatest blessings I've ever had. No matter what happens in the future, I want you to know that I always loved you. And I always believed God would bring us together again.

I had to make sure you knew this because of what I'm preparing to do. Cicely and I are going away. Right now I'm not sure if I'll ever see you again. I'll try to contact you, but if I don't, it's only because I don't want to put you in harm's way. Please don't worry about us. I'm taking us someplace safe. Someplace where no one will find us.

Our past has always haunted me, Sarah. Knowing that the people who killed our parents got away with it has never left me. I know you don't really want to hear this, but I have to explain so you won't think my leaving means I don't love you. My search for the truth made me stick my nose in places I shouldn't have. And now it's blown up in my face. Random thieves didn't murder Mom and Dad, Sarah. It was something else. Someone else. I know who it was, but I can't tell you. You might make the same mistake I did. It's just too dangerous. The conspiracy is huge. Much bigger than I realized. Too big for either one of us to handle.

Don't look for us, Sarah. I mean it. You will be putting all of us in terrible danger if you do. Leave it alone. Please. Just pray for Cicely and me.

Sarah, I need you to promise me something else. Never search for Cicely's father or look too closely at my past. I can't stress enough how important this is. Don't take this warning lightly. If you love me, if you love Cicely, you'll do as I ask.

I think I can get us out of here safely, but if anything goes wrong, if something happens to me, please take care of my daughter. As I already told you, you're the only person I trust to raise her the right way. We may have had tough childhoods, but somehow through it all, you retained your goodness and your sweet spirit. I know you'll pass that on to Cicely and you'll help her to become all God has created her to be. I'm counting on you, Sarah. I know you won't let me down. I've made out a will stating that you are to be Cicely's guardian. My attorney, David Rose, has a copy. His office is on 2nd Street in downtown Kansas City. His number is in the phone book. He doesn't know anything about my plans to leave Kansas City, so asking him where I am would be pointless.

After you read this, please destroy this note. No one else is to ever see it. Especially Cicely. Raise her up with joy and love, the way Mom and Dad raised us. They were such good people, Sarah. I want you to always remember that what happened to them wasn't their fault.

I really love you, Sarah. Please don't be sad. We've been apart before, but we will never lose each other. We'll be together again, either in this life or in the next. And someday we'll be reunited with Mom and Dad. What a great reunion we will have!

I will love you forever.

Remember me,
Hannah"

Janet dropped the letter as if it were hot. "Oh, Sarah. What are we going to do?"

All I could do was shake my head and cry.

CHAPTER FOUR

Two days later, I was packing to go to Kansas City. The police wanted to interview me before I picked up Cicely. A copy of Hannah's will had been sent to DCF, and it cleared the way for me to take her home. Even though I felt emotionally and physically drained, I kept pushing forward. There wasn't any choice. Cicely needed me. It was a little after seven-thirty in the morning when the phone rang. It was Paul.

"If you don't mind, I'd like to meet you at The Whistle Stop for breakfast."

"I'm not sure I have the time."

"It . . . it's very important. Please, Sarah."

I was quiet for a moment, trying to figure out if I could squeeze Paul in and still get on the road with plenty of time to get to the police station for the interview. He sounded so insistent I agreed to meet him at nine. As I hung up, I wondered what he could possibly want to talk about. At least this would

49

give me the opportunity to let him know about Hannah's letter. Janet and I hadn't told anyone else. To be honest, we weren't sure what to do about it. Hannah had warned me about getting involved in what had happened to her, but how could I let it drop? Was she really killed because she'd looked into our parents' deaths? Were the two cases related? If they were, what did that mean? I wanted answers, but I had serious doubts about Hannah's conclusion. No matter how hard I tried, I couldn't come up with any reason someone would wait almost twenty years after killing our parents to murder my sister. It didn't make any sense. Maybe the letter was just another sign of the fixation that had taken over Hannah's life. Because of that very real possibility, I had doubts about sharing it with the police. What if Cicely found out about it? It could frighten her unnecessarily.

I let Janet know I'd be gone for a while. Although she wouldn't admit it, I was convinced she'd been staying home in case I needed her. I appreciated it, but I knew how busy she was at the Sanctuary Animal Clinic. There were a lot of animals in Sanctuary. Not just pets but also many larger animals from nearby farms. Several other small towns in our area were without veterinarians, so they relied on Janet to help them. The woman who used to run the clinic had been sent to prison months earlier. Janet had been her helper, but since Rae's arrest, Janet had taken over the duties full time. Even though she loved animals, I knew she wasn't thrilled to be working so many hours.

I changed clothes three times. Maybe it was vain and silly, but for some reason I wanted to look nice for Paul. "This is just stupid. Paul Gleason isn't the least bit interested in you," I said to my reflection after finally picking out black slacks and a teal sweater that Janet had given me for Christmas. I usually wore subtle colors, especially at school. This was a daring choice for me, but Janet was right. The sweater looked nice with my red hair. Even though I'd tried to hide my freckles under some foundation and powder, they still peeked through. I'd never come close to being as pretty as Hannah, but I had to admit I didn't look half bad by the time I finished.

I decided to walk to The Whistle Stop, since it was only a few blocks away. It was cold outside so I bundled up. I actually found the winter temperatures invigorating. By the time I reached the restaurant, Paul's cruiser was already parked outside. I went in and found him sitting at a table in the corner. As I started toward him, someone tapped me on the shoulder. I turned to find Mary Gessner, the café owner, standing behind me.

"I'm so glad to see you, Sarah," she said. "Rosey and I are praying for you."

Although Sanctuary was full of good people, Mary and her daughter were special to me. Mary's gentle and loving nature not only drew people to her, but she was also known for her love of animals. Sanctuary's title applied to all of its residents, including all the unwanted pets that had been dumped off in the country by unfeeling, heartless owners. Mary never met an animal she didn't love. Her house was a happy, noisy, exuberant zoo, full of dogs and cats. From time to time, other animals had also taken up residence with her. Injured rabbits, squirrels, raccoons, deer, birds, frogs, and even possums had spent time recovering in her makeshift animal hospital. Janet used Mary as a foster home for abandoned animals that needed a place to live until they could be adopted. Somehow, Mary and Janet always found homes for their domesticated animal friends, while the injured wild animals were treated and released when they were well.

"Thank you so much," I said, giving her a hug. "It means more than I can say to know I have friends who are praying for me and for Cicely."

"You certainly have that. And if you need anything, please just let us know."

"I will. Right now, one of your fabulous breakfasts will certainly make me feel better."

She chuckled. "Well, I can't guarantee my food will cure everything, but at least today we can warm you up a bit. I'll give you and the deputy some time to decide what you want, and then I'll come and take your order."

"Sounds great, but on the way over here, all I could think about was a stack of your fabulous pecan pancakes."

Mary smiled. "Not a problem. They're very popular today. Must be something about pancakes and cold weather."

"Well, don't sell out before I get some."

"It won't happen. We have lots of batter and gobs of pecans."

"Good. See you in a bit." I headed for the table where Paul waited.

"Am I late?" I asked, approaching the table.

He shook his head. "Not at all. I'm a little early. I had to stop by Amos Peabody's farm on the way over. He'd called to report that his milk cow, Simone, had been stolen."

As I started to take off my coat, Paul jumped up and helped me. When his hand brushed my shoulder, it made me feel warm inside. I chided myself silently. My silly attraction for this handsome deputy could only lead to disappointment.

"And did you find Simone?" I asked as he took my coat and put it on the back of my chair.

"As a matter of fact, I did. She's decided she's in love with Boris Kirkendahl's bull. We found her hiding behind a small grove of trees next to Boris's fence. Unfortunately for her, I'm afraid her love will remain unrequited. Amos has no intention of allowing them to get together, and Boris's bull doesn't seem interested anyway."

"Poor Simone," I said and sat down.

Paul studied the menu. "Do you know what you want?"

I nodded. "Mary makes the world's best pecan pancakes."

"Sounds good." He closed his menu and stared at me. I'd started to feel a little uneasy when Mary suddenly stepped up next to our table.

"How about something to drink?" she asked.

"Hot coffee, please," I said. "I'm frozen."

"How about you, Paul?"

"Coffee sounds great. With cream, please."

"Need a little longer to decide what you want to eat?"

"I think we'd both like pecan pancakes," Paul said. "I'm told they're the world's best."

Mary laughed. "Well, we've never compared our pancakes with all the other pancakes on earth, but I don't think you'll be disappointed."

"Can you add a side of link sausage to that for me, Mary?" Paul asked.

"You've got it. Be back with your coffee in just a minute."

"There might only be two restaurants in Sanctuary," I said as Mary walked away, "but somehow we've managed to get the best cooks around. After I moved here, Janet and I used to go out of town for lunch on Sunday after church. But after a while, we decided it wasn't worth it. If you can't find what you want in Sanctuary, it probably doesn't exist."

Paul chuckled. "Sounds like a good town motto."

"You might be right. I love it here."

"I grew up in Fredericktown and really enjoyed it, but I have to admit, Sanctuary is

55

charming. I understand why you like it so much. I'm sure you're hoping Cicely will feel the same way?"

I sighed. "I do. Maybe it won't be the place she lives the rest of her life, but I hope she'll love it as much as I do while she's here. In the end, she'll have to find her own way, I guess. I believe God has a plan for each of us. I don't know what He has in store for Cicely, so I won't try to influence her to choose the same path I did."

Paul cleared his throat. "So how are you doing, Sarah?"

"I can't say I'm in great shape, but I'm hanging in there. Right now I'm concentrating on Cicely. That helps to keep my mind off myself and my own feelings."

"Most people would be pretty angry. Even mad at God."

Startled by his remark, I frowned at him. It was like he'd been peering into my soul. "In my heart I know He didn't have anything to do with Hannah's death, but . . . but I'm struggling some." I shrugged. "We live in a fallen world where there is evil, and sometimes it gets in. I can't say I understand why or how, but blaming God wouldn't make any sense. I have to focus on the person who killed Hannah." As I said the words, my heart convicted me. Even though my mind agreed with what I said, somewhere inside me there was rage that I couldn't deal with now, no matter what Jonathon said. This wasn't the time to let it out. If I did, I might completely unravel. Blaming God for what happened would go against everything I believed about Him. I couldn't lose my sister and my beliefs at the same time. It would be too much for me to endure.

"I understand. I may work for a small county in Missouri, but I've seen some things that really test my faith. People can do terrible things to one another. Sometimes it's hard to comprehend."

Before I had a chance to respond, Mary came back to the table with our coffee. After she left, I took a deep breath and let it out slowly, trying to calm my ragged nerves. "Frankly, I don't know that we'll always have the answers to everything. If we're not careful, we can drive ourselves crazy with questions."

"Have you asked God about it?"

I grunted. "No, not really. Maybe when I have a chance to catch my breath, I might do that. Right now I don't dare allow myself that luxury." I took a sip of coffee and then put my cup back on the saucer. "I'd be lying if I said I didn't have questions. But there is one thing I'm certain about. Hannah and I found each other for a reason. And that reason is Cicely. If Hannah hadn't located me, Cicely would have ended up in foster care. Maybe her experience would have been a good one. But maybe not. At least I know she will be with someone who loves her. Someone who will raise her up with a knowledge of God."

Paul didn't say anything for a few moments, just sipped his coffee. Finally he put his cup down. "I lost a brother when I was a teenager. Randy was a good kid, but he was reckless. Took chances. One night, he was in a car wreck. A friend of his was driving drunk. Randy tried to get out of the car before something happened, but the guy wouldn't let him out. When we got to the hospital, Randy told us he knew he wasn't supposed to go with his friend that night, but he didn't listen. He lived two days. His friend was killed on impact." Paul shook his head. "I believe God tried to protect Randy." He sighed as he stared at his coffee cup. "I think Randy would still be alive if he'd paid attention to his gut."

"I'm so sorry, Paul. God may have warned Hannah too. I'll probably never know."

"I guess we need to listen to those warnings," he said. "To be honest, I'm not sure if I know how to hear them."

"When Janet offered me the chance to come to Sanctuary and live with her, I didn't hear a voice, but I'll never forget the confirmation that bubbled up inside me. It was as if God was saying, 'Yes! Yes!' "

"Well, I'm certainly glad you listened." He frowned. "You told me your parents were murdered when you were young and after that you and your sister were separated. How does a child deal with something like that?" He stared intently at me. "I'm not just being nosy. I'd really like to know more about you. You can tell me to mind my own business if you want. I won't be offended."

I took a deep breath, trying to clear my head. At that moment, Hannah's death seemed to fill every corner of my mind. It was as if there wasn't room for anything else. But for some reason, I really did want to share my story with Paul. I took a deep breath. "After our parents' deaths, my sister and I went to live with an aunt in California for a couple of years, but she became very ill and couldn't take care of us anymore. She was our only living relative, so we were sent back to Missouri and went into foster care. Hannah and I were both taken in by a very kind Mennonite woman. Unfortunately, a year later Mrs. Johnson passed away suddenly." I realized I was talking quickly, but this wasn't a story I liked to repeat. "Not long after that, Hannah was adopted by a very loving couple. I stayed in foster care. Hannah was a beautiful child with blond hair and blue eyes. As you can see, I'm very plain, and I'm sure most adoptive parents weren't looking for skinny redheaded children with freckles."

Paul frowned at me. "I don't think you're plain. Not at all."

"Well, thank you, but you don't have to say that. Next to Hannah, I disappeared into the woodwork. She was very special. And not only on the outside. She was beautiful inside."

"So you were never adopted?" he asked.

"No. After being shuffled around to several foster homes, I ended up with a couple in St. Louis who were in the system only for the money the state paid. With all the moving around I did, Hannah and I lost contact. Though I asked repeatedly for help finding my sister, the people I lived with weren't interested. To them, I wasn't a child. I was a paycheck. They weren't physically abusive; they just didn't care about me. I never complained because I didn't want to move again, afraid if I did, Hannah would never find me. So I kept my mouth shut and put

60

up with the mistreatment."

"I'm sorry," Paul said. "Some people shouldn't be foster parents."

I nodded. "That's true, but actually I'm very grateful to them. You see, the family had two dogs that they treated better than their foster children. It was my job to take the dogs to the vet when they needed care. That's where I met Janet. She ran a veterinary office near our house. She was very kind to me. Not long before I turned eighteen, she told me she was moving to Sanctuary and asked me to live with her. Her sister owned the house where Janet lives now, but she'd decided to move to Florida. She offered Janet the house, and she accepted. As soon as I turned eighteen, I left my foster family and came to Sanctuary." I took a deep breath and then exhaled slowly. "I know that's the long answer to your question, but I don't know how else to explain it."

"And now you're a teacher."

"Yes. I'd wanted to be a teacher ever since we lived with my aunt. She was an incredible teacher. She not only gave me a love of learning, she showed me how teachers can make a huge difference in the lives of young people. Janet helped me obtain a scholarship, and I went to a small community college in Park Hills to get my degree. I worked hard and graduated in three years. My plan was to try to find a position near Sanctuary, but then the town approached me with the idea of opening a school here. I jumped at the chance."

Paul nodded. "So when did you and your sister reconnect?"

"Almost a year ago. After searching for me for a long time, she finally found someone who knew my foster family and remembered that Janet and I were friends. Hannah was able to track down an old friend of Janet's who told her she'd moved to Sanctuary. Hannah called Janet, found out I was living with her, and she and Cicely came to visit. I was so thrilled to have her in my life again." I looked away for a moment, trying to rein in my emotions.

"I'm sorry. Maybe we shouldn't talk about this right now," Paul said gently.

"No, it's okay. Although I loved seeing Hannah, she seemed almost obsessed with our parents' murder. You see, she didn't believe their deaths were the result of a burglary, the way the police had said. She'd been trying to find evidence to prove that ever since she was nineteen. Then a couple of months ago, a reporter, who was a friend of my mom's when she worked for a Kansas

City newspaper, contacted Hannah. The woman developed cancer and had to leave her job. She had a file about Mom and Dad's murders. She'd kept that information all these years because the killers had never been found. I guess she didn't want to destroy the file until she felt my parents had some kind of justice. Anyway, not long before she died, she gave the file to Hannah. Something in that file really stirred up my sister."

"Did she tell you what it was?"

"No. I told her I wasn't interested in talking about the murders."

"And did she back off?"

"Yes, but I knew she wanted me to . . . I don't know, get involved in whatever she was doing." I shook my head. "I just couldn't. I wanted to spend time getting to know Hannah again. And Cicely. The past was something I'd tried hard to put behind me. I didn't want to get pulled back there again." I shook my head. "I want closure too, Paul, but Hannah's claims were just too unbelievable. I couldn't allow myself to get sucked in. It . . . hurt too much."

"I understand," Paul said. "I'm sure I would have felt the same way."

"Hannah seemed to understand too, but I know she was disappointed." I took another sip of coffee before saying, "Paul, something's happened. Something I want to share with you."

"What's that?"

I picked up my purse, opened it, and took out Hannah's letter. I handed it to him and watched as he read it. His eyes widened with surprise. When he finished, he handed the letter back but didn't say anything.

"I know it sounds as if our parents' murders are connected to what happened to Hannah," I said, "but how could that be true?" I picked up my napkin and dabbed at my wet eyes. "What if I was wrong, Paul?" I said in a near whisper. "What if Hannah really did discover something important?" I put the letter back inside my purse. "And what if my reluctance to listen cost Hannah her life?" I gazed into dark brown eyes. "I don't know what to do."

"First of all, you're not responsible for what happened to Hannah," Paul said emphatically. "Don't do that to yourself. As far as the rest of it . . . I don't know. The police need to see this letter."

"No."

He looked confused. "I don't understand."

"I don't want them to know about it . . . yet. I'm afraid they'll think Hannah was delusional. And what if Cicely finds out about it?" I shook my head. "I intend to wait. If they find the person who killed my sister, I'm going to destroy the letter. Cicely will never know anything about it."

Mary walked up to the table with our plates, so we stopped talking. I hadn't been aware of how hungry I was until I was faced with Mary's marvelous stack of pancakes. We thanked her and she left to tend to other customers. I said something about how good our food looked, but Paul's face was tense and he seemed distracted.

"Have I upset you? Do you disagree with me?" I asked.

"No, it's not that." He picked up his fork and started eating.

I was convinced there was something else on his mind besides breakfast. Why had he wanted to meet me? We ate in silence until he asked me about school.

"I'm taking some time off," I said. "Reuben King has offered to fill in for me until I'm ready to return."

Reuben served as our town's mayor. Even though our Mennonite population didn't officially acknowledge his position, he was still able to represent their needs, along with everyone else's, with government officials. He'd done many things to help Sanctuary, and everyone admired him.

"That's great. He'll do a good job."

"You've been friends a long time, haven't you?" I said.

"Ever since we were kids."

"How are things going with him and Wynter?"

Wynter Evans was a reporter who had supposedly come to Sanctuary to do a story about interesting towns in Missouri. In truth, she suspected her kidnapped brother lived here. She was right. Wynter moved to Sanctuary not long after she found her brother, Ryan, who had been adopted by a Mennonite couple that had no idea their son had been abducted from his parents and sister. Wynter had fallen in love with Reuben, and now they were engaged. She'd left her job in St. Louis and moved to Sanctuary to do some writing — her real passion. She lived with Esther Lapp, an older Conservative Mennonite woman whose house was next door to Janet's.

Wynter's real name was Emily Erwin, but she'd changed it when she went into broadcasting. Although her family called her by her given name, everyone in Sanctuary knew her as Wynter, so the name had stuck.

"They're doing great. They're working on wedding plans, but they can't seem to agree on a date."

"Well, I hope they work it out. They're such a wonderful couple."

"Yes, they are."

That seemed to end our conversation about Reuben. Paul was quiet and still seemed preoccupied.

Finally I put my fork down. "Paul, why did you ask me to breakfast this morning? I've enjoyed our time together, but I got the impression you had something specific you wanted to talk about."

He drained the rest of his coffee and then poured himself another cup. After checking my cup, he put the carafe down. Then he wiped his mouth and put his napkin back in his lap. "I guess I'm thinking about our conversation. Sometimes we need to heed warnings. I wonder if I'm getting one now."

I frowned at him. "What kind of warning? What are you talking about?"

"A warning to walk away, Sarah. Not to pursue your sister's death too closely."

"Why? What's happened?"

"I don't want to make this more dramatic than it is. It's probably nothing. But . . . well, it bothered me, and I felt you should know."

"Should know what?"

"I heard back from my friend in Kansas City. He e-mailed me the initial report taken

67

at the scene of your sister's murder. Again, this may not mean anything . . ."

"Let me be the judge of that," I said.

"You mentioned something about flowers at the scene of your parents' murder. Is that right?"

I nodded. "White orchids." I thought for a moment. "Now that you mention it, I remember Hannah saying something about those flowers. That they weren't there before the murders."

"But you don't remember?"

"No. I saw them when we were taken out of the house, but I assumed Dad bought them for her. I do remember that he liked buying her flowers."

Paul picked up his coffee cup and stared at it, as if he couldn't stand to look at me. "I was able to see the report taken at your sister's crime scene. And it just seemed odd to me . . ."

"What? Tell me, Paul."

He looked up slowly until he met my gaze. "Orchids. There were white orchids scattered around your sister's body."

CHAPTER FIVE

The food in my stomach rolled over, and for a moment, I thought I was going to be violently ill. Paul must have been afraid I would faint again because he got up from his chair and came over to sit next to me.

"Are you all right, Sarah? You look so pale."

I nodded, but I couldn't find my voice. The room spun around me, and I felt as if I were looking at myself from somewhere far away.

"Do you want me to take you home?"

I shook my head. "No. Just tell me about the flowers." My dream from the other night came flooding back. In my mind, blood and flowers blended together in a kind of macabre torrent.

"There's not much more to say. There was a broken vase next to Hannah's body, and white orchids on the floor." He frowned. "The detective I spoke to is convinced the vase was knocked off the table during a struggle. The very same way it happened with your mother. But . . ."

"But what? Did you see something different?"

He nodded. "The flowers were not only on both sides of Hannah's body, they were on top of her. If the vase had been broken when she tried to fight off her attacker, she probably should have fallen on them. It doesn't make sense."

"Did you ask your friend about it?"

Paul sighed. "Yes, but after that he cut the conversation short. He wasn't supposed to let me see that report in the first place. Besides, I'm a deputy sheriff in a small county in Missouri. He works in Kansas City. I don't think he liked the idea of my questioning the work their detectives were doing."

"This is exactly what happened to my parents. How can that be?" My hand trembled as I picked up my coffee cup.

"It wasn't my intention to upset you," Paul said. "Maybe I shouldn't have . . ."

I shook my head and took a sip of coffee. "You did the right thing. This is *my* sister. *My* family. I need to know what's going on." I put my cup down and stared at him. "Was Hannah right, Paul? Was she killed because she found out something she wasn't supposed to?" I had to stop a moment to catch my breath. "Why didn't I listen to her?" I asked finally. "What have I done?"

"Don't go there, Sarah," Paul said sternly. "There was no way for you to know Hannah's claims had any validity. Besides, I'm finding it hard to believe that whoever killed your parents came back almost twenty years later to murder your sister. That's really farfetched."

"Maybe she uncovered something, Paul. Like she claimed. And the wrong person found out about it."

"But why didn't she just go to the police? If she had proof, they would have listened."

"I don't know," I said, "but if the killings are connected —"

"Are you basing this solely on the flowers? Couldn't Hannah have bought them?"

"That's impossible. We both hate white orchids. She would never, ever have them in her home. They remind us of the night our parents died."

Paul crossed his arms and fixed his gaze on some spot behind me. I could tell he was trying to make sense of the situation. I was dealing with several emotions at once. The terrible realization that the person who killed my mother and father may have just murdered my sister, guilt because I didn't listen to Hannah when she tried to share with me what she'd uncovered, and an underlying sense of fear. If the person who murdered my parents had come back for Hannah, how could I be sure he was through? Was Cicely next? Or me?

"Look, I'm going to do what I can to help you," he said finally. "But you've got to understand that I'm very limited. If the sheriff found out I was nosing around in a case from another county, he'd have a fit."

"Seems to me that people in law enforcement should care about justice."

"We do care about justice," he said soothingly. "Unfortunately, some departments are more committed to closing cases than finding the truth. But I care, Sarah. You won't be alone in this. I'll do my best to find out what really happened and who is behind it. You'll need to trust me. Can you do that?"

I nodded. "I trust you, Paul. You're the only person in law enforcement I do trust right now."

"Look, Sarah, most police officers are good people whose job is to bring justice to bad situations. Don't toss all of us out because of what happened with your parents. Right now the authorities in Kansas City know a lot more about your sister's case than I do." He frowned. "What will you tell the police when you see them this afternoon?"

I shook my head. "I honestly don't know. Hopefully, I'll find there's no reason to say anything. Maybe they've already arrested someone."

"Whatever you do, don't mention me. If you end up still needing my help, we can't let them know I'm stepping into their investigation."

"No problem. Again, thank you so much, Paul. This whole thing is so confusing, and I have no idea what to do next." I sought his eyes. "You said something about a warning. Do you think God's telling us to leave this situation alone?"

He stared back at me, his jaw working. Finally, he sighed. "I don't know if it's God or my own trepidation. Something's really off here, but I have no idea what's behind it. I don't want you or Cicely to get hurt. But . . ."

He stopped and stared down into his coffee cup.

"But what?"

"Look, Sarah. There's one thing I've learned from being in law enforcement. Something I believe with all my heart. Letting criminals go free doesn't help anyone.

No matter how scary it might be to confront them, getting them off the street so they can't hurt anyone else is always the right way to go. I just worked a rape case where the victim just wanted to forget what happened and move on with her life. Even though she said she'd told me everything about the incident, I knew she was holding back. She didn't want to go to trial, didn't want her friends and family to know what had happened to her."

"I can understand that."

"I can too. But what if more women are raped by this same man? What if someone gets killed? It happens. I wonder if the rest of his victims will understand? And what about their friends and families?"

I didn't answer him, but what he said made sense. Maybe Hannah didn't want me to go after the truth. But what if her killer hurt someone else? How could I allow that to happen? And how could I stand by and see her murderer get away?

"You see my dilemma," Paul said. "Do I stand by that belief, or do I tell you to stay out of it because I think it could be dangerous?"

I shook my head. "Look, we're making assumptions here. First, let's find out what the police say. Maybe they'll solve Hannah's murder and lay all our questions to rest."

I said the words and Paul nodded his agreement, but I could see in his expression that he didn't believe that any more than I did.

We finished our breakfast, and Paul gave me a ride back to Janet's. When we pulled up to the house, he got out of the car, came around, and opened the passenger-side door for me. Not used to that kind of chivalry, I thanked him.

"My father used to open the car door for my mother," I said. "Not many men still do that."

"Well, they should," he said with a smile. He closed the door behind me and then put his hands on my shoulders. I was surprised and jumped at his touch. When I looked up at him, I wasn't sure what I was seeing in his eyes. Was it concern? Or something more?

"Sarah, if the police try to tell you Hannah was killed by some random thief, and if they won't listen to you, I'm going to do whatever I can to help you find the truth," he said softly. "I won't let you down. I promise."

Before I had a chance to respond, he kissed me on the cheek. Surprised, I pulled away but immediately wished I hadn't. I gazed up at him for a moment but couldn't read his expression. Why had he kissed me? Was it just something he did with everyone, or was there more to it? My face felt hot, and I prayed he'd attribute my red cheeks to the cold air. Redheads blush easily, and I was true to the stereotype. My father used to tease me about it, calling me his "little beet." It was one of the things I remembered about him.

"Th-thank you," I said, embarrassed not only by my physical reaction but also for my emotional response. If I wanted his help, I couldn't risk acting like a silly schoolgirl. He would be uncomfortable, and I'd end up driving him away.

I turned away and practically ran into the house. It took effort to stop and wave goodbye, but I didn't want him to think he'd offended me. He waved back and got into his car. I stepped through the front door and closed it behind me. Then I slumped down and tried to calm myself. My cheek burned as if his lips were still pressed to it. I raised my hand and touched my face, remembering how it felt to have him near. I was glad Janet wasn't in the room to see how flustered I was.

CHAPTER SIX

I sat in a room at the Kansas City Police Department waiting to talk to someone about Hannah. After I was done here, I planned to go straight to her house. Tomorrow morning I was scheduled to pick up Cicely from Cora's. Before we left town, I'd decided I would take Cicely to her home so she could pack her things and say goodbye. But first, I had to make sure the house was presentable. I really had no idea what to expect.

I waited almost thirty minutes before the door opened and a man came in. He was nicely dressed in a dark suit and red tie. Handsome, with coal-black hair combed back from his face, his half smile looked practiced, and his overall demeanor was distant. I got the distinct impression that to him, talking to me was nothing more than part of his job.

"Miss Miller?" he asked.

I nodded.

"I'm Detective Sykes. I have some questions to ask, if it's okay."

"I understand."

He pointed at the cup sitting in front of me on the table. "Can I get you more coffee?"

"No, thank you. I'm fine."

He sat down at the table across from me, setting down his coffee and a file he'd carried in with him.

"I understand you live in a town called Sanctuary?"

"Yes. With my friend Janet Dowell. Well, I should say I *will* be living with her. My apartment is too small, so Cicely, my sister's daughter, and I will be moving in with Janet." I knew I was babbling, but I was nervous. Something about police stations and police officers.

"And Ms. Dowell will help with your niece's care?"

I hesitated for a moment. Why was he asking questions about Janet and Cicely? "Yes, I suppose, but I'll be Cicely's primary caregiver. May I ask why you're interested in my niece's living arrangements?"

"No reason. Just making sure the victim's daughter will be taken care of. I know it's not my job, but we're human beings, you know. Cases with children affect us."

"I'm sorry. I guess I'm a little on edge."

"Not a problem. People all act differently in these kinds of situations. There are no right or wrong reactions."

"I appreciate that." I tried to smile at him. "I'm sure you have a tough job. Having to deal with so many people who've gone through tragedy, I mean. Not everyone could do it."

He took a sip of coffee and then put his cup down. "It's not easy. I rarely get to stop something tragic before it happens. Usually I get a case after it's too late to protect the victim." He stared into my eyes. "I want you to know that I'm really sorry about your sister. We intend to do everything we can to find her killer."

"Thank you."

For some reason, I couldn't take my eyes off the green file folder the detective had placed on the table in front of him. Hannah's life had come down to a green file folder. Sadness flowed through me, and I fought to subdue the grief that threatened to turn me into a mass of blubbering emotions. This detective had a job to do, and trying to console me wasn't part of it.

"I'd like to ask you a few questions if you don't mind."

"Certainly," I choked out. "Anything I can do to help."

Sykes turned his attention to the file. He flipped it open and quickly perused its contents. "It looks like your sister was killed by a burglar. Quite a few things were missing. Money and possibly credit cards from her purse." He looked up and pushed a piece of paper toward me. "We checked your sister's credit. There are two cards listed. You need to contact them as soon as possible. Let them know the cards may have been stolen. And please let us know if either of the cards have been used. It might help us catch her killer."

I nodded. "I plan on going to her house when I leave here. Hannah was very meticulous about everything. I'm sure I'll find the information I need."

"Good." He went back to his list. "According to her landlord and her next-door neighbor, several electronics, including her laptop, were missing as well. We can't be sure there weren't more items stolen. Maybe you'll be able to tell us if anything else is gone?"

I shook my head. "I've never been inside her house. I'm sorry, but I can't help you with that."

"I guess the only person who would know

for certain is her daughter, but we couldn't ask her to go back into the house the morning we were there. She was just too traumatized. When she's doing better, you'll want to have her check the house. For now, we've pieced things together the best we could." He stared down at the paper in front of him. "Oh, and her jewelry box was emptied. I hope none of the pieces were family heirlooms."

I shook my head. "My mother wasn't big on jewelry. I have her wedding ring. As far as I know, there wasn't much else. Nothing very valuable."

The detective took a deep breath and let it out slowly. "What I'm getting ready to tell you next might be hard to hear. Stop me at any time if it's too difficult for you." He paused for a moment and stared at me.

"Go on," I said.

"Your sister was stabbed to death. Sixteen times. She put up a fight, but the coroner didn't find any DNA on her body. Not even under her fingernails. There wasn't any evidence at the crime scene that was useful. The only fingerprints we found in the room where she died belonged to Hannah and her daughter. The killer must have worn gloves." He sighed. "I want you to know that we're looking for her things, but to be honest, finding any of them is a long shot. Everything is probably gone by now. Either sold or pawned. We have a few pawn brokers who keep an eye out for stolen property, but most of them just don't have the time or the inclination to update us when something matching our list of items comes through their stores."

The gruesome details shocked me, but I was determined not to allow them to overwhelm me. Instead, I focused on something else he'd said. "Look, Detective —"

"I know this isn't what you want to hear."

I shook my head. "I'm not concerned about my sister's possessions. I am concerned about calling this . . . this crime . . . a burglary."

The detective's eyes narrowed. "I'm sorry. I don't understand."

"Are you aware that my parents were murdered almost twenty years ago?"

He nodded. "Yes. We found the case while we were researching your sister . . . and you."

My mouth dropped open in surprise. "You researched me? I don't understand."

"It's routine. When there's a murder, we check into all the close family members. Unfortunately, you and your niece are the only relatives we could find except for your sister's adoptive mother, who's in a nursing home. I understand she's in the last stages of Alzheimer's."

"And I'm happy to help you in any way I can. But I need you to understand why I don't believe this was a burglary." A battle raged in my mind. The warning from Hannah's letter versus Paul's admonition about bringing criminals to justice. But as I searched my heart, I realized I only had one clear choice.

His dark eyebrows knit together in a deep frown. "All right. Explain it to me."

I took a deep breath, aware I was getting ready to go down a road I wouldn't be able to come back from. "My parents were murdered in exactly the same way. Stabbed. It was staged to look like a burglary."

Sykes cleared his throat. "You were very young when this happened, weren't you?"

"I was six. But what does that have to do —"

"Six years old? Yet you know the murders were staged? And how would you know that?"

Anger coursed through me. "Because my sister was convinced of it."

"But what kind of proof did she have? Did she bring her concerns to us?" He flipped through the papers in the file. "I don't have any record of that."

"I . . . I don't know. But shouldn't you at least look into it? I mean if there's any possibility these murders are linked . . ."

Before the detective had a chance to respond to me, the door swung open again. A tall man with blond hair walked in. He frowned at Detective Sykes.

"Sorry. I thought you were in room B."

Sykes seemed to straighten up in the man's presence. "No, sir. Do we need to move?"

The blond man shook his head and smiled at me. He looked to be in his early fifties, and he possessed a quality that exuded confidence.

He held out his hand. "I'm Captain Anson Bentley."

"Sarah Miller," I said as we shook hands.

The captain looked at Sykes. "This is the Hannah Miller case?"

"Yes, sir. Sarah is Hannah's sister."

"I'm so sorry for your loss," the captain said. His words were said with the kind of sincerity that made tears spring to my eyes. I quickly blinked them away.

"Thank you so much."

"Detective Sykes is one of our best, but if there's ever anything you need and you can't get in touch with him, please call." He took a small brass cardholder from his pocket, withdrew a card, and handed it to me. "I can usually be reached at this number if you can't get me through the main number."

His kindness touched me, and once again I felt tears sting my eyelids.

He came over and put his hand on my shoulder. "I know it's hard, Sarah, but you'll get through this. I can tell by looking at you that you're a strong woman. And the entire Kansas City Police Department has your back, okay?"

Too choked up to respond, I just nodded.

He patted my shoulder then left the room.

"Nice man," I said to Sykes, my voice shaking.

He nodded. "Yes, he is. We're lucky to have him. He certainly knows how to solve cases. His father was also a very successful detective in this department years ago. Kind of a legend. Captain Bentley was named after him."

I was certainly impressed. "Will he be working on my . . . case?" To me, Hannah wasn't a *case,* but that's how the police saw her.

He shook his head. "Probably not. Although he oversees all our cases, he rarely gets personally involved. Not unless there's a problem."

I slid Bentley's card into my purse. "I'm sorry," I said. "What were we talking about?"

"You were saying you think what happened to your sister is somehow linked to the murder of your parents. Is there anything else that supports your belief?"

"Yes. The flowers."

Sykes didn't respond, just stared at something in his file. I could see it was a picture, but he was careful to keep it hidden from me. Looking at his expression, something dawned on me.

"You saw them, didn't you? You know about the white orchids."

"Yes, I saw them," he said hesitantly. "But I'm not sure it's enough evidence to connect the two . . ."

Without realizing it, I stood to my feet. "Enough evidence? My sister was convinced my mother did not have white orchids in her house the night she died. And my sister hated them. She never would have had them in her apartment. Don't you find that the least bit suspicious?"

Sykes raised an eyebrow. "You can sit down," he said quietly. "Look, I'm willing to listen to you, but I can't hinge a case on the victim's choice of flowers. If you're trying to get me to believe that someone killed your parents almost twenty years ago, for some reason left white orchids at the scene, and then a couple of days ago decided to kill your sister and leave the same flowers again . . . Well, it's an incredible story. I'm not dismissing your concerns out of hand; I'm just telling you that it's not enough to launch a full-scale investigation. I'd need more proof."

I sank back down into my chair. "My sister was convinced my parents' murder wasn't the result of a foiled burglary attempt. She spent a lot of years trying to prove it but never made much progress. Then a few weeks ago, a reporter who was leaving *The Kansas City Star* contacted her. Asked her if she wanted a file she'd started keeping ever since our parents died, hoping whoever killed them would be caught and she could write the story. Hannah met her and got the file. I have no idea what was in it. She tried to tell me, but I refused to listen. Hopefully, I'll find the file when I go to her house. If I do, I'll turn it over to you."

"I doubt it will have any information I don't have, Miss Miller."

"Maybe not. But I do have something you haven't seen." I reached into my purse and pulled out a copy of Hannah's letter. I held it out and Sykes stared at it a moment before finally taking it from my hand.

He quietly perused it before looking up at me. "This is certainly disturbing, but it doesn't prove anything."

"How can you say that?" I fought to keep my emotions in check. Why wouldn't he listen to me? Is this how I seemed to Hannah when she tried to talk to me?

He put the letter on his desk. "Look, Miss Miller. I don't want you to think I don't care about what happened to your sister. I do. I'm very interested in the truth, but . . ." He took a deep breath. "Look, I shouldn't be telling you this because we haven't had time to thoroughly investigate him, but we've picked up a suspect in your sister's murder."

For several seconds all I could do was stare at him. "You . . . you what?"

He leaned forward in his chair. "We've arrested a man who broke into a house the same night your sister was attacked. It was only three blocks from her house."

"B-but how do you know it's the same man?"

He straightened up and sighed. "We don't. Yet. That's why I didn't want to say anything until we're sure. But the evidence is pretty strong. I think he did it."

I didn't know what to say. Had Hannah been wrong? Was she just so obsessed that she saw things that weren't there? "Wait a minute," I said slowly. "But what about the flowers? How can you explain them?"

He shrugged. "Coincidence."

I pointed at his folder. "But the flowers are on top of her. Explain to me how that happened. If a vase of orchids was knocked off the coffee table during a struggle, wouldn't she have fallen on them? Why aren't the flowers under her? Did you find any underneath her body?"

Sykes's amenable expression changed as quickly as a pop-up thunderstorm. "How do you know where the flowers were found? Even if your niece or your sister's neighbor mentioned the flowers, I'd be surprised if either one of them looked closely enough to realize there were no flowers under the body. I'm certain no one from our department shared that with you."

Realizing I'd put my foot in my mouth, I struggled to find a way to explain. "Maybe I didn't know," I said after a few seconds. "Maybe I was just guessing and wanted to see how you'd react. It's obvious I was right." I forced myself to meet his steely gaze without flinching. The last thing I wanted to do was get Paul into trouble.

"All right," Sykes said slowly. "I'm going to assume you're telling me the truth. But a word of warning: interfering with our investigation won't help us close this case. It will only impede our progress."

Trying to keep my voice steady, I said, "Look, Detective. I appreciate knowing you're working your *case.* But this isn't just a case to me. This is my family. I've lost my parents and my sister. You can walk away from this when you go home at night. I can't. How can you tell me not to interfere?"

Sykes cleared his throat and stared down at his file, his jaw working furiously. It upset me to know that he was angry. I was the one who had the right to be enraged. Just when I was ready to chew him out again, he sighed and looked up at me.

"We deal with a lot of really bad situations, Miss Miller. Stuff you don't see living in some small rural town. The only way to survive is to try to keep some distance from the awful things people do to each other. I'm sorry if I come off as uncaring. I assure you it isn't true. I really am listening to you, but I have to stay professional. It's my job." He fingered my sister's file. "I see your point about the flowers. That bothered me too. Until we're sure we have the right guy in custody, I'll keep digging. Now, if I promise to look into any connections I can find between your parents' case and your sister's, will you allow me to complete this interview?"

"Of course."

He pulled a sheet of paper from the file and stared at it for a moment. "These questions are designed to find some connection to the burglary, in case the man we have in custody isn't involved. We want to be certain the person who broke in wasn't someone your sister knew. Usually, thieves break into homes where they know there are valuables that will make their efforts pay off. It appears your sister didn't have anything worth taking the risk of getting caught — let alone killing someone over. So let's do this. I'm going to ask about people she knew. Maybe we can find a reason someone might want her dead. Would that satisfy you?"

"I'm afraid I can't help you, Detective. I don't know any of her friends."

He shook his head. "How is that possible?"

I explained to him that Hannah had found me just a year earlier.

"Well, this is going to make things much tougher. I don't suppose you knew anyone she worked with either?"

"No. She was an administrative assistant

for a local law firm. I . . . I can't remember the name of the firm. I think Kennedy was part of it. I'm sorry. I guess I'm useless."

Sykes pulled out a piece of paper from his file. "Don't worry about it. I've got her employer's name right here. Kennedy, Worthington, Klemm, and Sparlin. We'll check with them. See if they can give us any useful information." He slid the paper back into the file. "From reading your sister's letter, I assume you have no idea who Cicely's father is?"

I shook my head. "The first time I knew she had a child was when we reconnected. I asked her about Cicely's father, but she told me it was a closed subject. I never asked again."

"Does her daughter know who her father is?"

"No. Hannah told Cicely that her father was someone who didn't want either one of them in his life, and they were better off without him."

He nodded and wrote something down in his small note pad. I wanted to yell at him. To tell him that Hannah was a wonderful woman. That she loved God and wasn't the kind of person who would sleep around with random men. But that was the Hannah I knew when we were younger. To be honest, I had no idea what kind of a life she'd lived during the time we were separated. It hurt that I didn't know more.

"Look," he said, "I want you to do something for me. I need you to make a list of people your parents knew." He raised an eyebrow. "You do remember some of them, don't you?"

"Not very many. I was only six."

The detective pushed a pad of paper and a pen toward me that were on the table.

I quickly wrote down the names I could recall and slid it back to him. "I'm sorry. That's it. If I remember anyone else, I'll call you."

He looked over the names I'd written down. "The Fergusons. The Bittners. And someone named Ray? That's it?"

"That's it. And the Bittners are probably dead. I think they were in their seventies when we knew them. I only remember them because Mrs. Bittner used to bring us taffy when she came over to visit."

"This isn't much to go on."

I sighed. "I know that. My sister would be able to give you more information. Again, I'm sorry."

"It's okay." He tore the piece of paper off the pad and put it in his pocket. "I'm still not convinced these two murders are connected, but I'll do some poking around. Just in case." He stared at me with his eyes narrowed. "But if we find proof that the guy we're holding was involved in your sister's death, all bets are off. You understand that, right?"

"Of course. If he did it, he did it." I waved my hand toward the file. "Then none of this will matter. Except my parents' case will stay unsolved. I guess I'm used to that." It wasn't true, but I knew there was no way to get an old case opened again unless I could give the detective a valid reason to do it. And I didn't have that. "I want you to know that I appreciate your help."

"Well, I haven't done anything yet. Let's see what happens."

He straightened up, slid the copy of Hannah's letter into the green folder, and closed it. "Is there anything else you can think of that I need to know?"

I hesitated a moment while Sykes frowned at me. "There's one thing, although I can't see how this would help you. Hannah and I heard two men at the house the night our parents were killed. One of them found Hannah and me hiding under the stairs. But instead of telling his partner, he closed the door and walked away. It's possible he saved our lives."

Sykes shook his head. "A killer with a conscience. It sounds strange, but I've run across it before. Some people don't mind killing adults, but they won't touch children. It's a twisted kind of moral compass." He frowned at me. "But doesn't that mean you saw him? That you could describe him?"

I shook my head. "He shined a flashlight in our eyes. We couldn't see a thing."

Sykes stood up. "That's too bad. A description would have been nice."

"I do have another question."

He nodded at me.

"As I said, I want to go to Hannah's house. I need to pack up some things for Cicely and for me. Is that all right?"

"Yes, we're through there. You can remove whatever you want to."

"If I find the file Hannah talked about, should I contact you?"

"Yes. As I said, I doubt a reporter would have access to anything I don't, but I'm willing to look at whatever information she obtained."

"Thank you, Detective." I stood up and faced him. "Am I free to go?"

"Yes. Can I walk you out?"

"No. I remember the way. But thanks." I held out my hand and he took it in his.

"Thank you for your time, Miss Miller.

I'll keep in touch."

"I really appreciate that. I hope I haven't offended you. It's just that I don't want Hannah's murder to be swept under the rug — if there's more to it. If it was just the unfortunate result of a break-in, I can live with that. And if the man you picked up is guilty, I'll be happy to know he's been caught. But until then, I think we need to do whatever we can to pursue the truth. I believe my sister deserves it."

"That's my job, Miss Miller. I'll do my very best for you and your sister." He took a deep breath. "I'm sorry I upset you when I asked you not to insert yourself into our investigation, but I was very serious. It could cause us real problems. Give me some time to see what I can come up with before you do anything on your own, okay?"

I nodded. "I have no plans to get further involved. I'm not a detective."

"I'm glad to hear that." He pulled the door open. "Good-bye, Miss Miller."

I said good-bye, walked out the door and down the hall. When I stepped outside, I found a nearby bench and sat down. The entire time I'd been inside the building, I'd felt smothered, as if I couldn't catch my breath. I had to pray the police wouldn't rush to judgment and blame the thief they'd picked up in Hannah's neighborhood. Although it sounded like a nice way to wrap everything up, it wouldn't explain the flowers. Or my sister's conviction that the murders were somehow linked. After a few minutes, I got up and made my way to my car. Had my visit with Detective Sykes helped or hurt? I had no way of knowing, but at least he'd listened to me. I hoped we were one step closer to catching a murderer.

CHAPTER SEVEN

After leaving the police station, I drove to Hannah's small rental house. Her landlord had promised to meet me and let me in. Sure enough, as I pulled up, an older man got out of his car and waited for me on the sidewalk.

"You're Hannah's sister?" he asked as I walked toward him.

"Yes. Mr. Hanson?"

He nodded. "I sure am sorry about Hannah. She was a real nice person and a reliable renter. Wish all my renters were like her."

"Thank you."

He walked up the steps of the bungalow and unlocked the door. Then he handed me the keys. "You keep 'em. When you're done, you can leave 'em in the house. The back-door lock is busted. Seems the guy who broke in came through there. I put a temporary latch on it. If you'd pull that latch

before you leave out the front, I'd appreciate it." He shook his shaggy gray head and
sighed. "You and Cicely take all the time
you need to get Hannah's stuff moved out.
I'm not in any hurry."

"That's very kind of you. We'll pack up
what we can tomorrow. I'm concerned
about the furniture though. We'll have
Cicely's bedroom furniture picked up and
delivered, but the rest of it will probably
have to be sold."

He thought for a moment. "Look, why
don't you let me put whatever is left in storage for you. I have plenty of room. That way
you can deal with it when you're ready. If
you still want to sell it, I'll help you. I've got
connections to local used furniture stores.
I'll call 'em up and see what they can do for
you."

Tears filled my eyes at his kindness.

"Aw, I didn't mean to make you cry." He
blinked several times, obviously emotional
too. He reached over and patted my shoulder. "She was a real special lady. If you're
her sister, I know you are too. You and that
little girl will be fine." He sniffed a couple
of times and wiped his face on the sleeve of
his coat. "You have my number. You call me
if you need anything."

I nodded. "Thank you so much, Mr. Hanson. I really appreciate it."

He turned and started to go down the steps, but then he stopped and swung back around. "I should warn you. I hired some folks to clean the place up some. But there's still a few stains on the carpet. I woulda cleaned it up more, but I had a water pipe bust in another house and couldn't get over here in time. There's all kinds of cleaners under the kitchen sink. Carpet cleaner too. I'm sorry I couldn't take care of it for you."

"I understand. I'll be fine."

As I went inside the house, I was grateful I hadn't brought Cicely straight home from Cora's. Truthfully, I wasn't certain bringing her here at all was a good idea, but neither was keeping her away. At least this way she could choose the things she wanted to bring with her. And I hoped it would give her some closure. Help her say good-bye.

It felt odd to enter Hannah's house for the first time. Hannah and Cicely had always come to Sanctuary to visit me, but I'd never made the trip to Kansas City because I didn't own a car. Janet had offered to let me use hers, but I'd been concerned she might need it. Hannah had told me it was easier for them to come to me, so I hadn't worried about it. Now I felt a little guilty.

The front door opened into a small but inviting living room. Hannah's personality was obvious. Framed pictures of her and Cicely adorned the fireplace mantel. I found a photo of Mom, Dad, Hannah, and me taken about a year before they died. I had no pictures of us, so I picked it up and put it inside a tote bag I'd brought with me. Although the living room and connecting dining room were in order, there was something that looked like dust covering almost everything. I realized it must be some kind of chemical used to capture fingerprints.

As I headed toward the dining room, I saw a large brown stain on the carpet. Someone had tried to clean it, but it was still visible. Too visible. I stood there for a while, staring at it. Hannah had died here, on this very spot. Even though I knew it would be hard to see the place where she'd breathed her last breath, the reality overwhelmed me, and I sank to the floor. For some reason, touching the stain made me feel closer to her. As I cried, it was as if she stood next to me, her hand on my shoulder, telling me everything would be okay.

"I'll take good care of Cicely," I whispered. "I promise. She will always know she's loved."

I finally got up, determined to get the

house and carpet looking as normal as possible before Cicely came home. After taking my coat off, I went to the kitchen and found the cleaners under the sink that Mr. Hanson had mentioned.

I scrubbed the carpet until the stain was almost invisible. Then I set about to clean the weird white dust off everything else. Warm water with a little dish detergent seemed to do the trick. By the time I finished, I was exhausted, but the house looked passable. Cicely's room was a little messy, but I left her things alone. My first instinct was to straighten up, but something told me she would want to find her room the way she left it.

I finally gathered the nerve to go into Hannah's room. Her clothes were hanging on a hook by the closet, obviously set out for the next day. Her bed was unmade. It appeared as if she'd heard a noise and gone to the living room to investigate. I walked over to a drawer in her nightstand that was pulled open. What had she grabbed before she faced her attacker? There were some papers in the drawer, a bottle of pain reliever, some keys, a pad of paper, and several pens. I looked in her closet and found a large, empty file box. I put it on the bed and began dumping things into it. The papers and the pad of paper from the drawer, and all the papers and files in her desk. I found another file box toward the back of the closet that was full of more papers and large envelopes. I pulled it out and put it next to the other box. I wondered if the file from the reporter was in one of these boxes. I didn't have time to look through everything now, but if possible, I wanted to find that file before I left town. On Hannah's desk there was a card file with bill information. I added it to the first box.

I'd decided to check the closet again when I noticed something sitting on a chair in the corner. When I realized what it was, I knelt down in front of it as tears rolled down my cheeks and dripped onto my shirt. My stuffed blue bunny. It was the last birthday gift I'd ever gotten from my parents, and I loved it more than anything I'd ever owned. All through the time we'd lived with my aunt and then Mrs. Johnson, I'd kept it close to me. It was a reminder of Mom and Dad. When Hannah and I found out we were going in different directions from the children's home, Hannah had been inconsolable.

"I'm supposed to take care of you," she'd said through her tears. "How can I do that if we're apart?"

"But we're sisters," I'd told her. "They won't do that." I'd handed her my bunny, Mr. Whiskers. "You keep him until we're back together. It will help you to believe."

The truth was that I'd been so afraid of losing her that somehow in my childlike mind I'd been convinced that if she had Mr. Whiskers, she'd have to return him to me. At that moment, without realizing it, I'd not only lost my sister but also my beloved stuffed bunny.

"I knew she'd bring you back," I whispered to him. Hannah had kept him in great shape. He looked almost exactly the way he had when I'd given him to her all those years ago. I picked him up and nuzzled him. My tears made his fake fur damp. Mr. Whiskers had been my best friend and confidant when I was a little girl, and if I'd ever needed him, I needed him now. Maybe crying over an old stuffed animal made me look immature and ridiculous, but at least for now, I found his presence comforting. It was as if Hannah were saying, "You keep him until we're back together again, Sarah. It will help you to believe."

I put Mr. Whiskers back on the chair and gathered myself together. Before I got up I noticed something on the floor, partially hidden by the bedspread. I reached over and picked it up. A single white orchid. Dead and shriveled. How had it gotten in the bedroom? I put it on the side table next to the bed. Then I got up and delved deeper into the closet. As I searched the upper shelf, I found a locked metal box shoved in the back. After taking it down, I decided to see if any of the keys in the drawer opened it. I sat down on the bed and tried sliding key after key into the lock. Finally I found one that fit, turned it, and the lock popped open. I gasped when I looked inside. A package of bullets. Hannah's letter came back to me. She'd armed herself because she really was afraid. Why hadn't she just gone to the police? Paul had asked the same question, and I couldn't answer it. If I'd been threatened, especially if I had a child, I would have contacted the authorities immediately. What was Hannah thinking? If she'd called the police, would she still be alive?

Suddenly, I remembered something. Sykes hadn't mentioned finding Hannah's gun. Tomorrow I'd call him and ask about it. A missing gun seemed like an important detail. Could that be why the drawer to the nightstand was open?

After going through Hannah's bills, I called the credit card companies, informed them of her death and told them her cards had been stolen. They gave me a list of things I'd need to do, including sending them copies of the death certificate. I was happy to find that no charges had been made since the cards were taken. If a thief actually had made off with them, it seemed to me he would have tried to exploit them by now. Of course, if the police actually had their man, it would make sense. He couldn't very well use Hannah's cards from jail. Sykes hadn't mentioned finding them on their suspect. Had he ditched them?

After I got off the phone, I carried out all the boxes and put them in the trunk of my car. I felt I should at least look through them before picking Cicely up in case there was something else I needed to do before we left in the morning. The amount of phone calls and paper work that stretched out in front of me seemed overwhelming. It would take a while to complete it all. Before leaving, I checked the house one last time. I found a couple of photo albums in a chest at the foot of Hannah's bed and grabbed those too. Although I didn't want Cicely to think I was stealing things from her home, I removed the framed pictures from the mantel and loaded those into my tote bag. After I made what was supposed to be my last trip from the house, I went back one more time and got Mr. Whiskers. There was no way I was leaving him behind.

After locking up the house, I drove to a nearby motel. Staying at Hannah's would have cost less, but I just couldn't do it. I knew I'd never be able to sleep. Fortunately, I was able to park right next to my room, so carrying in my suitcase and the boxes with Hannah's belongings was easy. Once I was settled in, I called Janet.

"I'm so happy to hear from you," she said. "I've had you on my mind and in my prayers all day long."

I told her about my meeting at the police station and then my time at Hannah's house.

"I'm sure that was difficult," she said. "I'm proud of you, Sarah. You're handling all of this with great strength."

"If you'd seen me collapsed on Hannah's floor, bawling like a baby, you wouldn't say that."

"Crying helps, honey. It's God's gift to help us get our feelings out. You cry all you want."

I grunted. "Not sure any of us could handle that."

"Well, I'm getting ready to welcome you and Cicely home."

"I can't thank you enough, Janet. If you weren't in my life —"

"I expect you'd do just fine. But I'm honored to be here for you, honey. I thank God every day that He brought us together."

"Hey, what do you know? We're thanking God for the same things."

"Thanks, sweetheart. By the way, Paul called today to see how you're doing."

"He did? Maybe I should have called him, but . . ."

"But what?"

I sighed. "I don't want to impose on him. He's already done so much."

"I don't think you'd be imposing on him. He's legitimately concerned about you."

"He's a very nice man."

"Yes, he is," Janet agreed.

"I plan to pick up Cicely in the morning, take her home, and help her pack. Then we'll get on the road. I'll call you when we're ready to leave."

"Sounds good. I fixed up the spare room, and I think it looks very nice. When her furniture gets here, we can put the other stuff in the basement. But for now, I think she'll be quite comfortable."

I told her about Mr. Hanson's offer to store Hannah's furniture and then said good-bye. After taking a quick shower, I riffled through some of Hannah's papers but decided to look at them more in the morning, since I couldn't keep my eyes open.

After falling into bed, I started dreaming. I stood in a field full of ripening corn. As I gazed around me I realized it was actually a corn maze. In front of me were two paths. One led to my left, the other to my right. The path to the right was clear. The corn had been pressed down flat, and I could see light shining on the path, as if it led to a way out. The other path was full of broken ears of corn that blocked my way. I could only see a few feet past the entrance because the pathway was dark. Although I couldn't see her, I could hear Hannah's voice.

"Take the easy way, Sarah. Please. We're all fine."

She didn't mention Mom and Dad, but I knew she was referring to them. I tried to explain to her that I couldn't walk away. That I had to know the truth, but just as soon as I opened my mouth, her presence was gone. I felt as if I were being drawn toward the left path even though another part of me yearned to go right. I woke up gasping for breath. When I looked at the clock I realized it was almost time to get up. I stared up at the ceiling. Today would be extremely emotional. I prayed for the strength to get through it.

"Please, God, help me today. Give me the right words to say to Cicely. Let her know she's loved, and that she'll be all right."

I stared at the ceiling for a while longer, and then sat up on the side of the bed. The curtains were open a crack, and I could see flakes of snow falling. After getting out of bed, I pushed the curtain all the way open. The snowfall was light, but I wondered if we were in for a storm that would make it hard to get home. The remote control for the TV was on the stand next to the bed. I turned it on and changed the channel until I found local news and weather. The announcer was talking about a murder on the city's south side. From there he switched to a gang shooting. I couldn't help but shiver at the violence in Kansas City and feel grateful for Sanctuary. Not sure how long it would be until the weather segment, I'd just decided to find my brush and work on my hair when the announcer mentioned a house fire in south Kansas City. Then they switched to video of the fire. I cried out and sunk back down on the bed as I watched a house partially engulfed in flames.

It was Hannah's.

CHAPTER EIGHT

"Oh, Sarah. What will you do now?"

All morning I'd been trying to stay calm, but hearing Janet's voice ignited a sudden rush of homesickness. I felt out of my depth in Kansas City. First Hannah's death, and now I was suddenly responsible for a young girl who'd just lost her mother. How would I find the words to tell her that her home was gone too? That all of her belongings were nothing more than ash?

"I called the landlord and talked to him. He told me fire-fighters pulled out some furniture, but it was water soaked and probably beyond saving. He offered to help me go through what was left if I wanted to look, but there's not much hope of retrieving anything else. The house is a total loss."

"Are you going?"

"I think I have to. How can I walk away without making sure there's nothing salvageable? Don't I owe it to Cicely?"

"I suppose so. Closing down Hannah's accounts and contacting creditors is going to be very difficult without a paper trail."

"Actually, I removed almost all her papers last night when I cleaned the house," I said.

"Well, that's a huge blessing."

"Yes, it is. I guess God knew I'd need them. Oh, Janet, what am I going to say to Cicely?"

"Just tell her the truth, honey. I'll be praying for you. For both of you."

"Thank you. I'm really going to need your prayers."

"So when will you come home?"

"I plan to drive back today as scheduled unless something comes up that keeps me here. I don't see why the fire would change my plans. Since it's a rental house, the landlord will probably be the person who takes care of the details."

"All right. You'll get through this, honey. You're not alone."

"I know. Thank you, Janet. See you soon."

"I love you, Sarah."

"I love you too."

After hanging up, I sat on the bed thinking. Cicely couldn't learn about the fire from someone else. I had to be the one to tell her. Picking up the phone again, I called Cora and asked her to keep Cicely away

112

from the TV. Cora was saddened to hear about the house and promised she'd keep Cicely from finding out about it until I could tell her.

Then I called Mr. Hanson and arranged to meet him at eleven. It would be very hard to see the charred remnants of Hannah's house, but I thanked God I'd gotten the papers, the photographs, and Mr. Whiskers safely out.

After talking to Mr. Hanson, I called Detective Sykes and was grateful when he immediately answered his phone. He seemed stunned to hear about the fire.

"Do they know how it started?" he asked.

"According to the landlord, it's way too early. He mentioned there had been a problem with the wiring and wondered if the electrician he'd hired had done something wrong."

Sykes was silent for a moment. In all the craziness of the last few hours, I hadn't realized that the fire might not have been an accident.

"You think someone set the fire on purpose?"

"I don't know," he said slowly. "I'd need some kind of proof to make that leap. It could take weeks to determine the cause. I'll contact the investigator in charge and ask to see the report when it's completed."

"Thanks," I said. "At least I got out all the important paper work."

"That's good. If you find anything helpful in her papers, let me know, okay?"

"I haven't had time to go through them. If I find the file that belonged to that reporter, I'll have to mail you copies from Sanctuary."

"Sounds good," Sykes said, "but don't worry about it for now."

"Actually, I have a question about something I found in Hannah's house yesterday." I told him about finding the drawer open next to Hannah's bed and the metal box with the bullets. "Do you have Hannah's gun?"

"No. It wasn't on the list of items removed from the house."

"Then the killer must have taken it," I said. "Did the man you picked up have it?"

"No, but he had plenty of time to ditch it. We'll certainly look for it. We just brought him in, so it will take some time for us to do a thorough investigation."

"I hope you won't focus solely on him," I said.

"Frankly, the missing gun makes this look even more like a burglary," Sykes said. "Why would someone who was targeting your sister spend time going through drawers? And why would he steal a gun?"

"I think Hannah heard a noise, grabbed her gun, and went out to the living room. She was afraid, Detective. I'm sure she had that gun for protection."

"Okay. So why would he take it?" Sykes sighed. "Probably either to sell or to use in his next break-in."

"Maybe."

"Look, Miss Miller, we'll keep an eye open for it. That's all we can do."

It was my turn to get exasperated. "How will you identify it? Do the bullets tell you what kind of gun it was?"

There was silence for a moment. "Sorry," he said finally. "Just looking through the report. In this case, the bullets help us narrow it down, but they don't tell us the exact model or make. And without the bullets themselves, if the gun is used, there's no way to say for certain it's your sister's gun."

"I'm certainly not an expert on guns," I said, "but isn't there some kind of, I don't know, license or something Hannah had to get to buy it?"

"Not in Missouri. Not unless she intended to carry it with her," Sykes said. "There should be a record of the sale though. We'll check it out."

I sighed. "I'm sorry. I know you're doing everything you can. I'm just frustrated."

"We're working the case, but it will take time. Don't give up on us. When do you plan to head home?"

"I intend to leave today. I don't know why I'd need to stay any longer, but with the fire, I guess that could change."

"I'll call you in a few days, after you've had time to get your niece settled. I hope by then I'll have some information for you. Is this number you gave me the only number I can use to reach you?"

"Yes, it's Janet's number."

"Do you have her phone with you?"

"No, it's a land line. In Sanctuary."

"Have you ever considered getting a cell phone? You're really doing things old school."

"Everyone I know is in Sanctuary, Detective. I don't need a cell phone. Or at least I didn't until recently. Once all this is over, and I'm home, I can talk to anyone I want to face-to-face — or on our home phone. Makes a cell phone kind of useless."

"I see your point," he said. "I guess life in a small town is a lot different than it is in Kansas City."

"Yes, and I'm thankful. This place isn't for me. Give me the peace and quiet of

Sanctuary."

"Every town has its challenges, Miss Miller. Evil can erupt anywhere."

"Maybe so, but I know I feel safer at home than I do here."

"Well, good-bye for now."

I hung up, called the front desk, and asked if I could stay another night if I needed to. Once I explained the situation, the manager assured me I could remain as long as I wanted. And if I decided to head home later today or tonight, I wouldn't be charged for an extra day. I thanked her for her thoughtfulness.

I dressed quickly and drove to Hannah's house. As I neared her street, two large fire trucks drove past me. When I pulled up in front of the ruins of my sister's home, I discovered another fire truck parked across the street. Mr. Hanson was standing in front of the damaged structure. Part of the house was still standing, but the roof had caved in and two sides of the building had partially collapsed. I got out of the car and met Mr. Hanson on the sidewalk.

He held out his hand, and I took it. "I'm so sorry," he said. "After everything you and Cicely have been through, this is just so awful."

"Thank you," I said. "But it's your loss too."

He shook his head. "I have insurance that will take care of everything." He frowned. "Hannah had renters' insurance, by the way. You should be able to get some money to help you take care of things you'll have to replace." He stared at the smoldering remains. "I guess all of Hannah's records are gone now, but I know her insurance agent. I recommended him when she moved in. At least I can point you in the right direction."

I was hopeful Hannah's policy was somewhere in the papers I had, but just in case I thanked him. Any information Mr. Hanson could give me would be helpful.

"Why is the fire department still here?" I asked. "It looks like the fire is completely out."

"They keep an eye on things just in case something ignites and starts the fire again. It's policy. After a while they'll leave, but they'll come back to check off and on throughout the day. Maybe tomorrow as well."

"You said on the phone that the fire may have been caused by a problem with the wiring?"

He nodded. "Seems like too much of a coincidence that we just had some wiring replaced a week ago and then the house catches on fire." He rubbed his chin with his hand, a thoughtful look on his face. "Does seem a little out of character for my electrician though. His work has always been so good. Don't see how he could have made such a huge mistake. 'Course, electricity is electricity. Can't always trust it. It will do whatever it wants to do."

I nodded and gazed around the yard. "So there's nothing I can salvage from the fire?" Mr. Hanson's assessment on the phone looked accurate. It was clear almost everything Hannah owned was gone, destroyed in the fire's rage.

He sighed. "I went through almost everything before you got here. Pulled a few things to the side, but the rest of it . . . Well, if it isn't burned, it's been pretty much waterlogged." He pointed toward a pile near the neighbor's driveway. "You can rummage through it, but I don't think you'll find anything you'll want to take with you."

It appeared that most of what remained came from the kitchen. If it wasn't broken, it was black with smoke. I'd told Mr. Hanson as much when I noticed something shiny a few inches away from my shoe. I bent down to pick it up and found a refrigerator magnet with the words *I Am With You*

printed on it. Below that was *Isaiah 43:2.*
The blue magnet with the silver lettering
was in excellent condition. Odd with the
state everything else was in. I slid it into my
purse.

"I don't see anything worth taking," I told
Mr. Hanson. "I really hate that Cicely lost
all her possessions. It will be devastating to
her."

Mr. Hanson snapped his fingers. "Where
is my brain? I'd completely forgotten about
Hannah's car."

I stared at the red Honda parked across
the street. "I did too. It will take some time
for me to get the title transferred, but maybe
I can sell it."

"Yes, that's true, but I'm talking about all
the stuff Hannah loaded into the trunk."

"Loaded into the trunk? I don't understand."

He crossed his arms and stared at me. "I
drove by last week and found her carrying
boxes to her car. I stopped and asked her if
she was trying to skip out on the rent. She
laughed and told me I knew her better than
that. Said she was taking some things to The
Salvation Army. It might be too late, but we
can sure look. Might be old clothes, but if
some of them belong to Cicely, it's better
than nothing."

I felt a little guilty knowing that Hannah had lied to Mr. Hanson. From her letter, I knew she was getting ready to leave town. However, I felt certain she would have tried to treat her kind landlord fairly.

"I'm sorry. I don't have copies of her car keys," I said.

"Maybe you don't, but I do!" he said with vigor. "She gave me one in case she locked herself out. Which she did more than once." He pulled a large key ring out of his jacket pocket and began to sort through it.

"Thank you for helping her," I said. "I'm relieved to know she had such a good friend in her life."

"You're welcome. My wife kept an eye on her too. Hannah reminded us of our second daughter, Becky."

I was touched to see how much he'd cared for my sister. I wondered if she had any other good friends. She'd never mentioned anyone she was close to. I still hadn't decided what to do about a funeral. I wanted to have some kind of service in Kansas City, but there wasn't time to do anything about it now. Cicely was my first priority. A local funeral home would get Hannah's body sometime in the next few days. Maybe I could set up a viewing in Kansas City and then have them ship her to

Sanctuary so we could bury her nearby. I figured it would be easier for Cicely if she had a grave to visit — a place where she could remember her mother.

"Here it is!" Mr. Hanson exclaimed finally. "Let's see if there's still something in the trunk that will help you."

I followed him over to the car and waited for him to open it. He unlocked the driver's-side door and pushed on the button that unlocked the trunk. I quickly scanned the inside of the car, wondering if Hannah had stashed anything there, but it was empty except for a few CDs. I scooped them up and put them in my purse. Then I checked the glove compartment. Just the car's registration, an owner's manual, and some napkins and condiment packages from a fast-food restaurant. I closed the small door and walked around to the back of the car, where Mr. Hanson pulled the trunk open. Inside were several boxes and two large plastic bags. I opened the bags and almost cried when I found clothes. Obviously, they were Cicely's.

"How wonderful," I said, choking up some. "At least Cicely didn't lose everything."

"Let me help you carry this stuff," Mr. Hanson offered.

Within a few minutes all the things from Hannah's trunk had been transferred to my car.

"Would you like me to keep the car at my place until you decide what to do with it?" he asked.

"That would be wonderful." I put my hand on his arm. "I honestly don't know how to thank you for everything."

He patted my hand. "You just take good care of that young lady. And maybe after things settle down, you could call me once in a while and let me know how you're both doing?"

I nodded. "You can count on it." After a quick hug, I said good-bye and got into my car, checking a map for directions to Cora's. Looked like I could get there without driving directly through busy Kansas City traffic. My years in Sanctuary had softened me to large, hectic cities. It took me about twenty minutes to find Cora's house. It was a nice two-story home in a lovely neighborhood. I parked the car and hurried to the front door. After I rang the bell, the door was opened by a pleasingly plump older woman with gray hair and a lovely smile.

"You must be Sarah," she said. "Please come in."

I stepped into a well-kept home with

comfortable furniture. Two small, friendly mixed-breed dogs ran up to me, wagging their tails. I leaned down to pet them.

"Meet Mutt and Jeff," Cora said. "The children love them. Pets make a home friendlier, don't you think?"

"I agree. We have a golden retriever named Murphy. He thinks he owns the house." I smiled. "I think he may be right."

"Cicely certainly loves animals. I'm so glad she'll have a dog." She reached out a hand. "May I take your coat?"

"Thank you." I slid it off and handed it to her.

"Why don't you have a seat? I thought maybe we'd talk a minute before Cicely comes downstairs. Is that all right?"

I nodded. "I think that's a great idea. Thank you."

I sat down in a comfortable overstuffed chair while Cora hung up my coat in the hall closet. "How about a cup of coffee?" she asked.

"That sounds wonderful. I'm chilled to the bone."

"I'll be right back."

Cora hurried from the room. It gave me a moment to look around a bit more. The living room looked lived in. It was clean and neat, but there were signs that children lived here. Scuff marks from little shoes were on the wooden frame of the couch. A stuffed animal's arm peeked out from underneath a chair. The coffee table had been cleaned, but it was obvious a child had not only colored outside the lines, he'd actually missed the paper. The house felt peaceful and good. Once again, I thanked God Cicely had found Cora.

"Here we are." Cora came in with two cups of coffee on a small tray. "I brought sugar and cream in case you use it." She smiled as she set the tray down on the coffee table. "I've got regular cream and my favorite pumpkin spice creamer. It's so good."

"Thank you." Although I usually drank my coffee black, I poured a little of the pumpkin spice creamer into my cup. A quick sip made me grateful I'd tried it. It was delicious.

"Cicely is packed and ready to go," Cora said, "but I wanted to talk to you before she leaves. Losing a parent is so traumatic. And in her case, since her mother was the only person she had, it's even worse. She wants to live with you because you're her only relative, but she's still frightened. Although she knows you, you two haven't had a lot of time to bond. It might be rough for both of you for a while."

I nodded. "She's lived in this city her entire life. She'll be leaving behind her friends, everything that's familiar to her." I sighed. "We were building a relationship, but as you say, we don't really know each other very well yet. If it were possible, I'd stay here with her. At least for a while. But it just won't work. I don't have much money, and my job is in Sanctuary. I have no choice but to take her home with me."

"I know that. And in her heart she knows it too. But don't be surprised if she acts resentful. You'll want her to appreciate you. Realize that you care deeply for her and that you want to give her a good home, but she probably won't feel that way for a while. Even though you're her rescuer, she has to find some way to release her pain and anger. You may be the recipient of most of those emotions. Just don't be hurt. Be patient and steadfast. No matter what she does, don't let it throw you."

"I understand."

Cora frowned. "I'm not sure you do. That's why I wanted to prepare you."

I took a sip of coffee and then put my cup down on the table. "You don't know my history, do you?"

Cora shook her head and frowned. "Your

history? I'm sorry. I don't understand."

"My parents were murdered when I was six. I spent the rest of my childhood being shuffled from one foster home to another. Although my sister, Cicely's mother, was finally adopted, I never was. When I say I understand how Cicely feels, I'm not being flippant. I truly do."

To my surprise, Cora's eyes grew shiny with tears. "You poor thing," she said. "I'm so sorry."

I shook my head. "Water under the bridge now. I have a wonderful life in Sanctuary with dear friends. Everything turned out great for me, and I'm believing the same will happen for Cicely."

"I'll be praying for the same thing," Cora said. "She's such a sensitive child. Very compassionate. I've found that sometimes the children who care deeply for others have a harder time adjusting. I'm not sure why, but I wonder if their ability to feel actually makes it more difficult for them. Hopefully, it won't be that way for Cicely."

"Were you able to keep the news about her house from her?" I asked, taking another sip of coffee.

"What about my house?"

I jumped, almost spilling my coffee. Cora

and I turned to see Cicely standing on the stairs, staring at us.

CHAPTER NINE

Telling Cicely about the fire was incredibly tough. Although she didn't cry, she looked like someone had punched her in the face. To be honest, I couldn't be sure she actually accepted what I'd told her. She was relieved to hear that many of her things were found in Hannah's car. I had no idea if she knew her mother had planned to leave Kansas City, and I didn't bring it up. The last thing I wanted her to know was that her mother thought they might be in danger.

"Do you want to stay in Kansas City tonight, or would you rather head to Sanctuary?" I asked her.

"I guess there's no reason to stay here anymore," she said. "Everything's gone."

The look on her face wreaked havoc on my already battered emotions. "Then let's get going. I know Janet can hardly wait to see you. She's fixed up a nice room that I'm sure you'll like."

Cicely didn't respond; she just nodded.

"Wait a minute," Cora said as we prepared to leave. She ran upstairs and then came down with a small bag. "I put some extra clothes and things in here for you." She handed the bag to Cicely. Then Cora reached into the pocket of her jeans and pulled out several sparkly blue hair clips. She smiled at Cicely. "I know you love these. I want you to have them. Maybe when you wear them, you can think of me."

Cicely held out her hand and took them. Then she wrapped her arms around the kind older woman. "Thank you," she whispered. "I won't forget you."

After saying a final good-bye to Cora, we got into the car and started for home. I hadn't driven very far before Cicely suddenly asked to see her house.

"I don't know if that's a good idea," I said. "Wouldn't you rather remember it the way it was?"

"It's *my* house, not yours. I want to see it."

Although her tone was sharp, the look in her eyes broke my heart. Against my better judgment, I turned around and drove back to the house. No one was there this time, so I pulled up right in front.

"I'm so sorry this happened, Cicely," I

said gently. "As I told you back at Cora's, your mother had already removed some of your things, so you haven't lost everything."

"Yes, I have," she said in a small voice.

"Honey, I know it might seem hard to believe, but things will get better. You're not alone. I'm here for you and Janet is too. You like Janet, don't you?"

She nodded. "She's nice."

"She's worked hard on your room. I really think you'll like it."

"I want my own room. And my own things."

"I know. If I could give them to you, I would. All I can do is tell you that eventually, the room at Janet's will feel like yours. And we'll buy you whatever else you need."

She turned to glare at me. "I need my mom."

I could feel her frustration but knew I couldn't take it personally. *Stay steady. Don't react.* "Cicely, we have a long and difficult road ahead of us, but we'll make it. I promise." I reached over and smoothed her hair. As I gazed at her, I saw myself. She even looked like me. Although her hair wasn't quite as red as mine, more of a strawberry blond, she had my freckles. Hannah had been blond, with perfect skin. She could have been a model. But Cicely and I

131

had inherited my mother's coloring. Even though I found my looks troubling, I could remember my handsome father telling my mother that she was the most beautiful woman in the world. It had always given me hope that someday I would be beautiful too.

Cicely pulled away from me. "I want to get out and look around."

It was getting a little late, and I really wanted to get on the road, but I decided it was best to let her face the reality of what had happened. I hoped it might help her to move on.

"All right," I said, "but you can't get too close. It's not safe."

She didn't respond, just opened her door and walked over to the sidewalk.

I left the engine running so the car would stay warm and followed her as she made her way into the yard.

"Isn't there anything left?" she asked, her voice so soft I could barely hear it.

"I'm sorry, honey," I said. "I went through it and so did Mr. Hanson. But I think you'll be happy to see what's in the boxes and bags in the trunk. I also took some pictures. We'll go through everything together when we get home."

"It's not my home."

"It will be." I sighed. "Look, Cicely. I realize how hard this is. I'm only trying to help. I loved your mother. She was my sister."

"If you loved her so much, then where were you all this time?" she fired back. "You weren't around when my mom needed you."

I frowned at her. "You know the answer to that. It wasn't my choice to be separated from your mother."

Even though she was ten years old, at that moment, Cicely seemed much younger. A look of defiance came over her, and she put her hands on her hips. "Mom didn't believe you, you know. She told me you didn't really want her in your life. That you could have found her a long time ago if you'd really wanted to."

At first, Cicely's pronouncement knocked the breath out of me. Had Hannah really believed that? But it was impossible. Sealed adoption records kept me from locating my sister, and a lack of information from my last foster home had left Hannah's search at a dead end until she located Janet's friend. There was only one reason Cicely would say those things to me. The realization made me feel like crying.

"That's not true, Cicely, and you know it." I put my hands on her shoulders and felt her tremble. Resentment flashed in her eyes. "Look, maybe you think I'm only taking you in because I have to. It's not true. You have my word. We're family, Cicely. We belong together. The same blood runs in our veins. When I look at you, I see myself. I see your mother. I loved her, and I love you too, honey. Can you understand that?"

She shook her head. "All I had was my mother and now she's gone."

"No. You had me from the moment you were born. You're a part of me, and you always will be." I gazed deeply into her eyes. "Things will change, but eventually, you'll be okay, Cicely. You have my word."

She wrestled away from me, tears streaming down her face. "I'll never be happy without my mom. Never."

I took a step back and stared at her. "I said the same thing after my parents died, but you know what? Life kept happening. The sun came up and went down. Every day I survived. Some days were good, and some were bad, but I kept breathing. Kept living. Then one day, something wonderful happened. Someone reached out and loved me. It changed everything. It took me a long time to find that person, but you don't have to wait like I did. I'm right here."

Cicely gazed at the remains of her home, grief etched in her childish features. "I feel like I'm leaving my mom behind."

"This was just a building, honey. A few rooms. Nothing more than a shell. What you loved in this house is still inside you. Your mother isn't here," I said, pointing at the ruined structure. "She's in here." I put my hand over my heart. "And here." I reached over and lightly touched her chest. "No one can take her away from us. No one has the power to do that unless we let them. And I don't intend to allow that."

"I won't forget her?"

I shook my head. "No. Some memories will change. Fade. But you don't have to worry. I believe God protects every good memory, every bit of joy, every laugh you shared. You'll see your mom again, and everything you shared will be there waiting for you."

"How do you know?" she whispered.

"I just do." I knelt down in front of her. "But now we've got to start building a new life with new memories." I put my hand on her cheek. This time she didn't pull away. "I'm not your mother, Cicely, but I promise you that I'll do everything in my power to make you happy again. Please give me a chance. If you can't do it for me, or for yourself, do it for your mom. You know it's what she'd want for you."

Tears slid down her face as she reached out to me. I let her collapse into my arms. She cried for a little while, but as the cold air bit through our clothing, we had no choice but to finally head back for the warmth of the car. I'd just closed Cicely's door and was walking around to the other side of the car when a sedan pulled up across the street. Before I had a chance to open my door, someone got out. I was surprised to see Captain Bentley. After checking traffic, he walked over to where I stood shivering.

"Captain Bentley," I said. "I'm surprised to see you."

"I heard about the house and came by to see it myself. I'm so sorry, Sarah. It's hard to believe."

"It's very difficult. Even tougher for Hannah's daughter. She's lost her mother, and now a lot of her belongings are gone."

He nodded. A few flakes of snow danced around his head. "I want you to know that I'm taking a personal interest in your sister's death." He nodded toward the house. "And this. If this wasn't an accident, I'll find out." He looked intently into my eyes, and I was temporarily shocked by the depth of emotion I saw there. He possessed a charisma that made him seem much younger than he was. Something about him made me feel a little shy.

"I'd like to meet your niece," he said, "unless you don't think it's a good idea."

"I'm sure she'd love to meet you too." I pulled my door open and he peered inside the car. Cicely stared wide-eyed at him.

"Hi, Cicely," the handsome detective said. "I work for the police department, and I just wanted you to know that we're doing everything we can to find the person who hurt your mother. Your aunt has my number, so if either one of you need anything or have any questions, you can call me anytime you want to. Okay?"

Cicely nodded. "Thank you."

"You're welcome."

He straightened up. "I understand you live in a small town near St. Louis?"

"Yes. It's called Sanctuary."

He frowned. "That name sounds familiar . . ."

"A few months ago a young man who had been kidnapped as a child was found living there. It was in the news."

His expression showed that he recognized the reference. "Yes, I remember now. I believe the FBI is still investigating, trying to find other children that were taken by the same couple."

I nodded. "Our small town was overrun with news media for a while, but things have calmed down again."

He patted my shoulder. "Well, I hope you and Cicely will find some peace there." He shook his head. "Look, we have a fund for victims. I'd like to help replace some of the belongings you've lost. Cicely will need clothes and other things. You shouldn't have to shoulder all the cost."

"Thank you, but I think we'll be fine. My sister had renter's insurance, and thankfully, I was able to remove some stuff from the house last night. This morning we even found some of Cicely's clothes in my sister's car."

"Do you have all the information you need about the insurance?"

"I have a lot of my sister's papers. I haven't had time to go through all of them, but I'm certain the insurance information is in there somewhere. If it's not, the landlord knows Hannah's. But . . . thank you. I can't tell you how much your kindness means to me." My last words were a little shaky because my lips trembled from the cold.

"Oh, Sarah. You're freezing. I'm sorry." He grabbed my door and held it open. "You'd better get on your way. It's not supposed to snow much, but later today the highways could get slick."

I slid into the car, thankful for the warmth awaiting me. "Thank you again. Good-bye, Captain."

He smiled at both of us. "Good-bye. You'll both be in my thoughts and prayers."

He closed the door and went back to his car.

"I like him," Cicely said after I got into the car.

"Yes, I do too."

Cicely was quiet as we headed out of Kansas City. On the edge of town I stopped at a convenience store and bought coffee for me and hot chocolate for Cicely. I wanted to talk to her but felt she might need some time to think. I'd brought a few praise CDs with me and slid one into the CD player.

"Who's that?" she asked when the music started.

"It's a group called Selah. I love their music." I glanced quickly at her. "Do you like it?"

She nodded. "It's nice. Mom played music like this. Wish I would have listened to it more."

"Cicely, open my purse and look inside."

She looked at me strangely but did what I asked. When she saw the CDs I'd taken from Hannah's car, her face lit up. "Where did you get these?"

"They were in your car. I took them before Mr. Hanson and I moved the bags and boxes from your mom's car into my trunk."

"That's awesome, Aunt Sarah. I'm so glad."

"Would you like to play one of them?" I asked.

Cicely was quiet for a moment. "No," she said softly. "Not yet."

"I understand." And I did. I remembered our aunt asking us about going through our parents' things after they died. It took us a while to be able to look at them. She wisely kept everything locked away until we were ready. I really missed her. Sometimes I wondered how Hannah and I would have turned out had she lived. But thinking about that was useless. At least I could use some of Aunt Barbara's wisdom now to help Cicely.

"Are you going to keep my mother's car?" Cicely asked suddenly.

I shook my head. "I don't need a car in Sanctuary. Whenever I need to leave town, I can borrow Janet's."

Cicely looked confused. "But how will I get to school?"

I smiled at her. "I showed you and your mom the school when you visited the first time, remember? It's only about two blocks away from where we'll be living."

Cicely's eyes grew wide. "I'll be going to that little school?"

"Yes, and I'll be your teacher."

She considered this. "That sounds okay. Sometimes I hate my school. Some of the kids are mean."

"It will be different in Sanctuary."

"Why?" she asked, sounding perplexed.

"Well, students are taught to respect their teacher. And each other."

I felt her staring at me. "Really? How many kids are there?"

"We have almost thirty students now." I smiled at her. "Of course, once in a while one of them can be mean too, but it's taken care of quickly. We don't allow that."

"What do you do to them?"

"We sit them down and talk to them. Along with their parents. We remind them of what God says about walking in love. And then we pray together."

She looked confused. "And that works?"

"Yes. Almost every time."

Cicely shook her head. "Boy, I can't see that working at my school."

I shrugged. "You never know."

I waited while she chewed on that.

"So how does that sound?" I asked after a short pause.

"Pretty good. I don't like it when kids talk bad about their parents or treat the teacher mean. It makes me mad."

"It makes me mad too."

Except for small talk and a stop for burgers, that was about it for conversation on our way to Sanctuary. As the miles slipped away behind us, I prayed that God would give us strength for the days ahead.

CHAPTER TEN

The next couple of weeks passed by in a blur. Although I'd thought about having a viewing in Kansas City for Hannah's friends, in the end I decided against it. A woman named Claire, who worked with Hannah, offered to hold a memorial at her church. She took care of all the details and told me I wasn't expected to attend.

"You take care of Cicely," she said. "I'll send you both some remembrances from the service."

I was very grateful to her and accepted her offer. Trying to figure out everything with the insurance companies, contacting all of Hannah's creditors, getting Cicely's school records, working with the funeral home, arranging a funeral in Sanctuary, and putting in a change of address was keeping me busy from morning to night.

Hannah's funeral was held at Agape, and Jonathon preached the service. He did an incredible job, and I know what he said touched and encouraged Cicely. The turnout was amazing. It was like the whole town took it upon themselves to give Hannah an unforgettable funeral. After the service, the women in Sanctuary held a dinner in the church dining hall. People went out of their way to greet Cicely and make her feel welcome. The people of Sanctuary made it clear that we were more than a town. We were a family.

Besides the renter's insurance policy, the human resources director from Hannah's job made sure I knew that there was also a small life insurance policy. It wasn't a lot, but it was more than enough to pay for transporting Hannah's body to Sanctuary, the cost for the funeral, and all of Hannah's final bills. In fact, there was enough left over that when things settled down, I could take Cicely furniture shopping for a bedroom suite that was more contemporary than the one she was currently using.

And we found most of Cicely's clothes in the boxes from Hannah's car. I finally asked Cicely if she knew why her mom had packed up so many of her things.

"I'm not sure," she said. "Mom mentioned we might go on a trip. I thought maybe we were coming to see you. She must have packed this stuff the day before . . ."

She didn't finish her thought, but I knew she meant the day before Hannah died. I had no intention of telling her the truth about Hannah's real plans. To do so meant I'd have to tell her about the letter, and I wasn't going to do that. Besides, although I felt there was a real reason for Hannah's suspicions, I had to admit to a seed of doubt, especially because of the man sitting in jail in Kansas City. If he proved to be Hannah's killer, my sister would look paranoid and unhinged. That wasn't the way I wanted Cicely to remember her mother.

The other boxes contained a mixture of things. Pictures, a couple of books, Hannah's clothes, makeup, more papers, a Bible, some jewelry, and a few other personal things. It was interesting to see what she planned to take and what she left behind. It was obvious these were the things she valued the most. I wondered about Mr. Whiskers. Had she planned to put him in the car too? I could only hope so.

My sabbatical was scheduled to end the first day of December. Including today, I only had four more days off. Reuben seemed to be holding his own in the classroom. I was a couple of months ahead in my lessons, so all he had to do was follow my plans. I'd walked over to the school a couple of times, and everything seemed to be going well. Cicely had elected to start school not long after we got back, and I was glad. It kept her busy instead of sitting around thinking about her mother. The other children were very kind to her, and she appeared comfortable in the smaller setting.

Paul had phoned to check on me since we'd gotten back, but I wanted to see him face-to-face, so I called to see if he had time to stop by. He seemed pleased to hear from me and agreed to come over. As I put the phone down, I thought about our relationship. I found myself wanting to see him more often, but I was afraid to tell him. What would he think?

When he arrived, I served us coffee in the living room. A fire crackled in the fireplace while we talked. I sat on the couch, my legs curled up beneath me, and Paul sat in the burgundy overstuffed chair. Murphy jumped up next to me and put his head in my lap.

I'd always felt peaceful in Janet's house and was secretly pleased to have moved back. I missed my cozy little apartment, but I was relieved to be at Janet's. She had gone out of her way to make Cicely's bedroom attractive. Although the first few nights were rough, now Cicely was sleeping better.

"So you told the detective about your parents' murder and about the orchids? How did he react?" Paul asked.

"He promised to look into it."

"You didn't tell him about me, did you?"

"I came close. I mentioned the flowers lying on top of Hannah before I realized it was something I shouldn't have known."

Paul's eyebrows shot up. "What did he say?"

"He asked me about it, but I covered it up. I told him I was just fishing for information."

Paul sighed and shook his head, his dark eyes troubled. "And he believed you?"

I shrugged. "He seemed to."

Maybe it was because I hadn't seen Paul for a while, but I was struck by how handsome he was. His kiss still lingered in my mind, and I found myself unconsciously touching my cheek.

I looked up to find him smiling at me. "You drifted away there for a moment. Everything okay?"

I nodded. "I guess. It's been tough. Dealing with Hannah's loss and adjusting to having Cicely in my life. It will take time, I guess."

"How's Cicely doing in school?"

"Pretty good. At least it's a distraction. She seems to appreciate the smaller class size. The school she attended in Kansas City was very large, and I think she felt a little lost. Besides, some of the other children were . . . rough. Although she tries to act tough, Cicely's a sensitive child. Easily bruised. The children here are very kind to her. I'm hoping she'll make friends. I think that would help her a great deal. She doesn't seem to have many friends in Kansas City. She has a cell phone, but she rarely gets a call, and when she does, she doesn't talk very long."

"Maybe she's on the phone more when you're not around."

I shrugged. "That's not impossible, but I don't think so. It seems to me that Cicely and Hannah spent almost all their time together. Neither one of them seemed to have developed close relationships in Kansas City."

"You have several Conservative Mennonite children in your class, don't you?"

"Yes. About half the class, although all the children are from Christian homes. Parents are reluctant to let their children go to the secular school in Barnes. It's actually a very good school, but they don't emphasize religion there. Because the Sanctuary

School is private, we can honor God in our curriculum. It's a good environment for Cicely. Hannah was a Christian, but I don't think she took Cicely to church a lot."

He frowned. "You're not Mennonite, are you?"

I shook my head. "No. I attend Sanctuary Mennonite Church some Sundays, but I'm a member of Agape Fellowship."

"Why do you visit the Mennonite church?"

"I guess it's because some of my students go there." I shrugged. "I enjoy both of the churches. The pastors are wonderful, and I like the people. I know Conservative Mennonites may seem a little strict to you, but I agree with many of their beliefs. One reason I love Sanctuary so much is because of the simplicity I find here. In my last foster home, the TV was on all the time. They never turned it off. Between all the yelling, kids running wild, and the constant noise from the television, I had very little time to study or to even think. It's quiet here. Peaceful. My life is very satisfying now. I wouldn't trade it for anything."

"I understand," Paul said. "I really do. My parents fought a lot while I was growing up. Especially after Randy died. When they divorced, at least the fighting was over, but the anger was never resolved. Taking the job with Sheriff Bradford and moving to Fredericktown gave me a chance to get away. To build the kind of life I want. My dad lives in Arizona and my mom lives in Iowa. And that's close enough for me. Besides, I love Missouri. If you want to enjoy life in the big city, you can drive to St. Louis. If you want to be out in the country, that's available too."

"I feel the same way." I smiled at him. "Paul, I want to thank you for everything you've done. You've been very kind."

"You're welcome, but I really haven't been much help yet, I'm afraid."

"I must admit I'm at an impasse. I don't know what to do next." I shook my head. "I want to trust Detective Sykes, but it's been two weeks, and I haven't heard from him. They have a lot of cases in Kansas City. Closing as many as they can is probably a high priority. I hope Hannah's murder doesn't fall through the cracks."

"On the phone you mentioned another police officer who took an interest in your case?"

"Yes. Captain Bentley. He was very nice. If Detective Sykes doesn't contact me soon, I might give the captain a call." I smiled. "That's one of the reasons I'm so grateful to you. You're the only one who seems really committed to uncovering the truth. I can't find my sister's killer by myself. I'm certainly not a detective. It will take someone smarter than me to find out what really happened."

Paul gave me an odd look. "You run yourself down quite a bit, Sarah. Why is that?"

Surprised by his comment, I shrugged. "I'm not trying to. I'm just telling the truth." I felt my face flush with embarrassment. "I . . . I don't know. Compared to my sister . . ."

"Why are you comparing yourself to your sister?" He leaned toward me. "Forgive me if this seems personal, but I have some experience in this area. I have another brother, Sam, who is tall and good-looking. He's also rich and successful, and people flock to him. I work as a deputy sheriff and live in a small town. I'm not the most handsome guy around, and frankly, I don't have that many friends. I used to feel like such a failure compared to him."

"But you have a wonderful job. You help people. Sometimes at the worst moments in their lives. And I think you're extremely handsome." Suddenly I realized what I'd said and put my hand up over my mouth.

My face felt hot enough to melt. I quickly stood to my feet. "If you don't mind, I need to . . . I've got to . . ."

Paul stood up and came over to me. He grabbed my hands, pulled me back down on the couch, and then sat next to me.

"I don't know you very well, Sarah, but I want to tell you what I see when I look at you. May I?"

I nodded dumbly, so mortified by my behavior all I wanted to do was run upstairs to my room.

"I see a woman who cares about children. A brilliant, compassionate teacher who makes a lasting difference in the lives of her students. Someone who didn't think twice about taking in her sister's child, even though it would completely change her life. Someone who is loyal and brave. And very, very attractive with beautiful red hair and deep hazel eyes. Unfortunately, she doesn't see herself this way, because when she looks in the mirror, all she does is compare herself to her sister." He sighed. "You're so unique, Sarah. God didn't want two Hannahs. He created one Hannah and one Sarah. He gave each one gifts and blessings. He didn't make one sister better than the other. He just made them different."

I wanted to stop him. Wanted to ask why

he'd say those things. I'd always felt I came up lacking when compared to Hannah. It wasn't that I was jealous. I was just . . . realistic.

"I don't mean to embarrass you," Paul said, letting go of my hands. "Maybe I've crossed the line here. If so, I'm sorry. It's just that I've been where you are. I wasted a lot of years under my brother's shadow. Years I can't get back." He smiled. "I love my job, and I love my life. Now that I can see things clearly, I realize I wouldn't want my brother's life even if I could have it. He may be successful, but he's been married three times. His job is so stressful he doesn't really enjoy it anymore. And he hardly ever sees his kids." Paul shook his head. "That's not what I want. And maybe, if you think about it, you may realize the same thing. That you'd never really consider trading your life for anyone else's."

"I don't know what to say," I said softly. "I'm sure you're right, but it's hard for me to see it. When we were placed in the children's home after our parents died, I overheard one of the women who worked there tell another staff member that she was afraid they couldn't place me because I was so plain." I shrugged. "You don't forget words like that."

Paul shook his head. "Yes, you do, Sarah. You forget them because they're wrong. I'm sure there was more to it than that."

"Maybe. I mean, it was hard for older kids to find homes. And I was incredibly shy. There were some couples who asked to meet me, but I didn't talk much. I'm sure that didn't help."

"I'll bet that was the main reason no one adopted you." He shook his head. "As you said, most people looking to adopt want babies or toddlers. Not sullen teenagers."

I understood what he was saying, but Hannah was six years older than me, and she'd been adopted.

I scooted back a bit on the couch. "Look, I really appreciate what you're trying to do, but I'd be much more comfortable if we could get back to talking about my sister's case."

Paul studied me for a moment. It made me uneasy, and I wondered if the friendship I thought we were developing was over.

"Okay," he said finally. "But if you ever want to talk . . ."

"I'll definitely let you know." I felt guilty saying that, since I had no intention of ever bringing the subject up again.

He got up and went back to the chair where he'd been sitting. "I'm trying to find

154

a way to help you, but I've looked into the case about as much as I can. I need more information. And by the way, anyone can be a detective, Sarah. It just takes a little common sense and a lot of determination. I'll keep working on my end, but I want you to do the same. If there's anything else to uncover, we can do it together."

"I'm not trying to solve my sister's murder," I said. "I just want to give the police a reason to look beyond the assumption that her death was the result of a burglary. Even if they have arrested someone. I'm afraid if they only look for a burglary suspect, they could miss the real killer. You understand that, right?"

"I heard about the man they have in jail. If they find evidence that connects him to Hannah's death, we'll have to let it go. I'm glad to hear you say you're willing to allow the police to do their jobs, because that's really all we can do." He took a sip of coffee and then put his cup down on the table. "Didn't you tell me you cleaned out some papers from your sister's desk?"

"Yes, but I haven't had a lot of time to go look at them. Trying to get Cicely settled and wrapping up my sister's business has taken almost every minute of my time."

"As soon as you can, why don't you sort

through her papers? We need more to go on. I'm not saying she knew the person who killed her, but usually murder is personal. The fact that Hannah was stabbed bothers me."

"Why?" I asked.

"Burglars usually carry guns. Mostly because they can use them to threaten their victims so they can make a getaway if they have to. Or if challenged, they'll pick up something that's handy to defend themselves. But not many thieves take a knife to a home they intend to rob. That speaks of premeditation. It doesn't point to a random burglary. According to the officer I spoke to, the knife didn't come from your sister's apartment, and it wasn't found at the scene. In my mind, killing her was his intention all along. I think the items that were stolen were taken just to throw off the police. You may not know this, but over seventy percent of all murders are committed by someone the victim knows. I think Hannah either knew her killer or knew the person behind the attack."

"Why do you see this but the police in Kansas City don't?" I asked, feeling bewildered.

Paul smiled. "You mean how can a small-town deputy sheriff be one step ahead of a big-city police department? First of all, Detective Sykes has probably seen the same things. Don't assume he hasn't just because he hasn't called you yet."

"I hope you're right. So far I haven't found anything that looks like a file from that reporter. What if it's not there?"

"We'll have to use whatever we've got. Look for names of people you don't know. Odd comments or notes. Anything that looks suspicious. If you come up with anything let me know. I'll see what I can do to follow up." He stood up again, this time picking up his hat. He ran his hand through his thick black hair before putting it back on his head. "Maybe it's time to talk to Wynter Evans, since she used to work in television news. She probably has some kind of connection I don't. Wynter might actually be able to get further with the police in Kansas City than I can. Even though I hope Detective Sykes is working hard on your case, we shouldn't put all our eggs in one basket. I would like to know what's really happening behind the scenes. If you hear from Sykes before you talk to Wynter, and he gives you cause to feel hopeful, then don't call her."

"All right." Wynter had been by a couple of times to check on us, and I'd been wanting to talk to her anyway. She understood childhood trauma, and I felt she was someone I could talk to about Cicely.

"We also really need to know more about the guy they arrested. Are they going to charge him with Hannah's murder or not?"

"I just hope he doesn't become a scapegoat. A way to close the case without looking for the truth." I thought for a moment. "Should I call Captain Bentley?"

Paul shook his head vigorously. "Not yet. As long as there's a chance Detective Sykes is working the case, I don't think we want to antagonize him by going over his head. Besides, Captain Bentley's got too much power. What if he shuts everything down? Contacting Bentley might open a door we may not be able to shut."

"You're right," I said slowly. "I have some time this afternoon. I'll start going through Hannah's personal papers with a fine-tooth comb. If I find anything interesting, I'll let you know."

"Good." Paul started for the front door but then stopped and turned around. "I don't suppose you've found Hannah's cell phone?"

"No. I went through her purse once, but I didn't see a phone. I'll look again. Why are you asking?"

"It might be good to see who she called. Find out who called her. Also check any text messages. Depending on what kind of phone she has, we might be able to check her e-mail. Whoever took her laptop may have been trying to hide something. I'd love to know what it was. And we should probably check to see if Hannah was on Facebook," Paul said. "It's possible we could learn something important. Find out who her friends were."

I shook my head. "I'm sorry. I don't have a Facebook account."

"That's okay. We'll take a look when I come back next time."

"Okay."

Paul paused for a moment with his hand on the doorknob, and I got the feeling he wanted to say something else. In the end he just said good-bye and left.

I sat on the couch for a while, thinking about what Paul had said concerning Hannah and me. It was easy for him to feel special because he was handsome, smart, and successful. Even in school, I'd been compared to my sister and had come up lacking. My parents had never treated me as less than Hannah, but it didn't make any difference. I knew they loved me, so I expected their approval. After Mrs. Johnson died, no one wanted me. It wasn't that I felt sorry for myself. I didn't. But I'd learned to face reality. Paul's comments were kind but misguided. Seeing myself unrealistically only brought pain. I was content knowing what I was — and what I wasn't.

I shook off our conversation and refocused on the situation with Hannah. Since I had some time to myself, I headed to the basement. We'd stored everything that belonged to Hannah downstairs until we decided what to do with it. It only took me a couple of minutes to find two boxes labeled Personal Papers. I carried them upstairs and placed them on the kitchen table. It was almost noon, so I fixed a sandwich and a glass of iced tea. As soon as I finished my lunch, I opened the first box.

Most of the papers inside were tax records and bills. I pulled several of them out, because I needed to make sure they had all been paid. One large envelope marked Important Records contained a list of Cicely's immunizations, information about Hannah's bank accounts, including her PIN number and account numbers. I'd been so busy paying off her bills and closing out her credit accounts, I still hadn't contacted her bank. She didn't have much money in either her checking or savings, but these accounts would still have to be closed.

After completely going through the first box, I put it down on the floor and picked up the second one. It was stuffed full of papers I'd quickly shoved inside when I was at Hannah's. This box was much more interesting. I found some personal letters and cards sent to Hannah by people I didn't know, but none of them were suspicious.

I also found some of Cicely's school papers and report cards clipped together. For the most part, the grades were good. They weren't spectacular, but none of them were lower than a C.

I put all the papers into stacks, trying to bring some order to the chaos. There were three more manila envelopes in the box, along with about a dozen loose papers.

Inside one of the manila envelopes I found a smaller envelope that contained birth certificates. I discovered Hannah's certificate and even a copy of mine. The next certificate I picked up was Cicely's. I looked at the space labeled Father, but it was marked Unknown. I stared at the box for a while, trying to figure out why Hannah was so committed to keeping Cicely's father a secret. No matter what Hannah told her daughter, someday she might want to know the identity of her father.

I also found Hannah's adoption papers. It was hard to look at them. Although I told myself I was happy she'd been adopted, it had always hurt that I'd been left behind. Hot tears filled my eyes, and I chided myself for being silly and childish. Maybe it took longer for me to find a home, but God was faithful, and I had everything I wanted. I put the papers back in the large envelope and continued on.

Among the loose papers I found a rental agreement for Hannah's apartment and some vacation brochures. Seems she was interested in going to Nashville and Branson. I wondered if she and Cicely had taken these trips or if these were plans they'd never get to fulfill. It crossed my mind that maybe Cicely and I could take them together someday. I set the brochures aside.

I picked up the second large manila envelope. It was marked Private. Feeling a little like an intruder, even though Hannah was my sister, I opened the clasp. Several things fell out, including a business-sized envelope. I turned it over and gasped at the message written on the front:

For Sarah, in the event of my death.

CHAPTER ELEVEN

I stared at the envelope for several seconds, almost afraid to open it.

"Don't be silly, Sarah," I said to myself. "It's probably a copy of her will."

I finally pulled open the seal and removed the folded papers inside. As I suspected, it was an informal will. She must have written this before the will she drafted with her attorney. There weren't any surprises. Basically, she left everything she owned to me, including Cicely. I folded the paper and put it back into the envelope. Then I opened another folded sheet of paper. It was a letter.

Dear Sarah,

I'm writing this after meeting you in Sanctuary today. What a wonderful day it was! Finding my sister again is the culmination of a dream. Sometimes I wondered if I'd ever see you again. But dreams can come true, I guess.

I don't expect to die for a long time, but when I do, I want you to know how much I love you and how much I've missed you. I also want you to know how sorry I am for allowing us to be separated. I know I was a child when it happened, but I was older than you. Maybe there would have been a way to keep us together. Perhaps I failed you. If so, I hope you'll forgive me. If it helps any, I want you to know that I tried many times to find you. My adoptive parents tried too, but there just wasn't a trace of you until we ran into someone who knew Janet. I'm so glad you two found each other. She's filled such a need in your life. Maybe she's not family by blood, but she's family through love. I look forward to getting to know her better.

Right now, I feel so hopeful about the future. Cicely and I haven't had anyone since Garret passed away and we had to put Betty in the care center. Betty doesn't remember me anymore, so I don't go to see her very often. To find my sister was a miracle. I just wanted you to know how important you are. I'm already planning things for the three of us to do. Vacations to Branson, Nashville, maybe a trip to Disney World? We'll have so much fun!

And, Sarah, thank you for not acting shocked when I introduced you to Cicely. I'm sure you wondered about her birth father. I made a mistake, Sarah. Got involved with a man who made me think he loved me. But I was wrong. He's not in my life anymore. In fact, he doesn't even know about Cicely, and he never will. Although falling in love with him was a mistake, if I had a choice, I'd do it all over again just to have Cicely. I know that sounds wrong, but she is the light of my life. God forgave me for my error of judgment. Instead of giving me guilt and condemnation, He gave me forgiveness. He gave me Cicely. I'm so grateful to Him for all my blessings.

For the first time since Mom and Dad died, my joy is full because I've finally found my beloved sister.

I love you so much,
Hannah

It wasn't until my tears splashed on the paper that I realized I was sobbing. What a wonderful gift Hannah had given me. My sorrow over her death left me grieving her shortened life. But at least now I knew that until recently she was happy, and that she had been reconciled to God. I wondered why she'd never mailed this letter. I'd probably never know, but I was grateful to find it now.

I couldn't help but compare this hopeful letter to the other one Hannah sent me. In a year's time, she'd gone from being upbeat and looking forward to the future to being so scared she'd planned to take Cicely and run away. What could have happened during that year to bring about such a change?

I picked up the scattered papers and repacked them. Then I carried the boxes back to the basement. There was still a stack of loose papers and one more envelope, but they didn't look like the file I was searching for. Where could it be? I gathered the remaining papers together, carried them upstairs to my room, and put them on the top shelf in my closet, intending to go through them later. After reading Hannah's letter, I needed a break. I noticed my hands shaking as I closed the closet door.

I remembered what Paul had said about Hannah's phone, so I retrieved her purse from the back of my closet and sat down on the bed. I'd gone through it once, but I'd been so upset maybe I'd missed something.

After dumping it out and going through the contents again, there was still no cell phone.

I picked up the purse, intending to put the things back that I'd removed, but somehow it didn't feel right. It was too heavy. That's when I noticed pockets on the inside. I hadn't seen them the first time because they were made with the same material as the lining of the purse. One pocket had lipstick, and another had a small phone book. Hoping it would be helpful, I pulled it out and put it aside. Then I dug into the last pocket and was rewarded with something smooth and hard. I pulled it out. Sure enough, it was a cell phone. I looked it over carefully. I had friends with cell phones and had a general idea how they worked, but I didn't understand the difference between smartphones, iPhones, and regular cell phones. This phone looked different from what I was used to. I was afraid I'd accidentally erase something important, so I decided it was best to leave it for Paul. Could there possibly be something on the phone that might help us find Hannah's killer? Had he looked for the phone and missed it too?

As I put the phone and the address book in my desk drawer, I made the decision to call Detective Sykes. Two weeks was long enough. I looked through my purse for the number. When I found it, I took a deep breath and dialed. He answered on the third ring.

"Detective Sykes, it's Sarah Miller. I'm sorry to bother you, but you said you'd call."

There was silence for several seconds. Had he hung up?

"Are you there?"

"Yes, Miss Miller, I'm here. If I had anything to tell you, I would have called."

"I . . . I understand, it's just that —"

"I'm sorry. We're doing our best. There just isn't anything new."

His abrupt attitude started to irritate me. "Look, you could have at least called to check in. You knew I was waiting to hear from you."

"I've got to go, Miss Miller," he said quickly. "Again, I'm sorry. But I don't have anything to tell you."

"But what about the man you arrested? Have you been able to connect him to Hannah? You need to —"

Sykes said something, interrupting me, but I didn't catch it.

"I'm sorry. What did you say?"

He cleared his throat. "I said he's dead. We found him hanging in his cell a few days ago."

I opened my mouth two or three times, trying to frame a response, but I was too flabbergasted to speak. The man was dead?

"But . . . does that mean you can't tie him to Hannah?" I asked when I could find my voice again. "Or does it mean you think he did it and killed himself out of remorse? I don't understand."

Sykes sighed deeply into the phone. "Look, I'm really sorry, but I can't talk right now. I'll call you back when I have more time." With that, he was gone.

I stared at the receiver in my hand. Had he really hung up on me? I suddenly heard the front door being slammed shut. A quick look at my watch revealed the entire afternoon was gone. It was a little after three o'clock. Cicely was home. I quickly put the phone down and went downstairs. Trying to regain my composure, I walked into the living room just in time to see her pulling off her coat.

"How was school?" I asked, trying to shake off my disturbing conversation with Detective Sykes.

"Pretty good. I like Mr. King. He's awesome." She wrinkled her nose the same way Hannah used to. "He's kind of cute."

"Yes, he is. And you probably shouldn't say that. Except to me."

Cicely smiled. Although we still had a long way to go, I could see some improvement. I sent up a silent *thank-you* to God.

"Why don't you come into the kitchen and have some cookies and milk?" I said. "Then you can tackle your homework."

She nodded and started to walk toward me. Instead of going to the kitchen, I stood my ground and pointed at the coat she'd left lying across one of Janet's chairs.

Cicely's eyes followed my finger. "Whoops. Sorry." She grabbed the coat and hung it up quickly in the front coat closet. Then she followed me into the kitchen. After a snack of chocolate chip cookies and milk, during which she told me about her day, she headed to her room to study.

I was cleaning up the kitchen when she came back into the room. "Aunt Sarah, can I ask you a question?"

"Of course." I sat down at the table. "What is it?"

She chewed on her lip for a moment while looking somewhat apprehensive. Finally she took a deep breath. "How old do I have to be before I can . . . go on a date?"

Her question caught me off guard. "Date? You mean with a boy?"

Cicely sighed dramatically. "Yeah, with a boy."

I stared back at her with my mouth hanging open. "I have no idea what to tell you, except that you're way too young. Surely young girls don't date until they're at least sixteen."

It was her turn to look shocked. "Sixteen? There were some girls at my old school who were married when they were sixteen!"

I didn't consider myself a prude, even if I did live in Sanctuary, but that information shocked me. "Sixteen? That's ridiculous." I reached over and took her hand. "Cicely, you're still a child. Besides, what boy are you referring to?" I couldn't think of any likely candidates in Sanctuary. Was she talking about someone from Kansas City?

The previous cheerful atmosphere we'd enjoyed since she came home evaporated, and she pulled her hand away. "Mom would let me date. I'm not going to live my life all alone, like you do."

I sat back in my chair, unsure of what to do or what to say. Maybe we hadn't progressed as much as I thought.

"I think you need to go to your room and do your homework," I said softly. "You're upset. Let's both calm down, and we'll talk about this later."

She glared at me. "You're not my mom, you know. I don't have to do anything you tell me to."

Even though my voice shook, I couldn't let her statement go unchallenged. "You're right. I'm not your mother, but you absolutely have to do what I tell you. As long as you're a minor and you live here, you have to obey me."

As soon as I said the words, I wished I'd used another term rather than *obey*. Perhaps it was archaic, but it was all I could think of at that moment.

Cicely's expression grew even stormier, and her eyes filled with tears. "My mom was so much better than you! Why couldn't you be the one who died?"

CHAPTER TWELVE

After yelling at me, Cicely grabbed her schoolbag from the kitchen counter and stormed out. I was left angry and wounded, but I knew in my heart she was right. Hannah was the golden child. Smart, beautiful, ambitious, and full of life. I'd lived in her shadow when we were children, and even now, her own daughter recognized her mother's value over mine.

"Stop it, Sarah," I said to myself. I was so immersed in my own pain I didn't hear Janet come in the front door. When she came into the kitchen, I was caught by surprise.

"For goodness' sake, what's wrong?" she asked when she saw me wipe away tears.

"I . . . I'm a terrible substitute for my sister," I said, my voice breaking.

Janet came over and sat down next to me. "Why would you say that?" she asked. "Did something happen?"

I quickly shared my emotional exchange with Cicely. When I finished, I was surprised to see her smile. She reached over and took my hand.

"I know you're hurt, Sarah, but Cicely doesn't know what she's saying. She's been through a terrible experience, and she misses her mother. I'm amazed she didn't say something like this sooner. It's coming out of her grief. You're just in the line of fire. Trust me, she probably feels worse than you do right now. She's a smart girl, and she knows you care for her. She also knows that without you, she wouldn't have a home." Janet squeezed my hand and then let it go. "You both need to calm down. When you talk to her again, don't let her know she upset you. Give her some slack and let her know you still love her. Even when she says something designed to hurt you."

"I guess you're right. Maybe I was hoping for too much too soon." I sighed. "It's not just Cicely. I finally called Detective Sykes."

Janet's eyes widened. "And?"

"I don't know what to think. It was obvious he didn't want to talk to me." I shook my head. "The man they arrested? The one they thought might have killed Hannah?"

Janet nodded.

"He hanged himself in his cell."

Janet's hand flew to her mouth. "How terrible. But what does this mean? Do they still think he was involved in Hannah's death?"

"That's just it. I don't know. I don't believe he killed her, but now that he's dead, will it be easy to blame him and move on?"

"Oh, Sarah. I can't imagine the police would do something like that."

"They did it in my parents' case, Janet. Once they decided they were killed by robbers, that was the end of it. They spent all their time looking for burglary suspects that never materialized."

She was quiet for a moment. "I saw something on TV the other day about a similar case. The police rushed to judgment and charged the wrong person."

I got a cup out of the cabinet and poured some coffee. "I know most law enforcement officials are thorough and work hard to find the truth. But it doesn't always happen that way. Kansas City police have their hands full. After talking to Doug Sykes, I have a real fear they'll hang Hannah's murder on the accused thief just so they can close the case."

Janet was quiet for a moment as she stared into her coffee cup. "Have you considered . . ." She paused and shook her head.

"What?"

"Nothing."

It wasn't like Janet to hold back her opinion. "Tell me what you're thinking," I said.

She looked up at me. "I don't want to put something in your mind that isn't true."

She had to be talking about the man who'd died in his cell. I'd been so busy thinking about Cicely, I hadn't considered a terrible possibility. "Oh, Janet. You're wondering if the man actually committed suicide or if he . . ." I couldn't finish the thought. It was too awful.

"It crossed my mind, yes," she said slowly. "But who would want him dead? And why?" She shook her head. "Just forget I said anything. It doesn't make sense. I'm sure he was closely watched, Sarah. No one from the outside could have gotten to him."

"I'm sure you're right."

I silently finished my coffee. Now a frightening scenario played in my mind. Was his death something more than it seemed? Was there a chance someone wanted to keep him quiet?

Janet stood up. "Why don't you get out for a while, Sarah? Go visit a friend."

I started to refuse her kind offer, but then

I remembered that I needed to talk to Wynter Evans. "Maybe I'll do that," I said.

Janet stood up. "Good. You need a break. It will do you a world of good."

I realized she looked tired, and I felt guilty leaving her alone to deal with Cicely. "You must be exhausted. Are you sure?"

"It was a long day, but I'm fine. Besides, there's still some spaghetti in the fridge. I'll just heat it up and pop some garlic bread in the oven. Easy." She smiled. "I haven't had to cook much with all the food people gave us. The freezer in the basement is still full. We'll be eating food brought by our neighbors for a long while." She sighed. "It's a blessing."

"Janet, are you ever sorry you took over the clinic?"

"No, I'm not sorry. But the property is still in limbo, which adds some strain to the situation." She sighed. "I decided today that I've got to have some help. I need someone to check in patients and help me keep the office organized."

"I think Cicely would love to help out after school," I said, frowning. "But that doesn't take care of your situation during the day."

"I think I'll pass the word around town," Janet said. "See if there's someone who'd like to step in."

"Wish I could help you, but I'm going back to school next week. Seems the girls in my class enjoy having Reuben as a substitute a little more than they should."

Janet grinned. "I can understand that." She pointed at me. "Now scoot. Go make that phone call."

I went upstairs to my room and dialed Wynter's number. It seemed odd, since she was right next door, but I knew she might be writing, and I didn't want to disturb her. However, she answered the phone right away. She seemed glad to hear from me and asked how Cicely and I were doing.

"Things have been a little rocky. This afternoon was the worst," I said. "Janet tells me I need to get out of the house for a while. I wondered if you might like to have dinner with me. There's . . . there's something I'd like to talk to you about."

"Sure," she answered. "Is it serious?"

I lowered my voice, since Cicely's room was right across the hall. "To be honest, I don't know. There's something strange about my sister's murder. I know I told you she was killed during a robbery, but now I'm not sure that's true. There are some similarities between her death and the way my parents were killed almost twenty years ago."

"That's interesting," Wynter said slowly. "I'm not sure what I can do to help you, but let's meet over at The Oil Lamp in about thirty minutes. Will that work for you?"

"Yes, that's perfect. I'll see you there."

When we hung up, I could almost swear I heard an odd click, like someone had been listening on an extension. There were only three phones in the house. The main line in the kitchen, an extension in the living room, and the phone in my bedroom. Cicely was in her room, so it couldn't be her. Maybe Janet had picked up the phone downstairs not realizing I was on it. I grabbed the phone again and called Paul. Unfortunately, I got his voice mail. I told him I'd found Hannah's phone, but I didn't say anything about the man who died in prison. That was something I wanted to tell Paul in person.

I quickly changed clothes and brushed my hair. As I checked my image in the mirror, I wondered if I'd look better with a little makeup. I rarely wore it, but I appeared washed out and tired. Although no one would object if I used a little mascara or blush, spending years living with Mrs. Johnson had discouraged me from straying too far from her simple Mennonite ways. And now, living in Sanctuary and teaching several students from conservative homes, it just seemed easier to stay makeup free. Many days I wore my hair in a bun or a long braid, but some days I wore it long. It was fine and straight, without much body. Hannah's strawberry blond hair had benefited from our mother's naturally curly hair, while mine mirrored our father's. It seemed that Hannah had gotten all our parents' best qualities, while I'd gotten their worst. As I stared at myself, I suddenly realized Paul was right. When I looked in the mirror, all I saw was Hannah. What she was. What I wasn't.

After putting on my coat, I said good-bye to Janet and went outside. The wind was icy, and dark clouds raced across the sky. It had already snowed once this winter, and I could tell we were in for another round. I loved the snow, but I only walked a short way to work. Janet had to drive out of town to the clinic, and I worried about her on slick roads.

The restaurant was just four blocks away, so I decided to walk. Cicely had mentioned more than once that she thought it was "weird" that we walked so much in Sanctuary. It seemed that Hannah had driven them almost everywhere. Even down the block from their apartment to get hamburgers. Janet had told me I could use her car whenever I wanted, but in Sanctuary, a car was rarely necessary, so there hadn't been much of a need. For a brief moment, I'd thought about taking Hannah's car so I wouldn't be forced to use Janet's sedan for those occasional longer trips, but I'd quickly dismissed the idea. I was afraid it would be too hard for Cicely to ride in her mother's car. Too many memories. I was happy that Mr. Hanson had found a buyer and was helping me get the title changed.

For some reason, Hannah's letter drifted into my mind. Asking me not to look for the truth. To let the past go. But how could I be true to her memory if I didn't try to get the police to search for justice? My sister's request was unfair. How could she ask me to turn a blind eye to her murder? As I thought about it, I started to feel a little angry with Hannah. Not just for dying, but for asking me to leave her murder unsolved.

A gust of wind swept past me, and I could swear I heard it whisper Hannah's words from the letter. *Remember me.* I almost turned around to see if her ghost stood behind me, begging me not to forget her. But it was absurd. I didn't believe in ghosts.

Not real ones anyway. I was certainly dealing with my own brand of ghosts though. Echoes from the past that wouldn't stay silent. Now another ghost joined the cacophony of voices. A man I would never know. Had he lost his life because of my sister? Because of my family?

Another strong blast of wind pushed me, as if trying to hurry me down the sidewalk. The streetlights in Sanctuary were on, but they only shone in the downtown area. Janet lived on the edge of town, so I had to walk in the dark for two blocks before reaching the safety of the lights. Although the few houses along the way had their porch lights on, it was still disturbingly dark.

Suddenly, I heard a noise behind me. The sound of something falling. I turned around and peered into the darkness, but I couldn't see anything. A feeling of panic seized me. There was only silence, but I swung back to see the lights from town ahead. I had an urge to run toward them, but a soft mewing behind me caused me to look back once more. A big golden cat sat in the middle of the street, watching me. Percy was owned by Martha Kirsch, who ran Sanctuary's library. He was always getting into trash cans when he was let outside to do his business. He was simply making the rounds before he and Martha left for home.

"You're a rotten cat," I scolded him. "You almost scared me to death."

He didn't seem the least bit remorseful, so I resumed walking toward town. Even though the source of the noise that frightened me had been discovered, I was still happy to reach the security of the yellow-tinged streetlamps. The Oil Lamp finally came into view, and relief flowed through me. The freezing wind only added to my desire to seek shelter.

I opened the door and stepped inside the restaurant. The warm air made me shiver with pleasure, as did the knowledge that I was finally safe. Hannah's letter made me feel as if someone were watching me all the time, though I knew that wasn't possible. Sanctuary was a small town, and there were no strangers here. Still, I couldn't shake the feeling. Maybe it was my own guilt causing me to imagine I was being stalked. Did I think Hannah was following me around, trying to warn me to leave the past alone? *Get control of yourself, Sarah. You're beginning to sound crazy.*

Gazing around the room, I spotted Wynter sitting against the wall on the other side of the room. The Oil Lamp wasn't a fancy restaurant, but Randi Lindquist had given it a quaint, homey feeling. It reminded me of a fifties diner. Mismatched vinyl tablecloths, red and yellow ketchup and mustard bottles on the tables, black-and-white checked laminate flooring, and pictures on the walls. Some of the pictures were decorative, but most of them were early photographs of Sanctuary. At the front of the restaurant was a counter where customers could sit on round stools if they wished. Some of our residents liked to talk to Randi or chat with the cook who stood at the grill. It always smelled good in The Oil Lamp. Even if I wasn't hungry, all I had to do was walk through the door and my mouth began to water.

"Thank you so much for having dinner with me," I said to Wynter when I reached the table. "I really appreciate it."

"Don't be silly," she said with a smile. "I'm looking forward to it. I haven't been out of the house much lately. Getting out was good for me."

I took off my coat and put it on the back of the chair before I sat down. Wynter's welcoming smile helped to chase away the disquiet that had trailed me from Janet's to the restaurant. Wynter was a beautiful woman with light blond hair and striking green eyes. The same feeling came over me that I'd experienced in front of the mirror. Next to her, I felt almost invisible.

Randi saw me from across the room and hurried over. "I'm so glad to see you, Sarah," she said. "We're all so sorry about your sister. How are you doing? And how's your niece?"

"We're getting along all right," I said with a smile, "but of course we miss Hannah. Cicely is in school and doing well. Thank you for the flowers and the food you sent over. It was very kind."

Randi put her hand on my shoulder. "Wish I could do more, honey. We're all praying for you."

Randi was a very contemporary woman with her own mind, and she didn't usually keep her opinions to herself. But she had a kind heart, and she loved Sanctuary. No one was more fierce in her loyalty toward her hometown than Randi.

"Thank you. We can certainly use all the prayers we can get."

She patted my shoulder. "So what can I get you two ladies to drink?"

At first I asked for just a glass of water but then quickly added coffee even though I knew it was a bad idea. I'd probably be up all night, but I was so cold, a cup of hot coffee sounded great. I could have ordered decaf, but I didn't care for the taste.

Wynter asked for water with lemon. Randi gave her a slight nod and walked away without saying anything.

"Is she still upset?" I asked when Randi was out of earshot.

Wynter nodded. "I'm afraid it will take a while for people in Sanctuary to forgive me for drawing attention to this town."

"*You* didn't draw attention to us. What Rae . . . I mean Marian Belker and her husband did brought the press here. I'm just grateful the media didn't hang around any longer than they did. Right now, everyone's more interested in locating the other children Joe and Marian kidnapped. Seems like you and your brother have finally become yesterday's news."

Marian Belker and her husband had kidnapped several children across Missouri and sold them to unsuspecting couples who thought they were adopting children legally. One of those children had been Wynter's brother, Ryan.

She sighed and shook her head. "I hope so. We made it clear we wouldn't give interviews. At first that made it worse. Reporters seemed determined to beat everyone else for the story, but after they found out we were serious, things finally started to

186

die down."

"There are a lot of people in Sanctuary who have secrets," I said. "We're all aware of it, but I don't know anyone except your fiancé who is privy to most of them."

Wynter shrugged. "And he isn't telling me. I guess that's what keeps us safe. A town full of people who are committed to keeping secrets . . . secret."

I nodded my agreement. Sanctuary was special, and I was grateful for it. Especially with what Cicely and I had been through. We both needed a secure haven where we could recover from the trauma of my sister's death without being bothered. I didn't watch much TV, even though Janet had one. But sometimes I saw the news and was horrified by reporters sticking a microphone in someone's face after the tragic loss of a loved one. The same question was almost always asked. "How do you feel?" As if the answer wasn't obvious to everyone watching. Although I was a peaceful person, I thought a good punch in the face would have been an appropriate response in most cases.

Randi came back with our drinks and took our dinner orders. For some reason, I was terribly hungry. After my confrontation with Cicely and the call to Doug Sykes, it was probably a yearning for comfort. Since I was too skinny for my five-foot-eight-inch height, an occasional indulgence wasn't a problem. I ordered a roast beef dinner with mashed potatoes and gravy, a side of green beans with bacon, and some of Randi's homemade rolls.

"Whoa," Randi said with a smile, "you usually order a salad or a bowl of soup. Nice to see you order some real food. Wouldn't hurt you to put some meat on those bones."

Although some people thought telling me I was skinny should make me feel good, it didn't. Just like most heavy women didn't want to be called fat, most thin women didn't want to be labeled as skinny. Either term was just another way to say you weren't "normal." Of course, I just smiled and didn't say anything. I knew Randi didn't mean to be rude.

Wynter asked for a bowl of chili and some corn bread. Randi scribbled the order on her pad.

"It might be a while," she said. "My new cook is a little slow, and we're really busy tonight. Is that a problem?"

"Not for me," I said. "I'm not in any hurry."

"Me either," Wynter said with a smile.

"We're both planning to enjoy a girls' night out."

Randi chuckled. "Only in Sanctuary would dinner in my restaurant be called a girls' night out." She winked at me. "You stay as long as you want. And if you manage to eat that big dinner you ordered, dessert is on me. Max may not be the fastest cook in town, but he makes a bread pudding that will make you beg for more."

"That sounds wonderful," I said with a sigh. "I'm out of the house, and there's the possibility of dessert. Life can't get any better than that!"

Randi and Wynter both laughed.

After Randi walked away, Wynter smiled at me. "So how are things between you and Cicely?"

I told her about the argument we'd just had. "Janet says Cicely just needs to blow up at someone because she's angry. I'm sure that's true, but I'm suffering too. It's hard to deal with my own feelings and take the brunt of her anger as well." I sighed. "I know how selfish that sounds."

"Believe me, if anyone understands, it's me. After my brother was kidnapped, I was furious with everyone. Even myself. I kept thinking that if I'd been home, he wouldn't have been taken." She shook her head. "I turned that into a reason to feel guilty. I shouldn't have been at a friend's house. I should have been with Ryan. As if sisters are supposed to spend their lives shadowing their siblings because something *might* happen. That's ridiculous. I imagine Cicely wonders if she could have done something to save her mother."

I blinked away the tears that filled my eyes. "Maybe she does. I've been doing the same thing. Trying to figure out if there was something I could have done to protect Hannah."

"And then Cicely tells you she wishes you had died instead of her mother." Wynter gazed into my eyes. "She didn't mean that, you know. Not really."

I shrugged and then quickly dabbed at my tears with my napkin. "I don't know. I think she did, actually. I mean, I know she doesn't want me dead. But if she could have chosen —"

"Stop that," Wynter said sharply. "That kind of thinking is ridiculous. We can't pick and choose those things. And if your sister could speak, I'm sure she'd tell you how thankful she is that you're here for Cicely." She sighed. "I used to think my father would have been happier if I'd been kidnapped instead of Ryan. That thinking was so destructive. It almost ruined me." She took a drink of water and stared at it after she put it back on the table. "Comparing ourselves to other people only brings unhappiness, Sarah. We almost always come up lacking. I think God hates it when we do that. He made each one of us special and unique. When we judge ourselves against someone else, isn't it saying that God didn't do a good job in creating us? Isn't it degrading His handiwork?"

I took a quick gulp of my coffee, not checking to see how hot it was. The steaming liquid scalded my throat, but Wynter's words already burned in my mind. First Paul and now Wynter. Was God trying to tell me something? I'd spent my life comparing myself to others, and I always came up short. My sister, my mother, and the other foster children I'd spent time with. In fact, I'd just compared myself to Wynter. I was so used to judging myself by the strengths and talents I saw in everyone else that it had become automatic. It had never occurred to me that my self-judgment was criticizing God. Is that what I'd been doing?

I nodded at her but didn't respond to her question, since I didn't have the answer. Not knowing what else to do, I quickly changed the subject and asked Wynter about her writing.

"It's coming along," she said. "To be honest, I spend most of my time planning the wedding and the honeymoon. I'm afraid writing will have to wait until we get back." Her perfectly shaped eyebrows knit together, and her expression grew rather solemn. "Now tell me about your sister's murder. What is it that bothers you?"

I took a sip of water in an attempt to gather my thoughts. Then I proceeded to tell Wynter why I was concerned about Hannah's death. The letter, the fire, and of course the flowers and their connection to my mother and father. As I told her about my conversation with Detective Sykes, she frowned, but she didn't ask any questions. When I finished, she leaned back in her chair and stared at me. Before she could say anything, Randi showed up with our food. After serving us, she scurried away to another table where someone had just spilled a drink.

"So you believe the person who killed your parents also killed your sister?" Wynter spoke softly so she wouldn't be overheard, but still, it made my stomach turn over to hear her say it out loud.

"I didn't at first, but you have to admit

that it's odd. Some reporter from *The Star* gave Hannah a file a couple of months ago. It contained information that really upset her. If I could find it, it might help me convince the authorities to take my concerns seriously. I thought Detective Sykes was willing to look a little closer, but now it seems he's dismissed any possibility the murders are linked. I truly don't understand why. The same flowers at both scenes. I'm about as sure as I can be that my parents didn't have orchids in the house before Hannah and I went to bed the night they died, and Hannah certainly didn't have them in her apartment. We both hate orchids. Especially white ones."

"Sarah, the police won't look at your sister's death differently because of similar flowers at the crime scene. I know it's significant to you, but it won't mean anything to them. They need real evidence. Remember, they're treating this as a homicide. Whether the killer was a thief or whether he broke in just because he was targeting your sister — it's still murder. I know this might not be what you want to hear, but I think you need to let this play out." She shook her head. "Are you absolutely certain the guy who hanged himself wasn't guilty? He was obviously distraught about something."

"Nothing is impossible, I guess. But why would some random guy leave orchids behind, Wynter? It doesn't make sense. Not unless he was working for someone else." The idea that the man who died might have been sent by another person hadn't occurred to me until that moment. Was it possible?

Wynter reached over and put her hand on mine. "Sarah, you're going to drive yourself crazy with all this conjecture. Is Hannah's death connected to your folks? Are the police really investigating? Did someone hire the guy who hanged himself? Did he really commit suicide? You have no evidence for any of this."

I chewed and swallowed a bite of roast beef. It was delicious, but I couldn't really taste much. My concern was more toward my conversation than my meal. "I understand what you're saying, but what if the police decide to pin Hannah's death on the man who died? They could miss finding the real killer."

Wynter studied me for a moment. "I'm not saying you're wrong. I don't suppose you know what they found at the crime scene? I mean, anything solid that could point to the killer or killers?"

"No. Detective Sykes told me there was no DNA evidence they could use. No fingerprints except Hannah and Cicely's. He said whoever broke in must have been wearing gloves."

Wynter frowned. "Didn't your sister have any friends? Visitors who could have left behind fingerprints or DNA?"

I shook my head. "Hannah didn't seem to have people over. In fact, it appears she kept pretty much to herself."

"Do you know why?" Wynter asked.

"No, not really," I said slowly. "I'm the same way though. Sometimes I think people who have been through something traumatic tend to be loners. It's not that we don't like people, it's just . . . a way of coping. Not allowing things into our life that we can't control. I know that sounds a little crazy."

Wynter shook her head. "It's not crazy. I was the same way. Not letting people in. I was the kind of person who would rather spend the evening alone at home with my cat."

"Trust me, I understand."

"Hannah was stabbed to death, wasn't she?" Wynter asked.

I nodded.

"I'm not a trained investigator, but it seems to me that there should have been

195

more evidence at the crime scene. Of course it's a moot point now since the house burned down. That certainly seems convenient."

"One other odd thing," I said. "I found a shriveled white orchid in Hannah's bedroom, lying on the floor. If the flowers were in the living room, what was that bloom doing in the bedroom? Oh, and the drawer to the small table next to her bed was open, and I found bullets in a locked box in her closet. I think she heard a noise, grabbed her gun, and went out into the living room. That's when she was attacked."

"Where's the gun now?"

I shrugged. "I have no idea and neither do the police. Detective Sykes said the theft of the gun made it look even more like a robbery."

"Maybe. Guns are stolen a lot. Seems odd though. I mean, why not get the gun from her and shoot her? Why stab her? It's messy and sometimes an attacker actually cuts himself and leaves evidence behind." She thought for a moment. "How close was your sister's house to the houses on either side of her?"

"Her house was on a corner lot, so there was only one house to the north side of her. It was fairly close, I guess. Cicely was at a slumber party there the night Hannah was killed."

"So a shot might not have been heard." Wynter said this softly, as if she were talking to herself. She stared down at her food for a moment before finally swinging her gaze up to me.

"What do you want me to do, Sarah?"

"Paul Gleason is trying to help me. Unfortunately, his hands are tied, since my sister's murder occurred in Kansas City. He mentioned that you have some contacts there. Someone who might be able to tell us what the police are actually thinking? I just want to know what's really going on." I shook my head. "Look, Wynter. I'm not trying to take over the police's investigation. Maybe they're on top of it. Maybe they listened to my concerns about Hannah's murder. I mean, if they're really investigating, then Paul and I need to stay out of the way."

"Very good advice," Wynter said, dipping her spoon into her chili. After taking a bite, she put her spoon down, and it clanged against the edge of the bowl. "What if we find out no one is taking your concerns seriously? That they've closed the case? What will you do? Try to solve this thing yourself? That's a terrible idea."

"That's not my intention. I just want the

police to do their job. Follow all the leads, not just narrow it down to their preconceived idea about some burglar. Any burglar." I stared at her for a moment. "You pursued the truth about your brother. And you found him."

"Yes, I did. And I almost got myself killed in the process."

"But —"

"But you have a young person to take care of, Sarah. Someone who is counting on you. Someone who would be lost without you." Wynter shook her head. "I think I know exactly what your sister would say if you asked her what you should do. And you do too, don't you?"

I nodded but didn't say anything. Part of Hannah's letter ran through my mind. *I'm counting on you, Sarah. I know you won't let me down.*

"Look," Wynter said, interrupting the continuing loop of Hannah's warning playing over and over in my head. "I'll make a call. There's a detective I trust in Kansas City. If the police aren't looking into the connection between your sister and your parents, maybe he can express some concerns about the similarities in the case and get someone to listen. But after I do this, that's it, Sarah. And the only way I'll contact

198

him is if you promise you'll back off after he rattles the cage down there a bit. Do you understand? You spend your time teaching those school kids and raising that niece of yours, okay?"

"I just want to know that the police are taking my concerns seriously." An idea popped into my head. "If your friend could find any records related to my parents' murders, I'd really appreciate it. Since they were killed when I was a child, I don't know much about the details. Hannah may have had some information, but if she did, I haven't found it yet."

She nodded. "I'll see what he can do. In the meantime, keep looking for the file from that reporter. We need to find out what was in it that upset your sister."

"I will. And thank you." I was relieved she'd agreed to help me, but no matter what she found out, I had no intention of backing off until I knew the entire truth. If Wynter wasn't able to get me the information I needed, or if her ability to open up a new round of inquiry wasn't accomplished, I'd have to find another way. Now, more than ever, I was determined to find the truth and bring justice to my murdered family.

CHAPTER THIRTEEN

Wynter drove me back to the house after dinner because it had started to snow while we were at Randi's. I would have asked her anyway, since I was still a little spooked by my walk into town. When I got home, Janet was curled up on the couch, sound asleep. The television was on, so I turned it off. I took the quilt from the back of the couch and covered her, and then I went upstairs to my room. The light was off in Cicely's room, so I assumed she was asleep. Good. I still didn't know what I was going to say to her when we faced each other again.

I went to my room, grabbed my pajamas and my underwear, and headed for the bathroom. I wanted nothing more than to soak in the tub for a while and let the hot water warm me. The freezing temperatures outside were nothing compared to the ice I felt in my heart. Wynter's admonitions were well intended, but I didn't want people telling me what I *should* do.

As I slipped into the water, I comforted myself with the knowledge that at least one person understood my situation. Paul. Even though he'd advised against it, contacting Captain Bentley was looking more and more plausible. First I'd wait to see what Wynter's contact had to say.

Paul still hadn't called me back, and I really wanted to talk to him about my conversation with Doug Sykes. I hoped he'd phone me in the morning.

I relaxed in the warm water and actually drifted off for a few minutes. When I woke up, I turned the hot water back on and decided to soak a little longer. I felt the most relaxed I'd been since my sister died. Finally I decided it was time to get out of the comfortable bathtub. It only took me a few minutes to dry off and slip into my pajamas. Then I hurried to my room and climbed into bed. Although I was tired, the day's events swirled through my mind. Wondering why I'd nodded off in the tub but couldn't seem to fall asleep lying in my bed, I tried to empty my mind and drift off. Unfortunately, faces kept coming to me. Hannah's face when we said good-bye the last time. Cicely's face when she'd told me she wished I'd died instead of her mother. And Paul's face when he encouraged me to stop comparing myself to Hannah. After about an hour, I finally dozed off.

When I woke up, I glanced at my bedside clock. It was a little after nine o'clock. I jumped out of bed, grabbed my robe, and hurried downstairs. Janet was already gone, but she'd left a note telling me she had an early surgery. I hurried back upstairs to check Cicely's room, but she was gone too. I usually woke her up to get her ready for school, but Janet must have taken care of her this morning so I could sleep. Or maybe Cicely got herself up because she didn't want to see me. Even if that were true, it was Friday, so she wouldn't be able to avoid me much longer. We had the entire weekend to work things out. Monday, I'd go back to school. Although I'd needed this time off, I was looking forward to returning to my class. Having something to think about besides Hannah would be a blessing.

After a quick breakfast, I called Paul. He answered his phone and told me he'd gotten my message about the phone. "Sorry I haven't called you back. Things have been pretty busy here. This morning is full, but I can get away for lunch."

"Why don't you come here, and I'll fix us something? I have a lot to tell you."

He agreed and told me he'd see me around twelve-thirty. I hung up the phone and had started toward the kitchen when the phone rang again. I turned back and picked it up. After I said hello, I heard a male voice I didn't recognize at first.

"Sarah, this is Doug Sykes."

I was surprised to hear his voice. "I wasn't sure I'd hear from you again," I said.

"Look, I'm sorry I was short with you. I need you to listen to me carefully. I don't have much time to talk."

"Okay," I said slowly.

"I've been told that Hannah's death is going to be blamed on Steven Hanks, the guy who died in his cell. And I've been ordered to close the case."

I felt the blood drain from my face. "But . . . do you think he did it?"

"I don't know. Something's going on here, Sarah. I'm not sure who's behind it, but . . . Well, I'm worried. I need you to be very careful. Back off this case. Drop it. For now anyway."

"Why? Are Cicely and I in danger?"

"I've got to get off the phone, but we need to talk. I may be able to drive down there next week."

"That . . . that's fine, but I go back to school on Monday. I'll be free anytime after three o'clock during the week."

"Okay. Whatever you do, don't call me. And do what I said. Back off and be quiet. If anyone asks you about the case, unless it's a close friend, tell them you believe Steven Hanks killed your sister. It's important, Sarah. More important than I can tell you right now."

"You're frightening me."

He sighed. "I'm sorry, but for now, it's probably good for you to be a little scared. Gotta go. I'll talk to you soon."

The phone disconnected, and I sat there and stared at the receiver for several seconds before putting it down. I wanted Detective Sykes to find something. To take my concerns seriously, but now that he had, my deepest fears suddenly felt real.

"Oh, God," I prayed quietly. "I want the truth, but I also want Cicely to be safe. Please watch over us. Keep us in your care."

Reality wasn't at all what I thought it would be. It was much scarier. I'd been feeling so much stronger. Like I was taking control of my life instead of allowing things to just happen to me. Suddenly Hannah's advice to leave this situation alone seemed to make sense. Had I done something foolish?

Although it was hard to think about

anything else, I forced myself to make tuna salad for sandwiches. Then I threw together a fruit salad as an accompaniment. There were still cookies in the cookie jar and a pitcher of iced tea in the refrigerator. Satisfied I could put together a nice lunch, I went upstairs to get dressed.

Looking through my closet didn't reveal anything I wanted to wear. I finally decided on a dark blue sweater and black slacks. It was cold and snowy outside, and I wanted to feel warm. I'd actually gotten compliments on the sweater because it went well with my red hair.

I tried to fluff my hair, but it just went flat. I remembered Hannah telling me once that if I'd pull the sides back and clip them, my hair would look fuller. I found one of Janet's hair clips in a drawer and tried it. It took a few attempts, but it really did seem to work. I put on some foundation and blush and then added a little mascara. Feeling brave, I also put on a small amount of lipstick. Satisfied with the results, I went downstairs.

When the doorbell rang a little after twelve-thirty, fear washed over me. Detective Sykes's warning about not sharing any information concerned me. But he'd mentioned people I didn't know. I knew Paul.

Besides, I trusted him. I took a deep breath and opened the front door.

"Wow, you look very nice," he said as he came inside. He colored and looked embarrassed. "I mean . . . you look nice every day."

"Thank you," I said. "I've got lunch ready."

"Sounds good."

He followed me into the kitchen and sat down at the table while I made the sandwiches and put the fruit salad into bowls.

"I hope I didn't offend you," Paul said suddenly. "I mean, how you look has nothing to do with what I'm here to talk about."

I finished pouring us glasses of iced tea and put them on the table. "It's all right," I said. "I'm not offended."

He smiled and took a deep breath. "You really do look good every day. I just think you look especially pretty today."

"Th-thank you," I said, stumbling over my words.

Paul bowed his head and began to pray for our food. I kept one eye open and watched him while he prayed. He seemed different today. Not as self-assured. Could he have feelings for me? I really liked him, but I didn't want to say or do anything stupid that might make it hard for us to work together. There was too much at stake.

Just as he said, "Amen," I closed my other eye. When I raised my head and looked at him, I found him staring at me. Immediately he picked up his glass of iced tea and took a drink.

"Paul, I have so much to tell you I don't even know where to start." First I told him about my original call to Doug.

He looked stunned. "The guy's dead? That's convenient, isn't it?"

"That's what I thought."

"So Sykes blew us off?"

I shook my head. "I don't think so. He's coming here next week." I quickly told him about the detective's phone call this morning, but I softened it some. If Paul thought Cicely and I were in danger, I wasn't sure what he'd do. Even with Doug's strange warning, I wasn't ready to walk away.

Paul frowned. "So what does that mean?"

I sighed. "I don't know what to think. But for some reason, Doug seems to finally believe Hannah's murder might be more than just the result of a robbery. He warned me to be quiet about the case. Not to talk about it with anyone I don't know."

"Did he actually find anything to connect Hannah and your parents?"

"I have no idea. He didn't stay on the phone long. I guess I'll find out when he gets here." I really wanted to tell Paul how much Doug's call frightened me, but I just couldn't. I needed his help. I'd wait until I talked to Doug in person before leaping to conclusions.

"Could I sit in on that meeting?" Paul asked.

"Absolutely. I'd certainly feel better if you were with me. Somehow this makes everything feel more real."

Paul frowned. "Look, try not to worry. We have no idea what Doug's going to say, so let's not overreact."

"I'll try." I tried to muster a smile and nodded at him. This was a good time to change the subject. "Oh, here's Hannah's phone," I said, taking it out of my pocket. "I didn't try to check it for calls because it's one of those fancy phones. I can use a regular cell phone, but something with all these bells and whistles scares me. I was afraid I'd accidentally lose something important."

"Good. Can I take it with me? I'd like to go through the calls tonight."

"Sure. I hope you'll find something useful." I pushed the phone book toward him too. "Maybe there's something in here that will help as well."

"Why don't you go through that yourself?"

he said. "Since I didn't know Hannah, you might see something that wouldn't mean anything to me."

"I already glanced through it once. There aren't many entries. Most of them were for businesses, the doctor, Cicely's school. I recognized a couple of the personal names, but there were a few that weren't familiar. I'll look through it more carefully and let you know if something sticks out."

"Good," he said. "Have you had a chance to talk to Wynter?"

"We had dinner together last night, and she promised to check with her friend at the Kansas City Police Department."

"Good. I'll be interested to see what she comes up with," Paul said. He stared at Hannah's cell phone. "After I go through this, we need to turn it over to the police. It's evidence."

"Should we wait and give it to Detective Sykes when he comes?"

"I guess so," he said slowly. "He's the detective assigned to the case. First I want to make a list of the calls and texts. That way we'll have all the information they do."

"All right. So now we wait on Sykes?"

Paul shrugged. "Unless I find something on the phone that troubles me, I think it only makes sense."

I nodded. We ate in silence for several minutes. "Look, Paul," I said finally, "I've thought a lot about what you said. You know, about Hannah and me." I sighed. "You took a chance bringing it up, and I know it was because you care. I hope we're still friends. I wouldn't want to do anything to hurt that."

"You haven't done anything to harm our . . . friendship, Sarah. Maybe I shouldn't have stuck my nose into your business. I have no right to get so personal with you."

"Well, that's what friends are supposed to do, right?"

He didn't respond, just stared down at his plate.

"Is there something wrong?"

Finally he looked up at me. "Are we really just friends, Sarah?" he asked softly.

"I . . . I don't know." I could feel my face grow hot. I cared for him. A lot. But right now finding out the truth about Hannah was more important to me than anything else. Complicating things with Paul could cause problems I didn't need. As I stared at him, I saw something in his eyes that almost took my breath away. He was such a good man, and I felt something for him I'd never felt before, but I was already keeping some things about Doug's call from him. For now, I had no choice but to hide my real feelings. "Of course we're friends," I finally choked out. "Is there any reason to think we're not?" I tried to smile, but I knew as soon as the words left my lips that it wasn't what he wanted to hear. His expression made that very clear.

He quickly finished his sandwich, and after a few minutes of uncomfortable small talk, he left. I stood by the door after he walked out and berated myself. There was a good chance this wonderful man liked me. As more than a friend. Had I just thrown something wonderful away?

Shaking my head, I went back to the kitchen, picked up Hannah's phone book, carried it upstairs, and put it on my desk, intending to look at it later. I was on my way down the stairs to clean the kitchen when someone knocked on the door. Had Paul forgotten something? I hurried over to the door, but when I opened it I found Reuben King standing there.

"Hi, Sarah," he said with a smile. "How are you doing? You look good."

"Thank you," I said, wondering why he wasn't at the school. "Is something wrong?"

"That's what I wanted to ask you. The kids are studying geography, so I ran over to check on Cicely. Is she okay?"

I frowned at him. "I'm sorry. I don't understand."

It was his turn to look concerned. "I assumed she was ill. She didn't show up for school today."

Chapter Fourteen

Reuben followed me as I ran upstairs to Cicely's room. A quick look revealed her schoolbag lying on the floor near her bed. I hadn't noticed it when I'd checked on her early that morning. Panic gripped my heart. Where was she? Had my sister's killer been here?

"We need to call the police," I said to Reuben, trying to catch my breath.

He grabbed my shoulder to stop me from running out of the room. "Before you do that, you need to know that Jeremiah Ostrander didn't show up either. Maybe we should check with his parents before we bring the police in on this."

"I don't understand. What does that have to do with anything?"

He let go of me. "Cicely and Jeremiah have developed a pretty close friendship. You know Jeremiah. He never misses school. Doesn't it sound like more than a coincidence that they're both gone today?"

I frowned at him. "Yes, as a matter of fact, it does." Suddenly Cicely's question about dating made sense. Obviously, she didn't understand that Conservative Mennonite boys don't just "date." Besides, Jeremiah was four years older than she. What was she thinking? I was certain the attraction was one way, and Jeremiah would be horrified to think Cicely had a crush on him. He was probably just trying to be friends with her for my sake.

I thought about calling Paul and asking him to come back to Sanctuary, but perhaps Reuben was right. A battle ensued in my mind between believing this situation had nothing to do with the call from Doug and the fear he'd instilled in me.

"Jeremiah's parents don't have a phone," Reuben said, "but I believe I saw his father going into the hardware store on my way over here."

I made a quick decision to talk to William before taking any drastic or unnecessary steps that could cause problems down the road. I grabbed my coat out of the closet, and Reuben and I hurried down the front steps and down the street to Ingalls Hardware. As the store came into view, I saw William Ostrander walking to his buggy.

Reuben called out to him, and William stopped. He looked a little alarmed to see us both jogging toward him.

"William," Reuben said when he reached him, "is Jeremiah ill today?"

William shook his head. "No, the boy is fine. Why would you ask?" The frown on his face deepened.

"He wasn't in school this morning," Reuben said. "And neither was Sarah's niece. Jeremiah and Cicely have become friends. It's odd that they're both missing. Could they have taken off together?"

"Cicely and I exchanged harsh words yesterday," I said. "Maybe she decided not to go to school today because she was still upset. But would Jeremiah leave with her?"

"It is not like Jeremiah to do something so foolish." William's Dutch ancestry was evident in his accent. He was tall and lean like his son, but that's where the similarities ended. Jeremiah's gentle countenance was in sharp contrast to William's grim demeanor. Although he'd always been polite to me, I'd felt something else brewing below the surface. A kind of quiet resentment. His next comment proved me right. "You need to learn to control your niece, Sarah Miller. She is not the kind of person I want my son to spend time with. She is worldly and vain."

215

My fear for Cicely's safety turned to resentment. "You realize she just lost her mother? She's hurting and needs help, William. Not judgment. You have no right to talk about her like that."

"I have no right?" he said loudly. "My boy never deceived us before he met your niece."

"Stop it, William," Reuben said sharply. "This isn't the time for blame. We just need to find them."

I trembled with rage at William's attack against Cicely, but Reuben was right. Our attention should be focused on finding Jeremiah and Cicely.

"Where would they go?" I asked. "Cicely hasn't been anywhere except my house and the school."

William turned pale. "The mine," he said, looking at Reuben.

"But we tell the children to stay away from there," I insisted. "I can't believe Jeremiah would take Cicely somewhere so dangerous."

Missouri was rife with abandoned lead and coal mines. At one time the state was a top producer of lead in the United States, but now many of the once profitable mines were closed. There was an old deserted mine just outside of Sanctuary, but most of our residents stayed away from it because it

216

was so unstable. Not only was the ceiling ready to collapse, there was an open shaft inside that was almost a thousand feet deep. Although Reuben had contacted the state many times, so far Missouri's reclamation project hadn't reached this area. Unfortunately, some of the town's teenagers liked to sneak over there from time to time.

"I heard the children talking about the mine the other day," Reuben said, his face pale. "But I had no idea any of them planned to go there."

William shook his head. "Jeremiah has been told to stay away, but his brother used to take him there without our permission."

Jeremiah's older brother, Joshua, had rejected his parents' conservative teachings and left Sanctuary almost two years earlier. I'd liked Joshua. He was a young man with his own mind who wasn't interested in the kind of life William planned for him. On the other hand, Jeremiah seemed committed to his church and to his parents. This was the first time I'd ever known him to be rebellious.

"I think we need to drive over there," Reuben said. "Then if we can't find them, we'll contact the police."

"The police?" William said. He glared at me. "This is what happens when you bring the world into our lives."

I struggled to hold my temper. Right now, all I cared about was finding my niece. If we didn't find Cicely and Jeremiah at the mine, I'd call Paul and ask for his help.

Reuben ran over to the library to ask Martha to watch the children, and then we all got into his truck. William sat in the truck's small backseat, while I sat in the front. No one said a word as we drove out of town. When we reached the road that led to the mine, Reuben instructed us to find something to hang on to. The road was strewn with rocks and vegetation that had grown after the mine closed. It was bumpy at best, and a couple of times we were jolted so hard I prayed I hadn't pulled a muscle. When the mine finally came into view, I searched for a sign that Jeremiah and Cicely were there, but there was nothing to indicate the children were anywhere around.

"I don't see them," I said.

"This is only the front of the mine," Reuben replied. "There's a lot more to it." He slowed down and parked. "I don't dare drive any closer. It's not safe."

The three of us climbed out of the truck. The entrance to the mine was carved into a hill. It had been repeatedly boarded up, but between young people from town and tourists who thought the mines were interesting, the boards frequently had to be replaced.

"Let's look around outside first," Reuben said. "If we can't find them, I'll go inside."

"No," William said emphatically. "You do not have a child at risk. If anyone enters the mine, it will be me."

Although Reuben didn't say anything, I was fairly certain his offer was made because he was younger and in better shape physically than William. It would be easier for him to stay safe inside the mine than it would be for the older man.

We each took a different area around the old shaft. Reuben went south and William went north. I searched the hill over the shaft, going away from the entrance. I was about to give up when I noticed something lying in the snow. I picked up a blue hair clip just like the one Cora had given Cicely. Feeling a twinge of hope, I scanned the area, but I didn't see her. I ran back toward the front of the mine, calling out Reuben's name. He and William met me a few feet from the entrance.

"This is Cicely's," I said, trying to catch my breath. "If they're not here now, they were at some point."

"William and I looked everywhere and

couldn't find them," Reuben said. "If they haven't left, they're inside."

"There were footprints in the snow where I found the hair clip," I said. "What about out here?"

We hurried over to the mine entrance. Sure enough, there were two sets of footprints going toward the entrance, but nothing coming out.

"I will go in and bring them out," William said.

"William, you need to let me go," Reuben said firmly. "I'm younger and stronger. The mine is dangerous. I know you feel responsible for your boy, but I'm the best candidate. The children are our most important priority. If you fall or get injured, it won't help them. I'm asking you to think with your head, not your pride."

It was evident that William struggled with Reuben's reasoning, but after a few moments, his expression became resigned. "All right, Reuben. But if I feel you need help or if you do not return in a reasonable time, I will come in after you."

Reuben nodded and looked at me. "And if that happens, you must get my cell phone and call the police. It's in the glove compartment."

"I . . . I will. Please be careful."

Reuben walked next to the entrance and began to pull away the rest of the old boards that covered the opening. Suddenly he stopped and leaned in, staring inside the shaft. Then he straightened up and turned to us.

"I see them. They're coming this way."

William and I hurried over to where Reuben stood. Sure enough, a light came from inside the mine. A few seconds later, Cicely stepped over the remaining boards, holding a flashlight. She was followed by Jeremiah. I ran to Cicely and hugged her.

"Thank God you're okay," I said, my voice shaking. "I was so worried."

She didn't respond at first, but then she raised her arms and embraced me. As I held her, I looked over at Jeremiah. He stood in front of his father, who didn't touch him. Instead, he just scowled at the boy.

"You have disobeyed me, Jeremiah," William said angrily. "You will be punished accordingly."

"Yes, Papa," Jeremiah said softly.

William whirled around and pointed at Cicely. "You are forbidden to have anything more to do with this girl. She is obviously a very bad influence."

I let Cicely go and confronted the furious William. "That will be a little difficult," I said. "They're both in my classroom. They will have to see each other."

William grabbed his son's shoulder and drew him roughly to his side. "He will see her only in class. If this is not done the way I have said, Jeremiah will be removed from the school altogether."

I saw a look of fear on Jeremiah's face and felt my own anger dissolve. "I'll make sure your rules are followed, William," I said as gently as I could. "You don't have to worry."

Now Cicely glowered at me. Maybe she'd expected me to stand up to William, but Jeremiah's future hung in the balance. I couldn't let him down.

We all got back into Reuben's truck, William and Jeremiah jammed into the backseat and Reuben, Cicely, and I in the front. No one said a word on the way back to town. Reuben let William and Jeremiah off in front of the hardware store, where William's horse stood waiting patiently for his owner's return.

Although William avoided eye contact, I saw Jeremiah looking at us as we prepared to drive away. He was clearly upset. I couldn't understand his rash decision to take Cicely to the mine, but neither could I turn my back on the boy. I gave him a small smile meant to reassure him, and a look of relief swept across his features.

Reuben drove back to Janet's house and let Cicely and me off. Cicely went straight into the house while I hung back to talk to Reuben.

"Thank you," I told him. "Pray for us, will you?"

He nodded. "Sarah, Cicely isn't really angry at you. Don't take it personally."

"I know. That's what Janet says, but at some point she needs to accept that this is her life now and that she's got to make an effort."

"It's hard telling how long it will take, but I know everything will work out. Just don't get weary in well doing." He smiled at me. "The whole town is praying for you, you know. I pray for you and Cicely every day."

My eyes flushed with tears of gratitude. "Thank you, Reuben. I don't know what I'd do without my friends. And I'm so grateful for your help at school."

"I've enjoyed it. It's given me a chance to connect with the children. Hopefully, our friendships will continue even after you come back."

"I'm sure they will."

"Call me if you need more help, or if you decide you're not ready to start back to school on Monday."

"I really appreciate that, but I can hardly wait to get back to my classroom. Sitting around here isn't good for me. I need to be with my students."

"I understand. God bless you, Sarah." With that, he rolled up the truck's window and drove back to the school. As I turned to go inside, flakes of snow began to swirl around me, blown by a sharp wind that hinted we may be in for rough weather. But I was more worried about the storm I faced inside the house than the one that might be forming outside.

CHAPTER FIFTEEN

When I opened the door, I found Janet sitting in the living room, a look of concern on her face. "Cicely just ran up the stairs without saying a word to me. What's going on?"

I quickly filled her in on the day's events. She reached over and took my hands.

"I'm sorry, honey. How frustrating."

"What do I do?" I asked. "I can't ignore this. Cicely could have been seriously hurt, Janet. I can't stand by and watch her make such bad decisions."

"No, I guess you can't. Part of showing love is correction, Sarah. God corrects us because He loves us, and you'll have to do the same."

I knew she was right, but this wouldn't be easy. Although there were times I'd had to handle behavioral problems at school, I had the parents to back me up. This time I *was* the parent.

"Well, I'd better get it over with. Pray for me."

"I always do, honey," she said gently. "Before you face Cicely, I need to tell you something." Janet got up from the couch, went over to the table that held the phone, and picked up a note pad she kept there to write down messages. She tore off the top sheet of paper and brought it to me.

"Detective Sykes called. Said he can't get away from work right now after all, but he's sending someone else. A Mike Templeton."

I took the sheet of paper and stared at it. "Is that all he said?"

"Yes. He said you'd understand."

I shook my head. "Well, I don't. He called this morning and claimed he'd discovered something important about Hannah's murder. And warned me not to talk to anyone I don't know. He really frightened me. Now he's sending someone else? A stranger? I don't like it." I frowned at her. "Did he say when this man will get here?"

"I asked him that, but he didn't know for certain. Just as soon as he can get away, he said."

"Okay." I folded the note and put it in my coat pocket. "Guess I'll wait for Mr. Templeton, but I'm really disappointed in Detective Sykes."

226

"At least someone is coming, Sarah. Maybe we should take that as a good sign."

"Maybe."

I had to push the phone call out of my mind for now and concentrate on Cicely. I walked slowly up the stairs, asking God to give me the right words to say. How could I punish her but still let her know I loved her?

When I reached her door, I took a deep breath and knocked lightly. No answer. I knocked one more time, but when there was still no response, I opened the door and went inside. Cicely was lying on her bed, staring up at the ceiling. Tears ran down her face and into her hair. I wanted to run to her. Gather her up in my arms, but something told me it wasn't the right thing to do.

"Cicely, I need to talk to you. About what you did today."

She turned away from me. "Well, I don't want to talk to you," she mumbled, her voice heavy with emotion.

I walked over and sat down on the bed next to her. "I can't imagine what you were thinking. That old mine is dangerous. You and Jeremiah could have been hurt. Going there was foolish. Jeremiah knows better. He shouldn't have taken you."

She flopped back over and sat up, glaring

at me. "Jeremiah didn't take me to the mine. I went there on my own. He went with me to try to talk me out of going inside."

My mouth dropped open. "Why in the world would you do that?"

"Some of the kids told me about it, and I wanted to see it. I asked Jeremiah to show me where it was, but he wouldn't, so I decided to find it myself. It wasn't hard."

"You walked there?"

She shrugged. "Yeah."

"And Jeremiah followed you?"

She nodded. "I told him not to, but he wouldn't let me go alone." The impudent look on her face slipped a little. "He shouldn't get in trouble for what I did. Please tell his dad that, okay?"

I sighed. "Well, I'd like to, but they don't have a phone. Your defense of Jeremiah may come a little too late."

"What will happen to him?" Cicely's sudden concern for her friend was real.

"I don't know, but if you care about him, you should have considered the consequences of your actions before you got him in trouble. Your choices today were very selfish, Cicely. Not only have they hurt Jeremiah and his family, they also hurt me. And Reuben had to take time out of his schedule to go after you. He was getting ready to go into the mine to look for you. What if he'd been injured? What if you and Jeremiah had gotten hurt? Besides being unstable, there's a very deep shaft inside. If you'd fallen down it —" My breath caught in my throat.

Her expression hardened again. "So what?"

"Cicely, how many times must I tell you I love you?" I shook my head. "I know you're hurting, but I can't let you make such terrible decisions. If anything happened to you . . ." I choked up again.

She raised an eyebrow and stared at me, a look of rebellion on her face. "So what are you going to do? Spank me? I'm too old for that."

I took a deep breath, trying to calm my jagged nerves. "I agree. So I'm taking your phone away, and you won't watch TV for a month. You will go to school and come home. When you're not in school, you'll sit in your room and study. Is that clear?"

She flushed with anger. "You can't have my phone! It's mine!"

"Really? And how do you propose to pay the bill?"

She didn't answer. I could see she hadn't thought much about it.

"If I have to pay for the phone, that makes

it mine. When you can pay for it, we'll talk."
The phone was lying on the bed next to her,
and I grabbed it quickly before she could
think to pull it away.

"Give that back!" she shouted.

Shaken by her obvious rage, I stuck the
phone into my coat pocket and walked to
the door. "You'll get your phone back when
I see some real changes in your attitude and
your behavior. And don't forget about TV.
Nothing for a month." I hesitated a moment
before saying, "I love you, Cicely." Then I
opened the door and stepped into the hall.
Once I pulled the door shut, I leaned
against it. "How am I going to do this,
God?" I whispered. "Help me."

Realizing I still had my coat on, I went
downstairs and hung it up in the hall closet.
I'd have to tell Janet about Cicely's punishment, since they were TV buddies. I found
Janet in the kitchen making dinner and told
her what I'd done.

"I think that was an appropriate punishment," she said. "I'll support you in it." She
stopped stirring the soup on the stove and
turned to smile at me reassuringly. "I know
it's hard, Sarah, but you did the right thing."

"I hope so. When I came here to live, I
wasn't like this, was I?"

Janet chuckled. "No, but you were older

than Cicely. Although you were very grateful for a home, you certainly tested me in your own way."

I shook my head. "I don't understand."

She went back to stirring the soup. "Your rebellion showed up in smaller ways. No matter how many times I asked you to wipe your feet before you came into the house, you almost never did. And then there was the whole towel fiasco."

I frowned at her. "What are you talking about?"

She laughed. "Every day I asked you to put your dirty towel in the clothes hamper, but every day I'd find it on your bed."

"I just forgot . . ."

She turned to look at me. "Now, Sarah. You're one of the smartest people I've ever known. Are you telling me you don't have the ability to wipe your feet or put your towel in the hamper?"

I looked at her in amazement. "You mean I was testing you?"

"What do you think?"

"Well, now that I think about it, it doesn't make much sense. I guess I was doing it subconsciously."

"Exactly. Just like Cicely. Her disobedience might be more extreme, but it's coming from the same insecurity. You hold the

231

line. Let Cicely know you can be counted on to stay strong. For both of you."

I sighed and shook my head. "You're a wise woman, Janet. You should be raising lots of kids."

"You're enough for me. No woman ever had a better daughter. I feel blessed every day."

I wrapped my arms around her. Her love for me was like a balm to my injured soul. "I don't know what I ever did to deserve you."

She patted my back with one hand while stirring the soup with the other. I heard her sniff. "You go on and get ready for dinner," she said, pushing me gently away. "Or I'll get tears in our supper."

I let her go and headed for the kitchen door. Before I left the room, she called out my name. "What about Cicely? Will she be joining us for dinner?"

"I hope so. I'll tell her it's ready, but the decision will be hers." I shook my head. "I would imagine she's starving. She didn't pack a lunch this morning."

"We'll be ready to eat in about thirty minutes. I want to pop some apple cinnamon muffins in the oven."

I grinned at her. "Cicely's favorite. Good thinking."

"Let's hope it works."

I went back upstairs. Cicely's door was still closed. After going into my room, I shut my door and picked up the phone. When I got Paul on the line I told him about Doug's newest call.

"I don't understand," I told him. "He acted like he really wanted to talk to me. Why would he send someone else?"

"I have no idea," Paul said slowly. "Maybe somebody higher up doesn't want him talking to you. What was this guy's name again?"

"It was Mike. Mike Templeton."

"Okay, let me see what I can find out about him. We need to figure out who he is before he shows up. When is he supposed to get here?"

"I have no idea. Doug just said he'd come when he could. I'd call Doug back, Paul, but I'm afraid he might get into trouble."

"Don't worry. Let me see what I can dig up. I'll get back to you."

I said good-bye and hung up. Then I pulled out Hannah's phone book. I began to look through it, page by page, searching specifically for people, flipping past numbers for fast-food restaurants, Hannah's doctor, the local pharmacy, the bank, work, and a couple of repair shops. I knew a few of the names because I'd met them at Hannah's funeral. Claire's name and number was listed, as was mine. There weren't a lot of personal entries. The remaining names didn't mean anything to me. There was one interesting note though. Just the initials *JR* and a big star drawn next to it. No address, but there was a phone number.

I slid the book back into the drawer, wondering if I should try talking to some of Hannah's friends. Maybe one of them knew something that might put us on the right track to finding her killer.

I was just getting ready to go downstairs when the phone rang. I picked it up. It was Wynter.

"Sarah, I talked to my friend in Kansas City. He told me that your sister's death has been blamed on a junkie named Steven Hanks. Seems he committed suicide in jail. Probably because he knew he wasn't going to get any more drugs. Is this the guy you told me about?"

"Yes." So it was official.

"I'm sorry. I know this isn't what you wanted to hear."

"I understand. Thanks for trying."

"Before you get too upset, why don't you wait to see why they believe this Hanks guy was involved? I expect they'll contact you soon to explain their reasoning."

"I guess, but it sounds like they're trying to close this case as quickly and conveniently as possible. I'd sure like to know why."

Wynter paused for a moment. "Why are you so convinced Hanks isn't guilty?"

I sighed. "I truly don't believe the person who killed Hannah was some out-of-control drug addict. Why would he leave white orchids on her body, Wynter? Whoever did that knew about my parents' murder. How old was Hanks?"

"I'm not sure, but I think he was in his twenties."

"Then he couldn't have killed my mother and father almost twenty years ago."

"I see your point," she said slowly.

I heard something odd in her tone. "Is there something else?"

"I don't know. Maybe it's my old reporter instinct rearing its ugly head, but my contact seemed . . . stressed. Like he couldn't get me off the phone fast enough."

"What do you think that means?"

There was a pause while I waited for her response.

"I don't know, Sarah," she said finally, "but I think it's time to let this go."

I took a deep breath and told her about my conversations with Doug.

Another pause. "Strange how things look so different on the other side of the fence. Now I know why people were worried about me." She sighed. "Look, keep me updated, okay? I can't call my contact again, but I might call a friend back at my old station. Have him nose around a bit. Find out what they have on Hanks."

"Are you talking about Zac?"

"Yes. He's great at uncovering things. Please be patient, Sarah. And be very careful, okay?"

I thanked her and hung up.

Wynter's friend, Zac Weikel, had come to Sanctuary with her while she was looking for her brother. He and Esther had formed a friendship, and now he returned every so often to visit his old friend, Wynter, and his new friend, Esther. I liked him but didn't know him very well. Wynter told me once that he'd been instrumental in helping her find her brother.

Now what? Maybe Mike Templeton would turn out to be the person who would turn things around. Unless Doug was sending him to let me down easy. If that was the case, I'd definitely call Anson Bentley. He might be the only hope I had left. All the doors seemed to be closing, but I was still convinced Hannah's death was connected to my parents'. I couldn't walk away until I knew the truth.

Janet called from downstairs to let us know dinner was ready. Steeling myself, I left my room and knocked on Cicely's door. Surprisingly, she flung it open, brushed past me, and went downstairs without saying a word. I guess her hunger was stronger than her dislike for me.

Conversation at dinner was limited to Janet and me. We talked about my return to school next week and how things were going at the clinic.

"I've taken your advice to heart about finding some help," Janet said. "If you think of anyone who might be interested in working part time during the day at the clinic, will you let me know?"

I nodded. "You know, Pastor Troyer's daughter, Ruth, might be willing to help you. She loves animals."

"She's not in school?"

"No, she dropped out when she turned sixteen. To be honest, I didn't fight it. She wasn't good in school."

Janet frowned. "She always seemed a bit . . . slow."

"She might be a little slower than some of my other students, but she's not stupid. She's just extremely shy and a little naive. I tried to get her interested in school, but it wasn't for her. I know that sounds odd coming from a teacher, but she had no interest in anything except reading and animals. She helps out at home, but I imagine she's bored silly. Working with you might be just the thing."

Janet nodded. "Do you want me to talk to her, or do you want to approach her?"

"We should probably ask her father first. I'll see him as soon as I can."

"Great. Let me know what he says." Janet looked sideways at Cicely, who was doing her best to let us know she wasn't the least bit interested in our conversation. "How about another muffin, Cicely? I kept them in the oven so they'd stay warm."

She nodded. "Yes, please. Thank you."

I had to suppress a smile, even though the whole situation with Cicely wasn't the least bit humorous. She wasn't usually this proper, and rarely did she thank anyone for anything.

Janet got up and took the remaining muffins out of the warm oven. She handed one to Cicely and then held the tray in front of me. I was tempted to say, "Yes, please. Thank you," but I didn't. Cicely would think I was making fun of her, and that wasn't my intention.

I put butter on my muffin and let the flavors of apples and cinnamon explode in my mouth. I wondered if I'd ever be able to match Janet's culinary skills.

An idea suddenly popped into my head. "I just had a thought," I said to Janet. "Why don't we go to Sanctuary Mennonite this Sunday? Then I can talk to Pastor Troyer about Ruth."

"Sounds good. I haven't gone to church with Esther for a few weeks. I've missed it."

That finally got Cicely's attention. Her head shot up and she stared at us. "Are you talking about that old-fashioned church? Don't we belong to Agape Fellowship?"

I struggled to force back a sharp retort. Since we'd been home, we'd only gone to church twice. One of those visits was Hannah's funeral. The other was a regular Sunday service, and Cicely had argued about going. Yet now she suddenly considered herself a member of my church?

"I belong to Agape," I said evenly. "I don't remember you placing membership. But I also visit Sanctuary Mennonite frequently. I have friends who go there."

"I'm not wearing one of those weird dresses or putting some goofy thing on my head," Cicely said in a whiny voice. "You can't make me do that."

"I have no intention of forcing you to do any such thing. Visitors don't have to wear prayer coverings or dress any particular way. However, we will wear modest dresses so our presence won't be distracting to anyone."

Her eyes widened. "But you let me wear jeans to Agape."

"Yes, it's okay to wear jeans there. But it's not appropriate at Sanctuary Mennonite."

She started to say something else, but I held my hand up to stop her. "You have a very nice dark blue jumper. Wear that with your white turtleneck. You look very pretty in that outfit."

Cicely's huge sigh showed her exasperation with my suggestion, but she didn't argue. Instead, she got up, carried her bowl and plate to the sink, rinsed them, and put them in the dishwasher. Then she flounced out.

"Well, it could have been worse," Janet said, once she heard Cicely's door slam upstairs.

"At least she's talking to me."

"I guess that's a blessing."

I popped the rest of my muffin into my mouth, sorry to be finishing it. "Janet, there's an odd noise on the phone," I said after I swallowed. "Have you noticed it?"

She nodded. "You mean that clicking sound?"

"Yes. I've heard it several times now. At first I thought Cicely was listening in on the extension, but she's not."

"I forgot to mention it, but I had a problem with the phones while you were in Kansas City. A guy from the phone company showed up and said they needed to upgrade our service. Something about new lines. He told me we might notice some noise until the work is completed." She frowned. "I'm not sure how long we have to wait, but eventually the line should clear."

I shrugged. "Okay. It's not interfering with anything. Just annoying." I picked up my dishes and took them to the sink. "You go watch TV and relax. I'll take care of the dishes."

"You know what? I'll take you up on that." Janet yawned. "For some reason I'm beat tonight." She smiled at me. "If I fall asleep, will you wake me up so I don't miss my favorite show?"

"I will. I promise. If I'm not too tired, I might even watch it with you."

Although I didn't watch much television, I enjoyed this particular show about a family of police officers. They prayed together, and I really liked the characters.

Janet left the room, and I began loading the dishwasher. It had been a long and difficult day. I prayed tomorrow would be better. But as I worked, I couldn't shake an odd feeling that something dark was lurking around the next corner.

Chapter Sixteen

Saturday was uneventful. I worked on lesson plans, preparing for school on Monday. The night before, a winter storm had swept through, dumping about six inches of snow. Several of the men in Sanctuary got out and began clearing sidewalks and streets. By Saturday afternoon, the snow had been pushed off to the side, giving everyone safe passage whether they drove a vehicle, a buggy, or made their way on foot.

Sunday morning Janet, Cicely, and I walked to Sanctuary Mennonite Church since it was close to our house. As we sat next to Esther, several of my students came over to say hello. We saw the Ostranders, but they didn't acknowledge us. William wouldn't look our way, and his wife, Trina, acted as if we were invisible. I caught Jeremiah's eye once and smiled. He gave me a brief nod but then turned his head. I had no idea what his father had said to him or what his punishment had been, but I prayed that the situation on Friday hadn't ruined our relationship or made it impossible for Jeremiah to continue his studies.

Even though she'd complained about going, Cicely seemed curious about the Mennonite church. The women sat on one side and the men on the other. Agape Fellowship had a praise and worship team with instruments, but there was only one person playing guitar in the Mennonite service. Cicely would have been shocked to learn that the guitar player had been added just six months earlier. At one time, the church taught that using instruments during worship was wrong, since they believed there was no mention of them in the New Testament. However, Jonathon Wiese had changed Pastor Troyer's mind about this point. Pastor Troyer had addressed the congregation before the change was made. "Why would God find instruments pleasant in Old Testament times and then suddenly not want them anymore?" he asked. "We must remember that the division between the Old Testament and New Testament was added by men. Even though we are now under grace through Jesus Christ, the story of God is seamless. We must not elevate traditions over the nature of God. There is nothing evil about instruments used to praise the name of the Lord."

Even though his explanation satisfied most of his congregation, at first there were a few older members who struggled with the change. Slowly but surely they began to accept it. Esther had been instrumental in bringing most of them around. One of the church's oldest parishioners, Gussie Brinkerhoff, even smiled now when the young guitar player came up to the platform. She'd been violently opposed to the change at first. The young man, Henry Shultz, played beautifully, and his soft strumming was so anointed it was hard to argue with his addition to the service.

Pastor Troyer's sermon was about love in action. "Love is not an abundance of words," he said. "Love helps. Love is there when a brother or sister has trouble. Love finds a way to hold them up and bring them through their difficulty. James points out that saying to someone in need, 'Depart in peace, be ye warmed and filled; notwithstanding ye give them not those things which are needful to the body; what doth it profit?' " He closed his Bible and looked out at the congregation. "How many times do we promise to pray for someone when the answer to their need is in our possession? Is it love to pray and not respond? I do not believe it is. God does not surround us with vain promises. He is our ever-present help in time of need. I encourage you to be the hand of God to your neighbors, and not just to those who attend your church or believe the way you do. Love doesn't ask for perfection before it reaches out. Remember that it isn't judgment that leads men to God. It is His love and forgiveness in action. For us to be like God, we must love the same way."

After the sermon one of the elders came up to give the closing prayer, and then we were dismissed. I went up to the front of the church to talk to Pastor Troyer. I waited until he finished talking to a couple who had reached him first. After they walked away, he smiled at me.

"Why, Sarah Miller. I am happy to see you. How are you doing?"

I smiled at the tall, thin minister with a salt-and-pepper beard that seemed to underline his wonderful smile. Although he couldn't really be called a handsome man, the love of God shone through him, making him someone people felt drawn to.

"We're doing okay, Pastor. Thank you. And thank you so much for all the wonderful food you and your wife brought to our house. I so appreciated your kind note. It meant a lot to me."

"I am glad. I left a message with Janet to tell you that if you ever needed to talk, I was here for you."

"I got it, and I appreciate it very much."

"Is there something I can help you with today?"

"It's about Ruth, Pastor. I know how much she loves animals. Janet could use some help during the day at the clinic. Is it possible that Ruth might be interested in working for her part time?"

Pastor Troyer's smile widened. "Oh my. I believe she would love that. She desperately needs something to do. I will talk to her this afternoon and then get back to you and Janet. Would that be all right?"

"Wonderful. Thank you."

I started to leave, but he stopped me. "Sarah, I am somewhat concerned about Jeremiah Ostrander. Is he doing well in school?"

I nodded. "As well as he can. I wish his parents would let me teach him sign language. It would help him to communicate better with the world around him."

He frowned. "I wasn't aware that Jeremiah was learning sign language."

"Only a few words so far. With all the

other children in class, I don't have much time to teach him. If his parents would help, it could make a huge difference."

"Thank you for sharing that with me. If you do not mind, I would like to talk to his parents about this issue."

I nodded. "That would be wonderful. Any help you can give would be greatly appreciated." I studied his expression. "But that's not why you asked about him, is it?"

"No," he said, shaking his head. "The boy seems morose and discouraged. Although I cannot point to any one example, I am concerned about the way his father treats him. William appears to be very harsh and critical of Jeremiah." He looked at me through narrowed eyes. "Am I wrong about this?"

Although I made it a policy not to talk about my students or their parents to others in the community, I made an exception and told Pastor Troyer about the incident at the mine.

"So Jeremiah was only trying to protect Cicely?" he said.

"Yes, but William was furious and intent on punishing him."

"He always seems angry with the boy. I confess I do not understand."

I hesitated a moment before saying, "I

think I do."

Pastor Troyer's forehead wrinkled with concern. "Will you please share your reasoning with me?"

I nodded. "Sometimes parents, especially fathers, carry guilt or anger if their children aren't perfect. Unfortunately, they can lash out at the child. I think that's what's happening here. One of William's sons left him and the other has hearing loss."

Pastor Troyer's eyes widened. "Oh my. That makes perfect sense. I must confess that sometimes I feel guilty about Ruth. I mean, I do not see her as disabled, but I wonder why she could not do better in school. And why she seems so withdrawn." He shook his head. "However, I do not feel anger. Just concern."

"William's concern comes out a different way. Unfortunately, it won't help Jeremiah. It only makes it harder for him." I smiled at him. "Ruth is a wonderful young woman. She just hasn't found her calling yet. Maybe working with Janet will spark something in her."

"I suspect you are correct." He patted my shoulder. "Thank you so much, Sarah. I must say how happy I am that you found your calling. You do so much to help the young people in our school. We are truly blessed."

"I don't seem to be helping my niece much. I covet your prayers, Pastor. She's hurt and angry, and I'm trying to find a way to help her."

"You will find it," he said with sincerity. "I have no doubt of that. But I will certainly pray for both of you."

"Thank you."

"About the incident at the mine. Have you explained the truth to Brother Ostrander?"

"That's my intention. If I can catch them before they leave, that is."

Pastor Troyer smiled. "But his busybody pastor is holding you up. I am sorry, Sarah. Please hurry along and speak to William. And if I can do anything to help . . ."

"Thank you. I'll certainly call on you."

"And I will let you know Ruth's response to your kind offer. I am certain she will be excited."

I said good-bye and joined Janet and Cecily. "He thinks Ruth will be very interested," I told Janet. "He's going to talk to her and let us know."

"Oh, thank you," Janet said with a sigh. "Maybe this will be a blessing for both of us."

We put on our coats and stepped outside. The Ostranders were just getting into their buggy. I took a deep breath, summoned up my courage, and hurried over to them before they could leave. Trina looked away as I approached. William, who was just getting into the buggy, glared at me. For a moment, I almost turned back, but my concern for Jeremiah kept me going.

"William," I said, trying not to be intimated by the look he gave me, "I need to tell you something. Cicely admitted that it was her idea to go to the mine, not Jeremiah's. In fact, he only followed her because he was concerned for her safety. I felt you should know that what happened wasn't his fault. He was just trying to help."

William's expression didn't change, but Trina turned around and met my gaze. Taking that as encouragement, I continued. "I want to apologize for my niece and ask for your understanding. Losing her mother was very traumatic. She . . . she's been making poor decisions, and it seems she pulled Jeremiah into this last situation. I hope you will forgive her. I want you to know that I'm trying as hard as I can to help her. I covet your prayers."

This time the compassion in Trina's face was clear, and I smiled at her.

"Jeremiah is a wonderful young man, and I'm sorry Cicely got him into trouble," I continued. "I . . . I guess that's all I have to say." I looked at Jeremiah, who stared at me with an expression I couldn't interpret. "I hope to see you in school tomorrow, Jeremiah." William just continued to glower at me, so I turned to go.

"Thank you, Sarah," Trina said. "It was good of you to explain the truth to us."

I looked back and found her smiling at me. "Thank you, Trina. Jeremiah has been a good friend to Cicely. I'll do everything I can to keep something like this from happening again."

"Your niece needs correction," William said gruffly. "You do not seem capable of providing it. Please keep her away from my son. As I've already said, if you cannot do that, we will remove him from your school."

With that, he urged his horse on and rode away. Every Conservative Mennonite family I dealt with through the school showed me nothing but Christian kindness, but William was another matter. His rudeness and judgmental attitudes were an antithesis to the gentle disposition of the other parents.

I went back to where Janet and Cicely waited for me. Esther stood next to Janet. When I reached them, Esther took my arm.

"I am so sorry William spoke so harshly," she said. "He is a man with a great burden."

"He's a jerk," Cicely said. She frowned at me. "Why did you let him talk to you like that?"

"My concern is for Jeremiah, Cicely," I said. "He loves school. Maybe William was wrong, but I had to decide what was most important. Protecting Jeremiah meant more to me than protecting my feelings."

Esther smiled at her. "Sarah is right, Cicely. And as far as William is concerned, remember that most of the time people who are 'jerks' are that way for a reason. Everyone has their own burden to bear." She pulled her cape closer as a cold gust of wind blew past us. "Perhaps we all need to get home."

"Why don't you come over and have lunch with us?" Janet said. "We'd love to have you."

"Oh, thank you, my friend, but Wynter and Reuben are taking me to lunch in Fredericktown today. Maybe another time?"

"Of course," Janet said. She gave her friend a big hug.

"Thank you for your kind words," I said. "And please keep us in your prayers. I don't want William's attitude to cause trouble for Jeremiah at school."

"You mean his father might really keep him out?" Cicely asked, her eyes wide.

I nodded. "Yes, Cicely. Sometimes our actions can hurt the people we care about."

She stared at me for a moment and then looked away. Another blast of wind convinced me we needed to get home. I gave Esther a quick hug, and we turned to leave. Suddenly, Cicely ran back and wrapped her arms around the elderly woman, who looked surprised and pleased by the touching gesture.

"You are a good girl," she said to Cicely after she let her go. "I am pretty smart about people, and I see what a wonderful heart you have. I am so glad we get to be friends."

"I am too," Cicely said. She turned and ran past us, headed toward Janet's.

We said good-bye to Esther and hurried toward home. Cicely's actions confused me. Why did she react that way to someone she didn't really know, yet she rejected me?

"Cicely and Esther have spent some time together," Janet said, as if she knew what I was thinking.

"When? Except for school, I've been with her almost all the time."

"Not when she takes Murphy out."

"She goes to Esther's?"

Janet nodded. "Esther gives her cookies and talks to her. Cicely thinks she's 'awesome.' That seems to be her favorite word."

I shook my head. "I'd noticed some of his walks were a little long, but I had no idea she was visiting next door."

"Esther is very supportive of you when she talks to Cicely. I think you should encourage the friendship."

"Of course I will. I love Esther to pieces."

"You know, Esther mentioned something interesting that Cicely brought up during one of their visits."

"What was it?" I asked.

"After your parents died and your sister was adopted, what was your biggest fear?"

I didn't even have to think twice about it. "Being alone again." As soon as the words left my mouth, I was shocked by my inability to see what was right in front of me. "I've been worried she doesn't believe I really love her. But she's afraid if she loves me back, something will happen to me and she'll be alone." I shook my head. "I should have seen it. When my parents died I went to live with my aunt. Then she got sick, and I had to leave her house. I ended up with Mrs. Johnson, who died a year after I moved in. After that, I lost my sister. When I came here to live with you, I kept wondering if you'd die too. I'd forgotten."

Janet nodded. "There's nothing you can do about it, Sarah. Time and patience will have to give Cicely the reassurance she needs. Just like it did for you."

"I still worry about what I would do if something happened to you, Janet. That fear has never really left me."

She gave me a tight hug. "I know. But you know now that God will never leave you, no matter what happens around you. You need to teach that to Cicely."

I sighed deeply. "As usual, you're right. So let's see. She's afraid I don't really want her. She's angry that her mother died instead of me. But she's also afraid I will die. Does that about sum it up?"

Janet laughed. "I know it's complicated, honey. But Cicely will work through all of it. You have my word."

I hugged her again. "Thank you. Now let's get inside before we both freeze to death."

When we reached the house, Janet opened her front door. The aroma of the pot roast she'd put in the oven before we left made me instantly hungry. Cicely wasn't downstairs, but her coat was draped over a chair in the living room. I remembered Janet's story about my towels and quietly hung up the coat.

After helping Janet set the table, I called

Cicely to come downstairs. She seemed to be in a decent mood, and although we only made small talk, the atmosphere wasn't as tense as it had been. We'd just finished lunch, and Janet had brought out a peach pie, when Cicely cleared her throat and looked at me.

"I wanted to know if I could help Janet after school," she said. "I know that other girl will probably help during the day and Janet might not need me every night. But if I get my homework done and keep my grades up, is it all right?"

I looked at Janet, who was smiling. "As long as your grades don't slip, I think it's a fine idea. But you'd better ask Janet too."

"Can I, Janet?" she asked. The pleading tone in her voice touched my heart.

Janet nodded. "I'd love it. Even with Ruth's help, I'll need some extra assistance. Maybe a couple nights a week? And Saturday if possible? It's my busiest day."

Cicely look back at me. "But I'm grounded, right? When can I start?"

"As long as you do your homework before you go, I'm willing to allow you to do this one thing."

Cicely's big smile told me my decision was the right one. "Awesome. Thank you, Aunt Sarah."

"I'm not sure how she'll get to the clinic during the week," I said to Janet. "When the weather is good, she can walk, but what about when it's bad out?"

Janet shrugged. "I'll run over and get her. Won't take more than a few minutes."

"Okay," I said, nodding. "I guess we have a plan." It was nice to feel I was no longer on Cicely's bad side. The pie tasted especially sweet. After we finished eating, Cicely and I helped Janet clean up. Then Cicely went upstairs to work on her homework. The job with Janet seemed to give her new energy.

"That was very wise," Janet said after Cicely left. "I know sometimes it may not feel like it, but you're doing a wonderful job with her. Just don't doubt yourself so much."

I sighed. "It's easy because I do doubt myself."

Janet patted me on the back. "Perfectly normal. I felt the same way when you moved in here. Even though you were older than Cicely, I still felt like a substitute mother. It was very intimidating."

I looked at her with surprise. "I never sensed you felt that way."

Janet grinned at me. "I didn't want you to know how afraid I was. I felt you needed someone stable and confident. So that's what I pretended to be."

I laughed. "I guess I need acting lessons. You may need to coach me."

She shook her head. "You're a natural. Just remember that when you're afraid, she'll pick it up. She'll be afraid too."

I leaned over and kissed her on the cheek. "Thanks. For everything."

"You're welcome. Now this old lady is going upstairs to take a nap. I'll see you later for supper. We'll have roast beef sandwiches, okay?"

"Sounds great, but to be honest, I'm so full right now, I doubt I'll be hungry the rest of the day."

Janet smiled at me. "I totally understand. I'm hoping when I wake up I won't feel like a stuffed zucchini." When she yawned, I realized I was tired too.

Not long after Janet went upstairs, I followed her. I still had papers to go through and wanted to look at them today, since I would be back in school tomorrow. After going into my room, I closed and locked the door. It wasn't that I didn't trust Janet or Cicely, I just felt the need to keep Hannah's personal papers to myself for now.

I got the last box of papers out of the closet and dumped everything on my desk.

Then I sat down and sorted out the loose papers. There wasn't anything too exciting. Two store lists, a list of Christmas gifts to buy, and a to-do list. I cried out softly when I saw what she'd written next to my name. *Get Mr. Whiskers cleaned and repaired. Sarah will love this!* I'd wondered why she hadn't given him back to me. I'd assumed he'd grown to mean so much to her she couldn't bear to part with him. Now I knew she'd been planning to give him to me all along. I looked over in the corner where he sat in my chair and smiled. I was so grateful to God that I'd found him and removed him from the house before the fire. I had to stop for a few minutes and have a good cry. When I could see clearly again, I started back through the papers.

The last envelope was full of lists. Things Hannah had wanted to accomplish but never got done. From stocking her pantry, to mending clothes, joining a gym, putting together photo albums, and cleaning her house.

That was it. I'd been through everything, but there wasn't any file from the reporter who'd contacted Hannah. Had someone found it? Taken it? I was starting to put some of the papers back in the box when I noticed something peeking out from underneath one of the box flaps that had been folded over another flap to close the bottom of the box. I reached down and pulled out a small manila envelope. I opened the clasp and dumped out the contents. Several old newspaper articles fell out. I removed a paper clip from them and realized several of them were about my parents' murders. This had to be the information from the reporter. I read through them quickly but didn't see anything new. Then I found an article about the robbery and murder of another couple in Kansas City. I looked at the date it was published. It had happened about a week after our parents were killed. I read the names, but they didn't mean anything to me, so I put it aside. Was the reporter investigating this case too?

I continued looking through the rest of the contents. There was a sheet of lined notebook paper with notes on it. Written in an unknown hand, I assumed they belonged to the reporter. There wasn't anything new, just a recap of basic facts from my parents' murders. But at the bottom of the paper Hannah had written, *J behind everything? Why? What is the connection to MLS?*

I picked up a letter-sized envelope and took out some folded pieces of paper. It was a police report. I began to read it but quickly felt sick to my stomach. It was from the day my mother and father were killed. Cold, clinical, and disturbing. I couldn't read the conditions of their bodies, so I skipped that part. Toward the end, someone had written, *Two children removed from the premises and turned over to CPS.* I recognized that as Child Protective Services. Images of horror from that day flashed in my mind like an out-of-control strobe light. I had to put the report down and catch my breath. I'd thought I wanted to see this, but I was wrong. It was too much to handle. I quickly put it back into the envelope. There didn't seem to be any new information that could help me now anyway.

"So what does all this mean, Hannah?" I said quietly.

I put everything back in the box except the last envelope and its contents. I found Hannah's first letter in my desk drawer, added it to the envelope with the reporter's information, and slid the envelope back into my drawer. Then I carried the box down to the basement. Hopefully, there was something important in the papers I was keeping upstairs, but as of yet none of it made any sense to me. I needed to go through everything more carefully, but the police report had upset me, and I wanted to take a break.

I was beginning to think I'd never uncover the evidence I needed to find Hannah's killer.

CHAPTER SEVENTEEN

I was up early Monday morning, feeling prepared to return to my class but a little nervous. My students had spent three weeks with Reuben. Would they want me back? I packed my satchel and headed over to the school at seven, an hour before my students were scheduled to arrive. I wanted some time to myself before facing them again. When I unlocked the door and went inside, I was surprised to find that they'd decorated the room. A large paper banner read, *Welcome Back Miss Miller!* And there were several pictures thumbtacked to the corkboard, depicting me returning to school. Their efforts touched my heart and made me feel even better about coming back. I'd missed them more than I'd realized.

I was ready for them when they began traipsing in a little before eight. Several of the children brought gifts from their parents. Homemade preserves, bread, and two pies. Mary Stoltz gave me a beautiful quilted lap robe sewn by her mother, Rachel. And David Ingalls handed me a large bag of popping corn. I smiled at him. It wasn't a secret that popcorn was one of my favorite foods.

Jeremiah came in after everyone else. He didn't have a gift, but that wasn't a surprise. I tried to catch his eye, but he wouldn't look at me. We'd always been close, so his reaction made me worry. Had the situation with him and Cicely caused irreparable harm? I could only pray it hadn't.

Cicely seemed fine throughout the day. She even laughed a few times and smiled at me more than once. I hoped we'd weathered our recent storm.

The day passed quickly, and I was pleased to find that Reuben had done an exceptional job with them. They were completely on track with the lesson plan I'd left. Before I knew it, it was three o'clock and time to send the children home.

As they were leaving, I asked Jeremiah to stay. Cicely shot me a strange look, but I waved her on. I wanted to talk to Jeremiah alone. She left but stood outside, in front of the window, watching us.

I motioned for Jeremiah to come up to my desk. "I need to make sure you're all right," I said. "I also want you to know that

I appreciate what you tried to do for Cicely. It may not have been wise to follow her, but your heart was in the right place. I'm just sorry you got in trouble for it."

His eyes finally met mine. "It's okay, Miss Miller. I knew my father would be upset, but I was afraid Cicely might get hurt. That mine is dangerous."

"You were willing to risk your father's anger to protect my niece." I shook my head. "That was a very brave thing to do."

"My father says it was very foolish." He sighed. "I let him down a lot, even though I try hard to please him."

I hesitated before replying. William had already driven one son away. Would Jeremiah be next? "Your father loves you, Jeremiah. Sometimes parents don't know exactly how to show their love. Some are too lax and some are too strict. I'm sure he was upset because you were in danger. I hope you're able to forgive him."

Jeremiah's eyes grew bright with tears. "I'm trying."

I stood up. "If there is anything I can do . . ."

He shook his head. "Father is looking for a reason to take me out of school. If you want to help me, it would be best if you don't challenge him." I noticed the boy was clenching and unclenching his fists. "I want an education so I can go to college."

"I think that's wonderful, but I know your parents expect you to work on the farm after graduation."

He thrust his chin out and a look of defiance changed his usually meek expression. "If I tell you something, will you keep it to yourself?"

I nodded. "Of course."

"I read some books in the library about men and women who design buildings. Big buildings."

"You're talking about architects?"

His eyes sparkled. "Yes. More than anything, I want to be an architect."

His revelation amazed me. A Mennonite boy who had probably never been to a large city wanted to design the kind of buildings he'd only seen in books.

"I'll do everything I can to help you, Jeremiah." I frowned at him. "You realize your father probably won't support your choice."

"I know that, but when I'm a man, I'll make my own choices. Like my brother did."

I stared at him, praying God would give me the right words. "I lost my parents when I was a child. All I had was my sister, and now she's gone." I gazed into his brown eyes. "Even though I support your plans, I would encourage you to do everything you can to keep your relationship with your parents strong. Family is something we all need."

"I . . . I guess."

I smiled at him. "It may not sound like good advice now, but maybe someday it will mean more to you. In the meantime, if my niece decides to get herself into any further trouble, will you come to me instead of trying to handle the situation alone?"

His lips quivered and the sides of his mouth turned up slightly. "I think that might be a good idea. Cicely is a really good person, but she's also . . ." He seemed to struggle for a word.

"A handful?" I finished for him.

He laughed. "Yes."

"Thank you for being her friend, Jeremiah. She needs one. But if your friendship causes you trouble at home, Cicely and I will both understand if you need to pull back."

He shook his head. "We can be friends at school. My parents never come here during the day, and I ride home with Peter Johanson's parents. They would never tell my father anything that might get me in trouble."

"Okay, but please be wise in your decisions. And if you ever need my help, I'm here." When I said the word *help,* I made the sign for it.

Jeremiah smiled. "Thank you, Miss Miller." He turned to leave but stopped halfway to the door. "I think you're a wonderful teacher. I'm glad I know you." Without waiting for a response, he hurried out the front door.

Cicely met him outside and they talked briefly. Then Jeremiah climbed into the Johansons' old station wagon, and they drove away. I'd hoped Cicely would come back inside and walk me home, but I watched through the window as she ran down the street toward Janet's.

I quickly gathered up my planning book, the students' papers, and the gifts the children had brought. I loaded them into an old milk crate, put it on the front porch, and locked the door before picking it up again. Carrying everything proved to be more difficult than I'd anticipated. I was only halfway home when the crate became too heavy. I set it down to catch my breath before going the rest of the way.

"Let me help with that," a deep male voice said, making me jump.

I looked up to see a man I didn't recognize. He wore jeans, a black leather coat, and looked to be in his fifties. He had dark eyes and black hair. His white teeth were a startling contrast to his ebony complexion.

"Thank you, but I don't believe I know you," I said.

His smile widened. "I'm Mike Templeton. From Kansas City. I think you're expecting me?"

Surprised, I stuck my hand out. "Yes. Yes, I was, but I had no idea you'd be arriving today."

After shaking my hand, he reached down and picked up the crate. "Sorry. I probably should have called. Look, let's get you home. It's pretty cold out here."

"I'm sorry. You're right." I pointed toward Janet's house, which was only about a block and a half away. "I'm headed that way."

"Then let's get going, shall we?"

I nodded and picked up my satchel, relieved that I didn't have to carry the crate anymore. I snuck a few looks at Mike on the way home. He had a kind face, but there was a toughness about him that made me a little uncomfortable. Paul had promised to check him out, but I hadn't heard back from him. I felt a little uneasy about letting someone into my life I knew nothing about.

When we reached Janet's, she was waiting on the front porch. "I see you met Mike," she said as we approached.

"You two know each other? When did you get to town?" I asked him.

"Been here a couple of hours. Janet fixed me lunch and kept me company. She's a fine woman."

Janet laughed. "He just likes my tuna salad."

Mike shook his head. "Actually, it was the chocolate cake that sealed the deal."

"Your chocolate cake *is* incredible," I told her. I sighed and shook my head. "Now *I* want a piece of cake."

Janet laughed and waved us both inside. "It's freezing out here. Come in where it's warm."

I excused myself and went upstairs to put my things away and change clothes. Cicely's door was closed, but I knocked and opened it. She was sitting at her desk with her books open.

"Just checking on you," I said. "Need anything?"

She shook her head and pointed at a cup sitting next to her. "Janet made me a cup of hot chocolate. I'm good." She frowned at me. "Who's the guy?"

"He's here from Kansas City. A detective sent him."

"About my mom's murder?"

"Yes. I just want to make sure we do everything we can to find out what happened. This man is here to help us."

"Can I come down and listen?"

I shook my head. "I'm sorry, Cicely. It would make him — and me — uncomfortable to talk about certain things in front of you. I'm just trying to protect you."

"But this is about *my* mother, you know."

"I know that. I promise to keep you updated. You have my word. But for now, please stay in your room and do your homework. I know it doesn't seem fair, but if you could just trust me a little . . ."

"I trust you, Aunt Sarah," she said quickly. "I . . . I'm sorry for what I said about wishing you'd been killed instead of my mom. I didn't mean it."

I smiled at her. "Yes, you did, honey. But it's all right. Any child would feel the same way. I don't blame you. I guess you have to realize that we don't have the ability to make that trade though. Frankly, if it were possible, I'd change places with your mom too."

Cicely's eyes flooded with tears. "I thought you'd hate me for saying that."

I closed the door and came over to her. "I will never hate you, Cicely. Never."

She grabbed my hand and held it, wiping

her eyes with the fingers of her other hand. "I'm going to try to act better, Aunt Sarah. I promise."

I let go of her hand and put my arms around her. "I don't want you to 'act better,' honey. I want you to be honest about how you feel. The best thing you can do for me is to let me help you and remember that I'm on your side."

"Sometimes I feel so mean," she said through her sobs. "And I don't like it."

"It's just anger, and it's completely natural with what you've been through. Talk to God about it, Cicely. Ask Him to help you, and He will."

"Aren't you mad too?"

I sighed. "Yes. Sometimes I feel so mad I can't stand it. But I guess I'm taking my anger out in a different way. I want to catch the person who did this. I want him to pay for his crime."

Cicely frowned. "Jeremiah told me that being Mennonite means you don't fight back when other people do wrong things to you."

I nodded. "Yes, that's part of their religion. And I respect them for it."

"Then why do you want the person who killed my mother to be punished?"

"I know I'll have to forgive whoever did

273

this someday — when I can. But I still want them caught before they hurt someone else. Mennonites don't believe in payback, but they do believe in justice. That's all I want."

As I said the words, I knew they weren't completely true. I wanted revenge. In fact, the need for revenge burned inside me. It was wrong, but it was there and it was too strong for me to ignore. I'd just told Cicely to be honest about how she felt, and I recognized that I had to do the same thing. God would have to help both of us to deal with the rage we had inside.

"You think the person who killed my mom killed my grandparents too." Cicely's statement was said matter-of-factly. I was stunned. How did she know?

"Where did you get that idea?"

"Mom was trying to find the people who killed them. She tried to hide it from me, but I knew." She looked up at me. "I know about the flowers. I mean, that they were there after your mom and dad were killed."

"And how did you find out about that?"

"I heard my mom talking to someone on the phone about it once. It was John. John Smith. About a week before she died."

My knees felt weak and I sat down on her bed, a few feet away from her. "What did you hear, Cicely? Can you remember?"

She stared down at her books. "She said someone found white orchids when her mom and dad were killed. And then there was something else . . ." Cicely sighed. "I can't quite remember."

"But you knew there were white orchids at your house. I mean, when the police arrived, right?"

She nodded. "I saw them when I found Mom. They were everywhere. I wondered how they got there. I told the police I didn't remember seeing any flowers before I went next door for the sleepover."

"Did you tell them about overhearing your mom's phone conversation?"

She shook her head, her eyes wide. "No. For some reason I forgot about it until just now."

"Cicely, if you recall anything else from that conversation or something you might have overheard about my parents, would you tell me? It might be important."

She nodded. "I'll try. I don't know why it's so hard."

I stood up. "It's the shock, honey. It's normal. Don't feel stressed about it, but if something pops into your mind, let me know. Okay?"

"I will."

I gave her a quick hug. Then I went back

downstairs.

"I'd almost given up on you," Janet said when I came into the kitchen. She smiled at me and got up from her chair. "If you'll excuse me, I've got something to do upstairs."

"You can stay if you want, Janet," I said. "You know everything anyway."

"I realize that, but I'd like to make sure no one upstairs is listening. You can fill me in later." She smiled and pointed at the table. "I got you a piece of cake. It took some effort, but I talked Mike into another piece too."

"Yes, she strong-armed me," Mike said, grinning. "I finally gave in."

"She can be very persuasive." I gave Janet a quick smile. "Thank you."

"Do you want to talk here?" I asked Mike when Janet left. "Or would you rather go into the living room? It's more comfortable in there."

"This is fine. There's something about a kitchen that I find comforting."

I sat down in the chair across from him. Even though he had a rough edge, there was a quality about Mike that made me want to trust him. Something in his eyes. I needed to focus on him, but my mind was still processing Cicely's information about John

Smith. Was this the *J* mentioned in Hannah's notes? I didn't know Mike well enough to share this information with him, but I needed to let Paul know as soon as possible. Maybe it would lead to something.

"I like a cup of tea in the afternoon," I said. "How about you?"

"Actually, that sounds wonderful."

I got up, grabbed the teapot, filled it with water, and put it on the stove. Then I opened the cabinet door. "We have Earl Grey, chai, Constant Comment, and English Breakfast tea." I turned and smiled at him. "I also have chamomile, but I usually drink that at night."

"Constant Comment, please. That's what I drink at home."

"Sounds good. I'll join you." I leaned against the counter, waiting for the water to get hot.

"Doug Sykes told me a little about your situation," Mike said. "I'd like to hear it from you though, if you don't mind. I want to hear your view of things."

"It's not complicated. My parents were killed eighteen years ago by two men. They left white orchids at the scene. My sister, Hannah, was murdered about three weeks ago. White orchids were left with her as well." I took a deep breath. I didn't want to tell Mike too much. I still didn't know him, and I had no reason to trust him. "She'd been looking into my parents' deaths. Something she discovered frightened her. Unfortunately, she wasn't able to get away in time. Whatever she found got her killed. The police believe her death was the result of a robbery that went wrong. They blamed it on a man named Steven Hanks, a drug addict who was picked up a few blocks from my sister's house the night she was killed."

His eyebrows shot up. "And you don't think he did it?"

"No. Why would some thief trying to steal things for drug money leave white orchids around my sister's body?"

"Maybe someone else sent him there."

"If I wanted someone dead I wouldn't hire a down-on-his-luck drug addict. Besides, as far as I can tell, they don't have any direct evidence tying this guy to my sister. And certainly not to my parents. They were murdered almost twenty years ago. Steven Hanks would have been in elementary school. How could he be connected to us?"

"And these flowers are the only thing you have to go on?" Mike shook his head slowly. "It's not enough, Sarah. It's clear to me why the police didn't take your concerns more seriously."

"There are . . . other reasons." I took a deep breath. "A reporter from *The Kansas City Star* gave Hannah some information that convinced her the two cases are connected."

"Can you show me that information?"

"I . . . I don't know. Maybe. I'm sorry, Mike. I just don't know you well enough yet to —"

"Trust me?" He smiled. "I understand, but at some point, I'll need to see what the newspaper reporter gave your sister if you want me to help you."

I didn't answer, just nodded. "There's more. Whoever killed her also burned down her house, hoping to destroy evidence. Thankfully, it didn't work. I have most of her personal papers. I'm going through them, looking for something that will explain why someone wanted Hannah dead."

"And what is it you want me to do?" Mike asked, frowning at me.

"I want you to find the truth. I need the police to take my concerns seriously."

"Even though you think the truth got your sister killed?"

I nodded. "Yes. Look, I'm not a risk to anyone. I just want the police to do their jobs. And I want justice for my family."

"But what if pursuing this puts you and

your niece in danger, Sarah? How do you feel about that?"

His direct challenge startled me. Why did he think I might be in danger? "If I really thought something could happen to us, I wouldn't pursue this. But I'm in Sanctuary, Missouri. A town so small no one except the people who live here even knows it exists."

"That doesn't mean you can't be found, you know."

"I realize that. But I'm convinced the truth is the only thing that will keep us safe." I sighed. "I know my story might sound fanciful, but Detective Sykes believes me. Surely he explained all of this to you. He wouldn't have sent you if he didn't think there was a good reason."

"He didn't actually send me."

I frowned at him. "I don't understand. He called and left a message saying you were coming."

Mike stared off into the distance for a moment. "That wasn't Doug. That was me. Doug did mention your case to me. He'd been told to leave it alone. Quit investigating. The powers that be are sure your sister was killed by Steven Hanks — or some other random burglar. I guess she lived in an area where there'd been quite a few break-ins. Addicts looking for anything they could sell to feed their habit."

"But . . . but Doug called me. He was concerned about the case . . . and about us. Wanted to talk to me." I started to tell him that Doug had warned me to stop talking about the case and act as if I believed Steven Hanks killed Hannah. Obviously, talking to Mike meant I wasn't following Doug's instructions, but if he sent Mike, shouldn't it be safe?

Mike nodded. "Yes, he was concerned, Sarah. That's why he asked me to help him with this case. But it was my decision to come here. I told your aunt I was Doug so you wouldn't be shocked when I showed up."

"I don't understand."

Mike looked away from me and shook his head. Finally he said, "I'm afraid I'm all you have, Sarah. Doug Sykes can't help you anymore."

"Why not? He promised . . ."

The expression on Mike's face pulled me up short. For a few seconds I couldn't breathe.

"I'm sorry," he said slowly. "Doug Sykes is dead. He died a few hours after he last talked to you on the phone."

CHAPTER EIGHTEEN

I realized I was holding on to the counter for dear life. "What?" I said. "How could he be dead?" I walked over to the kitchen table and sank down into a chair. "What happened?"

"He and his partner were investigating a case. The guy they were questioning had a gun. He shot Detective Sykes and Sykes's partner shot him. They both died at the scene."

I stared at Mike for a moment before saying, "Don't you find this a bit suspicious? Detective Sykes calls me to tell me he's found something about my sister's case, and then he's shot and killed the same day? And what about Steven Hanks? Bodies certainly seem to be piling up, don't they?" I felt devastated and angered by Sykes's death. He'd listened to me when no one else would. Had I caused his death?

"Look, Sarah. It happens. It's unfortunate,

but Doug died in the line of duty. It has nothing to do with you. And Steven Hanks hanged himself because he faced the rest of his life in prison. Without drugs. He couldn't handle it." He shrugged. "He's not the first junkie to kill himself in jail."

"I find it hard to believe in all these co-incidences."

"If I didn't think there was some merit to your concerns, I wouldn't have come. Especially if I'm not being paid. I'm trying to honor my friend. I want to make sure every stone is turned over, and there isn't a rush to judgment when it comes to your sister's death. But we need to stay focused on the real facts. Doug's death was caused by a drug dealer with a gun. That's it."

"I understand what you're saying, but I still find it very convenient."

"Killing a law enforcement official is extremely serious. The investigation into an incident like this is beyond thorough. If there were any reason to be concerned, I would have heard about it. There's no ques-tion. Doug was killed in the line of duty."

I stood up from my chair as the teakettle began to whistle. "I realize Doug's death is serious. So is murdering three people, Mike. And burning down someone's house." I took the kettle off the burner and put the tea bags in our cups. My hands trembled and my knees felt weak. No matter where I looked, I could see Doug Sykes's face. I felt a hand on my shoulder.

"Come over here and sit down," Mike said. He propelled me gently back toward my chair. "I'll finish getting the tea."

"Thank you." I sat down and tried to calm myself. "I just can't seem to grasp it."

"Can you remember what he said when he called?" Mike brought our cups to the table.

"Yes. He said that he'd discovered something. That he didn't want to talk over the phone." I sighed. "He told me to be careful. Not to talk to anyone I didn't know about the case. To make people think I believed Steven Hanks killed Hannah."

"And did you do that?"

"Yes. I've only talked to people I trust."

"Except me."

I nodded. "Except you. He also said he planned to come to Sanctuary, but he said he'd call back and let me know when."

Mike grunted. "I wish I had more information, but I don't. He died before we had a chance to talk again. All he said was that he had reservations about Hannah's murder. He wanted me to help him figure out what really happened."

"Why would he ask you to help him?"

"We were friends, and he needed someone who could fly under the radar. Bucking your own colleagues' theories isn't the way to win friends and influence people at the department. Before I retired, Doug and I used to work together. He trusted me."

"So he might have made someone angry? Someone who didn't want him to get involved in Hannah's case?"

Mike sat down next to me. "Look, Sarah, you've got to listen to me. If Detective Sykes was murdered, his partner would know. He was right there. He said a guy high on drugs pulled out a gun and shot Doug. Not a hit man. Not someone who knew your sister."

"All right." I was confused. Was Mike right? Was I trying to create a connection where there wasn't one?

"Let's talk about your sister's murder. Doug and I never got the chance to get into the specifics. I have some sketchy details from a media liaison at the police department, but they're not very helpful. Basically all I have is . . . nothing."

Mike took a sip of tea. If it had been any other afternoon, I might have found it almost amusing to see this large, tough-looking man sipping tea from a small china cup. But right now, I wasn't in the mood to be amused.

"I want to hear in your own words why you think your sister's death wasn't the result of a burglary," Mike continued. "The last thing I want to do is cause you any more pain, but you should know right up front that unless I find credible evidence that there's really something here beyond an unfortunate burglary, I'm done. And I'll encourage you to let it go. Do you understand?"

I frowned at him. "Before I answer your question, I have to ask you one. You don't look old enough to retire."

"I retired because I was injured. However, I like to keep my hand in law enforcement, so I decided to become a private investigator. I haven't actually put out a shingle. I only take cases that interest me. Like this one. Maybe."

"You look healthy. Can I ask . . . ?"

"Sure. I was chasing a guy one day and fell jumping over a fence. Tore my ACL. I can still get around, but my insurance wouldn't cover me in the field anymore. Instead of sitting at a desk, I took my pension. I do PI work when I need a little extra money. That's all there is to it."

I nodded. "Okay. I'm sorry you were hurt." I took a drink from my cup and put it back on the saucer. His story had lessened my concerns somewhat. After taking a deep breath, I began to recount my reasons for believing my sister hadn't been murdered by Steven Hanks or any other burglar. I told him about Hannah's letter, but I didn't mention her phone or anything else I wasn't confident Paul wanted me to share. For now, the phone would stay between Paul and me, since the police could say we withheld evidence. Besides, it would soon be on its way to Kansas City. If Paul wanted to tell Mike what he'd found on Hannah's phone, he'd have to do that on his own.

Mike stopped me several times and asked questions. When I finished, he was silent for quite a while. I picked up our cups and made another cup of tea for both of us.

"I'll look into this more carefully," he said finally, "but I'm not completely convinced."

I sighed as I brought our cups back to the table. "So you think finding the very same flowers at both crime scenes, my sister sending me a letter telling me her life might be in danger, and then her house burning down is all coincidence?"

He studied me for a moment, obviously trying to come up with an answer. "I can't explain it. Janet tells me you're friends with a local deputy sheriff? A Paul Gleason?"

"He's trying to help me, but since he has no jurisdiction with the police in Kansas City, his assistance is more moral support than anything else."

"Still, he's a professional. If he has concerns about this case, I'd like to hear them."

"Then you'll look into it with an open mind?"

He nodded. "I'd like to stay in or near Sanctuary for a few days. I'll do some poking around. See what I can find. I also want to go over your parents' murders carefully. Hear everything you can remember. What your sister told you she remembered. And I'd like to talk to her daughter. Is that possible?"

His request caught me up short. I was trying to protect Cicely. Did I really want to pull her into this?

Mike noticed my indecision. "I realize it may be hard for her, but she spent more time with her mother than anyone else. She might know something that could help. If it makes you feel any better, I know how to talk to kids. We're trained to handle them. You can trust me."

I sighed. "It isn't you. It's just . . . well, this has been so traumatic for her. I'm afraid talking to you could send her spiraling away from me again."

"The decision is yours, but it could be very important."

"Will you let me think about it?"

"Sure. Why don't we call it a night? I'd like to talk to you more tomorrow. I need you to gather together any papers or anything else that might be important to this case. I want everything you've got. Something that doesn't seem important to you might be a clue that could send me in the right direction." He took a sip of tea. "Did your sister have a cell phone?"

I took a quick breath before answering. "She did, but the police didn't find it at the crime scene." It wasn't a lie.

He looked at me through narrowed eyes. "Most thieves wouldn't steal a cell phone. Unless it's one of those high-dollar jobs, they're not worth much."

"I'm sorry. I don't own a cell phone so I don't know much about them."

He nodded. "I understand. Her laptop was missing?"

"Yes. Have you seen all the reports?"

"Doug gave me access to them, but I only had time for a brief look before he was killed. The police won't be any help from here on out. I'm afraid we're on our own."

"You think everyone in Kansas City accepts that Hannah was killed by some guy who thought her little rental house in a lower-middle-class neighborhood looked like someplace to score a fortune?"

He shrugged. "It looks that way. Steven Hanks fits the bill perfectly."

"But what about evidence?"

"They probably have it."

My mouth dropped open. "What are you talking about?"

He shrugged. "They wouldn't close the case without some kind of proof. Just because they haven't shared it with you doesn't mean they don't have it."

"But this is my sister. Why wouldn't someone contact me?"

"I suspect they will. With Doug's death, everything's been pushed back."

I blinked back tears. "I'm not trying to be difficult, Mike. I just want some answers. Some justice for my family."

"You might not get it, Sarah," he said gently. "You should be prepared. But before we worry about that, let's see if we can at least find out what really happened to Hannah."

"Okay."

He sighed. "Now I need to find a motel nearby."

"Esther Lapp, the lady who lives next door, would probably put you up. She loves company."

Mike grinned. "I think I saw her out on her front porch earlier. Pretty sure she and I wouldn't make good roommates. Janet told me there's a nice motel in Fredericktown. It's not too far away. I'll go there."

"We'd let you stay here, but the only room we have is used as a sewing room. If you'd be happy on a cot . . ."

"Thank you, Sarah. Really. But I like to smoke a cigar in the evenings, and I'm not opposed to a couple of drinks before bed. Don't think I'd fit into the Sanctuary mold. Better for everyone if I stay somewhere else." He frowned. "You teach tomorrow?"

I nodded. "Yes. School lets out at three. I can talk to you after that."

"Okay. I really want to pick your brain."

He stood up, so I walked him to the door.

"Can you ask your friend Paul to meet with us too?" Mike said.

"I guess, but I don't want him to get in any trouble."

"Talking to me won't cause him problems. Remember, I'm not the police. I'd just like to hear what he thinks."

"Okay. Why don't I ask him to dinner tomorrow night? You can talk to him afterward."

"Sounds good."

I followed Mike to the door. As he put his hand on the doorknob, I decided to ask him a question that had been bothering me ever since he'd told me about Detective Sykes.

"Mike, if you're wrong and Doug Sykes *was* killed because he started digging into my sister's case, doesn't that mean you might be in danger as well?"

He turned around and frowned at me. "Actually, that would mean we're both in the line of fire, wouldn't it?"

With that he walked out the door and went to his car. His words reverberated in my mind as I watched him drive away.

CHAPTER NINETEEN

I called Paul as soon as Mike left and told him about Doug Sykes's death, my meeting with Mike, and Cicely's information about John Smith. "I found something in Hannah's papers that referred to a *J.* Could *J* be this John guy?"

There was silence on the other end of the line. "Maybe. Boy, that's a pretty common name," Paul said finally. "I don't think we can draw too many conclusions about it yet, but I'd certainly like to know who John Smith is."

"Me too. Hey, Mike wants to know if you'll come over tomorrow night."

"I suppose so," Paul said slowly. "I still can't believe Detective Sykes is dead."

"Mike is convinced it has nothing to do with Hannah's case."

Paul was quiet. "I hope he's right," he said softly. "Let's proceed carefully with this Mike guy, Sarah. Okay? I called and left a message with someone who should be able to tell me more about him. I'd hoped to hear something before he showed up."

"I think he's all right, Paul. In fact, I think you'll like him. But I didn't tell him everything. Like Hannah's phone. I figured you'd want to keep that between us. I agree we should be cautious."

"Good girl. Speaking of Hannah's phone, do you mind if I drop by tonight for a bit? I've gone through it — as much as I could. I'd like to share what I found. Unfortunately, I couldn't get anything from her Facebook page. Its privacy settings kept me out."

"I'm sure it's okay, but let me check with Janet first." I put the phone down and found Janet in the kitchen. She was more than happy to have Paul join us for dinner. I told Paul and asked him to come over around six.

After we hung up I rushed upstairs to grade papers and prepare for school the next day. Around six o'clock I heard the doorbell. I'd just finished making out my lesson plan, so I quickly slid everything into my satchel and put it next to my desk.

"It's Paul," Janet called up the stairs.

I glanced in the mirror. It had been a long day, and I looked tired, but there wasn't much I could do about it. When I got downstairs I found Paul in the kitchen talking to Janet.

"Something smells good," I said as I came in. "What's for dinner?"

"Nothing fancy," she said with a smile. "Chicken and dumplings. Just seemed like a chicken and dumplings kind of night."

The wind outside howled as if it agreed with her. I snuck a look out the window. It wasn't snowing, but the trees frantically danced and swayed back and forth.

"Temperatures are dropping," Paul said. "I'm afraid we're in for lots of snow. With the wind, we could end up with a blizzard."

"Oh dear. I hope that won't keep Mike from making it back tomorrow. I knew he should have stayed here."

Janet laughed. "He seems like the kind of guy who won't let a little snow hold him back. Besides, I'm sure that SUV of his has four-wheel drive. If anyone can make it through the snow, he can."

"I hope so."

Janet pointed a big spoon at me. "I know we can't talk about what's going on in front of Cicely, but I want an update later on."

I nodded. "Nothing to tell you yet. Mike's here because Detective Sykes felt someone needed to dig a little deeper into Hannah's murder."

I knew I'd have to eventually tell Janet that Detective Sykes was dead, but I couldn't do it now. I was afraid she'd assume what I had. That Doug Sykes was dead because he'd offered to help me. I didn't want to frighten her.

I called Cicely down for dinner, and we spent the next hour eating and talking. Cicely and Paul chatted easily and appeared to be very comfortable with each other. She seemed drawn to him, probably because she had no father figure in her life. He went out of his way to include her in our conversation and asked questions that made it clear he was really interested in her. I watched her respond to him and was once again grateful for his involvement in our lives. I was thinking about Paul when Janet's voice cut through my reverie.

"Did you hear me, Sarah?"

Startled, I looked over at her. "I . . . I'm sorry. Were you talking to me?"

She smiled. "You drifted away again. I'd ask you what you were thinking about, but you won't tell me, will you?"

I could feel myself blush. "It wasn't very interesting, I'm afraid."

She shook her head. "Why don't you and Paul go into the living room? I'll bring you both a piece of cake and a cup of coffee." She pointed at Cicely. "Is your homework finished?"

She shook her head. "Not yet but almost. Can I take my cake upstairs so I can eat it while I work?"

Janet looked at me.

I nodded. "Sounds fine. Let me know before you go to bed so I can say good night."

"I will." She smiled at Paul. "Good night, Paul. I'm glad you came over."

"Me too. When the weather gets better I'll teach you to ride, okay?"

"Awesome. I can hardly wait."

Cicely almost skipped as she followed Janet to the kitchen to get her dessert.

"Wow. What's that about?" I asked Paul. "You certainly made her happy."

"Boy, you really did wander away." He grinned. "Seems your niece is crazy about horses. I have two. Told her I'd teach her to ride."

I frowned at him. "I didn't know you had horses."

"There are a lot of things you don't know about me, Sarah."

"Oh, Paul. All we do is talk about me and my situation. I'm so sorry. I almost never ask you about yourself. You must think I'm very self-centered."

"I don't think you're the least bit self-centered. Right now what's going on in your life is much more important than getting to know me better." He smiled. "But someday when we have all this behind us, I'd love to show you where I live. I built my own cabin in the woods, not far from a beautiful creek. I have two horses, three dogs, and two cats. Oh, and a fox that I've raised since he was abandoned by his mother. Rover thinks he's a dog, and I've never tried to set him straight."

"You named him Rover? How funny."

He grinned. "Well, it seemed to fit."

"It sounds wonderful. Cicely will love it. She adores animals."

He gave me an odd look, and I wondered if I'd said the wrong thing.

He stood up. "Let's go into the living room and get to work," he said gruffly. "That's why I'm here, right?"

I watched as he left the kitchen. I'd upset him, but I had no idea how.

"Sarah, you're one of the smartest people I know, but you're also one of the most clueless women I've ever met."

I whirled around to find Janet standing in the doorway, holding two plates of chocolate cake.

"What are you talking about?"

She put the plates down on the dining room table. Then she put her hands on her hips.

"I'm talking about Paul's feelings for you. Are you seriously so blind that you haven't realized how much he likes you?"

Startled, I couldn't think of anything to say. Had I been right? Was he interested in me?

"Look, I know you loved Hannah with all your heart. But you've spent your life comparing yourself to her and coming up short. She was bright, beautiful, intelligent . . . all those things. But you are too. We can't see ourselves clearly when we're standing in someone else's shadow, honey. You'll never be Hannah because you weren't made to be Hannah. God created you to be Sarah, and it's time you realized that you're an incredible woman. Paul sees it. I see it. Now it's time for you to believe it."

I shook my head. "That's exactly what Paul told me. But Hannah . . ."

Janet came over and put both of her hands on the sides of my face. Then she looked deeply into my eyes. "But Hannah is gone, Sarah. Are you always going to compare yourself to her? Even after she's dead?"

"I don't mean to. It's just . . ."

Janet let her hands drop and took a step back. "Do you realize you've built a life around one comment a careless social worker said years ago? One comment. What about all the positive things that have been said about you? By me? By Paul? By all the people who love you? Why is that careless woman's opinion more important than everyone else's?"

"It's not. I wasn't adopted. She was right."

"No, she wasn't. You weren't adopted because God loved you so much He wanted you here, Sarah. With me. With Cicely. And now with Paul. If you'd been adopted, you wouldn't be in my life." Her eyes filled with tears. "I can't imagine my world without you in it. And what about Hannah? It might have been impossible for her to find you. And right now, Cicely would be alone. Don't you realize you're exactly where you're supposed to be? Oh, honey. You're beautiful, compassionate, brave, strong, and full of the love of God. I brought you into my life because I saw how valuable you are." She sighed and shook her head. "It took me a long time to realize that I was special and unique to God. Please don't waste as much time as I did."

Janet's past was troubled. She'd gotten involved in an abusive relationship and finally had to run away from an ex-husband who had a violent and criminal past. I'd always been shocked that anyone could be mean to her. Janet was the most compassionate, loving person I'd ever met. Suddenly, it was as if the Holy Spirit started speaking to me. *You were never second to Hannah. You were framed by me to be my special, unique, and blessed daughter. When will you trust me?*

I stepped back from Janet, stunned by the words that drifted into my spirit. I felt like a shock of electricity had gone through me.

"Are you okay, Sarah?" Janet's eyes were wide with concern.

I felt overcome by the love of God. All I could do was nod, but I couldn't tell Janet what I'd heard. Had God really just spoken to me? I believed God still talked to people today, but I'd never heard Him this clearly before.

"I have to . . . I need to . . ."

I turned and ran to the bathroom. As I tried to stop the tears that streamed down my face, I couldn't help but stare at myself in the mirror. Before dinner I'd only noticed how tired I looked. Now I saw something different. A woman loved by God. If God wasn't looking at my imperfections, why was I?

"I'm so sorry, God," I whispered. "Help me to see myself the way you see me, and thank you for not allowing me to be adopted. I wouldn't want to be anywhere else other than where I am."

Although I'd been crying only moments before, now I felt like laughing. It was odd, disturbing, and exhilarating all at the same time. When I finally left the bathroom, I found Janet waiting in the kitchen, her expression tight with worry.

"Are you all right, honey? Do you want me to tell Paul to come back some other time?"

I shook my head and smiled. "No. I'm fine. Thank you so much for what you said. You're right, Janet. I've been stupid."

I picked up the plates of cake from the table and headed to the living room. Paul sat on the couch, his laptop on the coffee table. He looked up when I came in. I went over and sat down next to him, handing him a plate.

"I have a question," I said as he took the plate from my hand.

"About the case?" He stuck his fork into the cake and took a bite.

"No, not about the case." I waited until he looked at me. "About us. I may be a little dense, but Janet tells me you care for me. Is that true?"

Paul's eyes got wide and he started to choke on his cake. A little frightened, I pounded him lightly on the back to make sure he was okay. Finally he held his hand up as a signal to stop.

"Boy," he said, his voice gravelly from coughing, "when you decide to change directions, you should at least give a guy a warning. I could have gotten whiplash."

"I didn't mean to upset you."

He coughed a couple more times but then gave me a thumbs-up. "I'm not upset. I'm happy. To be honest, I was about to give up."

"I know I probably seem rather slow to you, but being insecure means you don't trust things that may seem obvious to other people. There's always an excuse to turn a positive comment into something else. You've said a few things that lead me to believe you like me. I mean, beyond just regular friendship. Am I misreading you?"

"No, you're not misreading me." Paul gazed into my eyes. "I think you're incredible, and I'd like to get to know you better. I realize this is not the right time. You've been through a terrible tragedy, and your life has been turned upside down. But when your situation settles down, I'd like to ask you out. On a real date, I mean. What do you think?"

I gave him a slow smile. "I think that would be lovely. And I like you too. Very much. Just so you know."

He blinked several times, whether it was from surprise, shock, or just being grateful he could breathe again remained to be seen. But his smile made it clear he was pleased. A wave of happiness flowed through me, and even in the midst of darkness, a light shone through. *Hannah would be delighted.*

I cleared my throat. "Now, maybe we should get back to the reason we got together tonight."

He looked confused for a moment. Then realization dawned. "Oh yes. The phone."

"Why don't we finish our dessert, and then we'll talk about the phone?"

Paul nodded his agreement. He still looked a little thunderstruck. I knew the feeling. Being so bold wasn't usual for me, but I felt pretty good about it.

"Coffee?" Janet's smile as she carried in our coffee made it clear she'd overheard at least part of our conversation.

"Thanks, Janet," Paul said. "This cake is delicious."

"Thank you, Paul. I'm going upstairs to watch TV so I won't disturb you." She pointed toward the window. "You might keep an eye on the weather. Snow's moving in. I'd hate for you to get trapped here."

Paul cleared his throat. "No, we wouldn't want that. I might have to eat another piece of cake."

Janet laughed. "If it gets too bad, you're welcome to the couch."

"I appreciate that," he said with a grin, "but the chief isn't too compassionate about bad weather. He'd rather have me stuck out in a storm, trying to get to work, than somewhere else where I'm safe and warm."

"Then I'd make it fast, you two."

"We will," I said.

Paul took a sip of coffee and stuck the last bite of cake in his mouth. "Okay," he said, putting his fork down, "first of all I want to talk about your friend Mike. I heard back from my contact at the police department right after I talked to you. Mike's an ex-detective with the KC police. Had to retire because of an injury. He definitely does some private investigating. I heard very good things about him."

"I thought your contact wasn't talking to you anymore."

"I didn't ask any questions about your sister's case, so he opened up some. I don't intend to push him any more right now. I

305

might need him down the road."

"Mike told me exactly the same story. Do you feel better about him now?"

"Well, let's just say I'm glad to know he's who he says he is. As far as the rest of it, we'll see."

"You're very suspicious."

Paul's eyebrows shot up. "With everything that's been going on? You bet I am. Better safe than sorry." He got up and got his jacket, pulling out a note pad and a pen. He sat back down and flipped the pad open. "Now, about the phone. First of all, I was able to figure out Hannah's voice mail code." He shook his head. "Using your child's name and the numbers of your address is pretty standard. People really need to work harder to create codes that aren't so easily cracked."

"If I ever get a fancy cell phone, I'll remember that."

He smiled. "I'll make sure you do." He glanced at the notes on the pad. "There were calls to work, a couple of calls to Cicely's school. I've written down the others. Have you gone through her address book?"

"Yes. Do you want me to get it?"

He nodded. "In a minute. But first I want to show you something." He reached into his pocket and pulled out his phone. "You know, you really need to get a cell phone. They can come in handy."

I started to protest, but then I remembered being at the mine. Reuben had told me to use his cell phone to call for help if anything went wrong. Although I'd told him I would, what if he had an iPhone or something beyond a simple phone? I wasn't completely certain I could have figured out how to use it. The only other person who could have helped was William, and I was pretty sure he knew even less about electronic devices than I did.

"I know how to use a regular cell phone," I said. "I'm just not sure about these newer models."

"It's the same principle," he said. "You just take a different route to get there." He turned it on and then showed me how to find the application for phone calls. It was easier than I thought it would be.

"I guess I've been letting all the fancy applications scare me off."

"There are a lot more things you can do like access the Internet, take pictures, you can send text messages . . ."

"Whoa," I said, laughing. "This is enough for now. Let's leave all that for another lesson, okay?"

"All right." He put his phone away. "Why don't you go and get that phone book?"

I hurried up the stairs, got the address book, and came back, handing it to Paul. Suddenly, the wind shook the house, rattling the windows. Murphy, who had curled up on the floor by Paul's feet, raised his head and barked at the sound.

Paul frowned at the book and then shook his head. "I may have to leave sooner than I planned. Why don't you take this list of phone calls and match the numbers from Hannah's phone to the numbers in her phone book? Can you get it done so I can pick it up tomorrow?"

"Yes. I'll work on it tonight. Where's the cell phone now?"

"It's at the office. I'm going to contact the police in Kansas City and tell them we found it. Then I'll send it on to them. I got everything I needed from it, and I can't hold on to it any longer, since it's evidence."

"I understand."

"Here are the numbers I'd like you to check out." He tore a page out of his note pad and handed it to me. Then he took his laptop out of its bag and put it on the coffee table. After a few strokes on the keyboard, he brought up a page with Hannah's name and picture on it.

"I couldn't read anything on Hannah's page, because I don't have access, but I could see her friends. There aren't a lot of them. I wrote down their names. You can go through this list and see if anyone pops out. Also check to see if any of these people show up in her address book." He took another sheet of paper from his notebook and handed that to me too.

I took it from him, then scooted closer to peer at the computer screen. "What am I looking at?"

He pointed to the screen. "This is Hannah's Facebook page. As I said, we can't see her posts because she hasn't friended us."

"Did you just say 'friended'?"

He grinned. "Yes. I know it's not a real word. If you were on Facebook, you'd understand."

I wanted to ask why I'd have to butcher the English language if I wanted a Facebook page, but I kept my opinion to myself.

Another strong blast of wind from outside got Paul's attention. "I'm sorry, but I need to get on the road before this storm hits."

"I think we need to find John Smith," I said. "Hannah was talking to him before she died, and in her notes she said, '*J* might be behind everything.' "

"I agree, but I have no idea where to

start," Paul said, frowning. "Without some kind of clue, I don't know how to proceed. Let me think about it some."

"I guess we don't have much of a choice."

I stared down at the phone book. "Oh no," I said. "What is wrong with me?" I flipped the book open and searched until I found what I was looking for.

"What's wrong?" Paul asked.

"You said something about John Smith being a common name. Maybe that's why I forgot."

"Forgot what?"

I handed him the small address book. "Look. A number for John Smith. I can't believe I forgot about it."

"You've had a lot on your mind," Paul said gently. "It's understandable." He brought up a page on his laptop and asked me to read him the number. "I'll see what I can find out. Might as well give me the number for *JR* too."

I read both the numbers to him.

"If John Smith was meeting with Hannah before she died, he may be the person who can help us."

"Or the man who killed her. Please be careful, Paul," I pleaded.

He smiled at me. "I will. Don't worry. I'm going to check him out before I call. I don't want to scare him away." He closed his laptop and slid it back into its bag. "So you think this Mike guy is on the level?"

"I think so. Doug obviously trusted him too or he wouldn't have told him his concerns about Hannah's murder and asked for his help. Mike didn't have to come here, Paul. He could have just walked away."

Paul frowned. "If Sykes's death had anything to do with Hannah's murder, couldn't Mike be in danger?"

"Maybe. I don't know."

Paul stared at me, his expression serious. "We can stop at any time, Sarah. We don't have to do this. We can just leave everything with the Kansas City police and take our chances."

I shook my head. "I think we have to do everything we can to find the truth. Taking a chance that a murderer could walk free to hurt someone else is too dangerous." I smiled at him. "A very smart sheriff's deputy told me that."

Paul grunted. "I'm not so sure how smart he really is. Sometimes I wonder if he should have kept his mouth shut."

"Look, all we have to do is let Mike figure out what's going on. Then he can contact the Kansas City police and urge them to rethink Hannah's case. He was a detective.

They'll listen to him. Isn't that all we've wanted from the beginning?"

He nodded. "You're right. Sykes's death makes me nervous though. I want you to be especially careful, okay?"

"I'm fine. Besides, with Mike nearby, I have even more protection." I put my hand on his arm. "You be careful too. I couldn't stand it if anything happened to you."

He put his hand over mine. "Please don't worry. I know how to protect myself."

"I'm sure Doug Sykes thought the same thing."

Paul grunted. "*If* his death had anything to do with Hannah, he probably didn't see it coming. I'm taking special precautions, because I know we need to be careful."

"Good."

Paul stood up, got his coat, and walked to the front door. I went with him, looking out the window first. The snow was just starting to come down. The wind was so strong, it blew the snow sideways.

"I'll try to find out something about this John Smith tomorrow," Paul said. "If nothing concerns me about him, I'll call the number."

"I'll start trying to match the numbers and names you gave me to the information in Hannah's phone book," I said. "Maybe we'll find someone else she was talking to before she died, and it will lead us to something that will help us. Again, I'm sorry I spaced on John Smith's name. I don't know how I did it."

Paul shook his head. "Sarah, you're operating under extremely stressful conditions. I think you're doing a wonderful job. Don't worry about it."

I smiled at him. "Okay. I hope we can get together tomorrow night. Call me so we can make different arrangements if the weather is too bad."

"I will." He zipped up his coat and then leaned over and kissed me. This time I didn't pull back.

I watched through the window as he drove away. My feelings for him were stronger than ever. Was it love? I wasn't sure. I wanted a relationship with him, but what if death was the only thing binding us together?

CHAPTER TWENTY

I spent some time sitting at my desk, working on the list of phone numbers Paul gave me. I was able to match several of them, including two from John Smith. I prayed Paul would be able to find him. I had some questions for him. It crossed my mind that once we found John, we should turn over his name and location to the police. What if he was dangerous? I was glad Paul said he would be careful making contact with him.

I also matched calls to Cicely's school. Hannah had called a Dr. Wentz several times. The doctor's office called back once, the school called back twice, and someone from work called her several times. I'd talked to Hannah on the phone around the dates listed. She'd been home, sick with the flu, and then Cicely had come down with it. These calls made sense in the light of those circumstances.

There were a couple of calls I couldn't

figure out. I did a quick Internet search and found that one was a pizza place near Hannah's house. The other belonged to a local pharmacy. I also matched several calls to Claire Freeman, the woman who had put together the memorial service for Hannah. I found a call from Hannah's boss, Tom Sparlin, during the time she was sick. I think he'd helped Claire with the memorial service, but I was still in shock when we talked, so I wasn't completely certain about that.

I decided to give Claire a call tomorrow. I thought if anyone could provide additional information about Hannah, it would be Claire. I'd wait and talk to Paul before phoning anyone else. Especially people I knew nothing about. I was just about to quit when I realized one of the numbers on Paul's list that I hadn't matched looked familiar. I checked Hannah's phone book again. Sure enough, it was the same as the number written next to *JR,* the entry with the star. I'd missed it my first time going through the list. I made a note to tell Paul about it. I was tempted to dial it just to see who answered, but I didn't want to risk doing something wrong, since Paul already planned to check out the number. I searched the number online, but nothing came up.

By the time I finally quit working, it was almost one in the morning. For almost another hour I lay in bed thinking about Paul. It was hard to believe he liked me, but knowing he did made me almost giddy with happiness. God's words kept running through my head. *You were never second to Hannah. You were framed by me to be my special, unique, and blessed daughter. When will you trust me?*

At some point I fell asleep and then woke up with a start. When I looked at my alarm, I realized it hadn't gone off. I'd slept an hour later than I should have. Wondering what happened, I jumped out of bed, grabbed my robe, and practically ran down the stairs. Janet sat at the kitchen table drinking coffee. She smiled as I rushed in.

"Jonathon and Pastor Troyer called off school today. There's too much snow for the kids who live out in the country to get to school safely."

Since most of the children lived outside of town, when the snow was especially deep or the roads icy, the churches closed school. All the families of schoolchildren had home phones except for three. The neighbors of those families had phones, and they would let them know there was no need for them to make the trek into town.

"Did you turn off my alarm?" I asked.

Janet nodded. "I heard you up late and thought you could use the extra sleep."

"Thank you." I nodded toward the stairs. "You turned off Cicely's alarm too?"

Janet chuckled. "No, she did. She heard the phone ring and ran downstairs to see if the call was about school. Once she found out she didn't have to go, she said that was 'awesome' and went back to bed."

"Children are so funny. Even when they love school, they get excited about snow days. It's hard to figure."

"You did the same thing when you were in college."

"Yes, but that was because I had an extra day to study. I'm pretty sure none of my students will be doing much of that today. I bet we'll see quite a few snowmen before the day is over."

Janet smiled and nodded in agreement. "So what will you do with your day off?"

"I'm not sure. I might make a few phone calls." I grabbed a cup of coffee and sat down at the table while I told her about my findings of the night before.

"So you think Claire might know something about Hannah's death?"

I shrugged. "I don't know, but I intend to find out. She may have been closer to Hannah than anyone else in Kansas City. I'm hoping she'll be up-front with me. There are a couple of other numbers that I'm going to give to Paul to follow up on. Hannah called them before she died."

"You might be able to enter the numbers into a search engine and see if it matches anything."

"I did that. Nothing came up."

Janet got up and went to the oven. She opened it and took out a pan of cinnamon rolls.

"I thought I smelled something good," I said with a smile. "Yummy."

"I figured you and Cicely would enjoy these."

"Janet, have you ever heard of Facebook?"

She laughed. "Of course. You mean you haven't?"

I nodded. "People at school talked about it, but I never got involved with it."

"You know, Facebook can tell you a lot about a person. You could use it to look up some of the people you're interested in. Like this Claire person."

"I might do that. Do I have to sign up for it?"

"Probably. But you can use my account if you want. Just enter my e-mail address and then Murphy Dowell 1234. No spaces though."

"You use Murphy's name as a password?"

"Sure." She smiled. "I bet most people either use their pet's name or their child's name."

"Paul said crooks can gain access to our information because people use their addresses and their children's names for their passwords. I imagine the same holds true for pet's names. Maybe you should pick something else."

She frowned at me. "Good point. After we're done, maybe I'll change it. Of course, the harder I make my password, the more difficult it is for *me* to remember it."

I grinned at her. "I guess it won't do you much good if you lock yourself out."

"You're right about that." She sighed. "Now, back to Facebook. You'll be able to read some of the pages, but there are others you can't read unless you're that person's friend. I know it sounds confusing, but if you need help, let me know. I'll walk you through it."

"Thanks. I appreciate it."

After eating two cinnamon rolls, I went upstairs. As I passed Cicely's room, the door opened and she came out.

"No school today," she said with a smile.

"I know. Now you have time to catch up

on your homework."

Her mouth dropped open and her face fell. "I . . . I thought I *was* caught up."

I pretended to look confused. "Oh, that's right. Well, then, I sentence you to help me bake chocolate chip cookies and play Scrabble with Janet and me this afternoon."

She grinned. "I like that kind of homework." She came over and hugged me. "Thanks, Aunt Sarah. That sounds awesome."

"First of all, you'd better get a couple of cinnamon rolls inside you to warm you up. It's cold outside, and the house is still a little chilly."

Cicely wrapped her arms around herself. "Sure takes this house a long time to heat up."

"I know, but it will be better soon."

Janet always turned the heat down low at night to save money. The old, drafty house took its sweet time warming up in the morning. Until then, a thick robe and hot coffee was my only defense.

I went to my room and changed clothes. Then, after gathering together all the notes I'd made the night before, I sat down at my desk and turned on my laptop. It didn't take me long to find Facebook. I logged in using Janet's account. There was a spot at the top of the page where I could enter names. On a hunch, first I entered Hannah's name. Sure enough, at the top of a list with several Hannah Millers, I saw my sister's picture. I couldn't read anything on her page. I could, however, see the list of "friends" Paul had mentioned. I opened the list and found Cicely. She not only had a Facebook page, but I could see pictures and posts. Wondering if someone her age should be on a social page that could be accessed by scores of strangers, I searched for information about age limits. When I found the answer, I quickly got up and went to her room and knocked on the door.

"Just a minute," she called out.

I waited until she opened the door. She'd changed into jeans and a sweatshirt. I crooked my finger at her and asked her to follow me. As she walked into my room she looked surprised to see her Facebook page up on my computer screen.

"I don't know much about Facebook," I said, "but I do know someone your age shouldn't have a page. The rules state you're supposed to be thirteen or older. I'm surprised your mother let you have a Facebook page. Did she know there's an age limit?"

Cicely shook her head. "No, I didn't tell her. A few days before she . . ."

"Before she died?" I said gently.

Cicely nodded. "She told me to shut down my page. I told her I would, but I didn't. I'm sorry about it now."

"Look, Cicely. It's just not safe. Besides not being old enough, you have your page set so anyone can see your posts. There are lots of bad people out there. The rules are for your safety." I could see the challenge in her expression, but I had no intention of backing off. "I need you to remove your page, honey. And please be cautious about the places you visit on the Internet. Until we know what happened to your mother . . . and why . . . I need you to be really careful."

She considered this. "Okay, Aunt Sarah," she said finally, her shoulders slumping. "I guess I can e-mail or chat with my friends. I don't have to be on Facebook to do that."

"That's fine. Just people you really know though, Cicely. And before you delete your account, I want to see any friends who signed on a month or two before your mom died."

Her eyebrows shot up with alarm. "You think whoever killed my mom might be one of my friends?"

I shook my head. "I don't think so, but I imagine there are people out there who could use information posted on your page to find out where you are. Right now, it's not a good idea. Can you understand that?"

She nodded slowly. "Yeah. I'll make a list of new friends and then I'll take it down."

"Thank you. Now I have another question. Is there any way I can see your mom's page?"

She nodded. "I can log on and show it to you."

"That would be great. Can you do that without getting in trouble?"

She flashed me a quick smile. "Are you asking if the Facebook police will throw me in Facebook jail?"

I laughed. "I told you I don't know much about Facebook. I just proved that, didn't I?"

"It's okay, Aunt Sarah. You know a lot of stuff other people don't know."

I wasn't certain whether I should be offended by her patronizing comment or touched that she felt she needed to defend me. I decided to go with the latter response.

"Do you want me to go to my room and use my laptop, or do you want me to do it here?" she asked.

"Why don't you do it here? I'd like to watch you. I'm not saying I'm ever going to have a Facebook page, but I'd like to understand something about it if you're going to be involved with it when you're older."

I stood up and let her slide into my chair. As she started clicking keys, something occurred to me. Where did Cicely get her laptop? Was there any chance it was one of Hannah's old ones? If so, could it have information that might help me find out what happened to her?

"Cicely, where did you get your laptop?" I asked. "Isn't it unusual for ten-year-olds to have their own computers?"

She laughed. "Boy, you really don't know much about kids, do you? All of my friends have either a laptop or an iPad. My school in Kansas City has a Web site where they post stuff for our parents and us all the time. We can even get homework assignments." She stopped typing and looked at me. "I got my laptop from a friend at school. Her folks got her a new one, and she gave the old one to me." She shook her head. "I'm really glad I had it in my schoolbag and took it with me to Cora's. It could have gotten burned up in the fire."

I nodded absentmindedly and smiled, but I was disappointed the laptop hadn't belonged to Hannah.

"Hey, what's everyone doing?" Janet had come in the door and was smiling at us.

"Cicely's signing on to —"

"Logging in," Cicely corrected.

"Oh, sorry. Cicely is *logging in* to Facebook. I want to read Hannah's Facebook page."

Janet frowned. "Cicely's too young for a Facebook page."

Cicely let out a big sigh. "She knows that. I have to take it down."

Janet nodded. "Good. I love Facebook, but I'm very, very careful with my privacy settings. And I don't accept friend requests from people I don't know. It can be dangerous, and kids shouldn't be on it." She put her hand on her hip. "But maybe it's time *you* got a Facebook page, Sarah."

I shook my head. "I don't think so. I like keeping my life private."

"We'll see." Janet kissed Cicely on the head. "Bet you one week of doing the dishes she'll change her mind within a month."

"I don't know," Cicely said. "Aunt Sarah's pretty stubborn."

"I beg your pardon?" I said. "Stubborn? Me?"

Janet snorted and Cicely giggled.

"You people obviously don't know me." I winked at Janet, glad she was able to make Cicely laugh.

"Here," Cicely said. "This is Mom's page.

She hardly ever posted on it. She only had a few friends, mostly people she went to school with. They didn't post much either. It was usually just me and Mom. I haven't been on it since . . ."

I put my hand on her shoulder. Maybe I shouldn't have asked her to bring up Hannah's page. "That's good enough, Cicely. Why don't you let me take over from here?"

When she didn't respond, I peered over her shoulder so I could see why she'd suddenly grown silent. At the top of Hannah's page was the last comment she'd typed late the night she'd died.

I am feeling grateful tonight. Grateful for my wonderful daughter, Cicely, and for my incredible sister, Sarah. My life is so rich because of them. No matter what happens in the future, I consider myself very, very blessed.

CHAPTER TWENTY-ONE

"I'm so sorry, Sarah. That must have been tough," Paul said when I told him of Hannah's last Facebook posting.

"It hurt, but yet it helped too. She spent her last night on earth counting her blessings." I sighed. "It upset Cicely though."

"Probably made Hannah's death seem more real."

"I think you're right. Her mother's last words."

"I'll pray for her."

"Thanks, Paul. Are you coming over tonight?"

"I'm going to try, but I'm not sure yet. Some people don't know how to drive on snow and ice. I've spent most of my time helping people get their cars unstuck. It looks like I'm going to be pretty busy. Have you heard from Mike?"

"No. Janet thinks he'll be here because he has a big SUV with four-wheel drive."

"Yeah. I've pulled a couple of those out of snowdrifts so far."

"I should have asked where he was staying. I know he said he was in Fredericktown. There aren't that many motels there. I suppose I could start calling them."

"There are only three motels in town, and I'll be driving right past them. Might be easier if I just stop by. I want to meet him anyway. What color is his SUV?"

"Black."

"If I can't find him, I'll let you know. As far as tonight, I'll call you, but the roads don't scare me. I plan to be there as long as the rest of the county can stay out of snowdrifts."

"Great, but be careful."

"I will. Do you have time to make a list of everyone whose name starts with *J* in Hannah's phone book or among her Facebook friends? I don't want to assume *J* is John Smith. It wouldn't hurt to look at all the people whose names start with *J.*"

"I looked through her friends list. Only one name started with a *J.* Julia. According to what she says about herself on Facebook, she worked with Hannah. She looks older, and I doubt she's the *J* Hannah was talking about. I'm afraid her list wasn't very helpful. Hannah only had a little over twenty friends, and as Cicely said, they rarely posted."

"But maybe one of them knows who *J* is."

"That's possible. I'll ask Janet how to contact them. It won't hurt to ask."

"By the way, have you found anything in the address book that matches the *MLS* in Hannah's notes?"

"No, nothing," I said. "That's still a mystery."

"Okay. I'm checking out our John Smith. Hopefully, I'll have something soon." I heard someone talking in the background. "I've got to go, Sarah, but I'll call you later. Do you all need anything?"

"We're fine. Janet is always prepared for storms. I think we could ride out Armageddon with all the supplies she has."

"Good. I'll talk to you soon."

I said good-bye and hung up the phone. Even though he seemed confident about his ability to drive on icy roads, I took a moment and prayed for his safety.

"Everything okay?" Janet stood at my bedroom door.

"Just talked to Paul. I'm still not sure he and Mike will get here tonight, although Paul doesn't seem to think it will be a problem."

"I'm making beef stew in the Crock-Pot.

There will be plenty if they make it. If not, we'll have leftovers."

"That sounds great."

Janet came over and sat down on the bed, next to my desk. "I wasn't actually asking about dinner. How are *you*?"

"You mean after seeing Hannah's message?" I sighed. "It made me sad and happy all at the same time."

She reached over and took my hand. "Sarah, I want you to know how proud I am of you. I know you've wondered more than once whether you should just walk away from what happened to Hannah or keep fighting for the truth. You know, I wasn't the first person my ex-husband abused. I put up with him for several years, praying he'd change. Unfortunately, things just got worse. What made me finally decide to get out was finding an old letter written by his previous wife." She shook her head. "It was a shock to discover he'd been married before. I had no idea. But it was seeing what she wrote to him that finally made me understand what was really happening — what I'd become and where I was going if I didn't get out. That woman's letter changed my life. I never got to thank her or tell her how much it meant to me. Because she stood up to him, she saved me. Her bravery helped me to find freedom. Finding out what happened to Hannah may save someone else, you know. Someone who will become the next victim unless you make sure the person who did this faces justice. You may not be fighting just for you. You might be fighting for someone you don't even know."

"Paul said the same thing."

She let go of my hands. "He's a smart man."

"He must be. He likes me."

"Yes, he does." Janet's smile slipped, and the corners of her blue eyes crinkled with concern. "So what will you and Paul do next?"

"Cicely mentioned a man named John Smith who was talking to Hannah. We're trying to find him. Hannah made notes about a *J* someone and something called *MLS.* Maybe this John Smith is the *J* she mentioned, but I'm not certain about it. We're still looking for people whose names start with *J.* Can you help me contact Hannah's Facebook friends? Ask them if they have any idea who *J* is? There aren't many of them."

She frowned. "I can try, but I might need to log on to Hannah's or Cicely's account to access her list."

331

"Thanks. I'd do it but —"

"It would take you forever. I know Facebook. I can do it."

"I appreciate it, Janet."

She left, but I sat there awhile longer, thinking about Cicely. I finally got up and headed to her room, still unsure what to say. I knocked on her door and heard a muffled, "Come in."

She was lying on her bed in a fetal position, her head on her pillow.

"Hi, honey," I said gently. "I just wanted to make sure you're all right."

She wiped a tear from the corner of one of her eyes. "I . . . I thought I was. But I keep wondering what Mom thought about. If she —" A small sob cut off her next words.

"Her message from that night made everything seem more real, didn't it?"

She nodded.

"I understand. It made me feel the same way."

Cicely slowly raised herself up to a sitting position. "Why did I have to go to Brenda's that night, Aunt Sarah? Maybe I could have helped my mom. Maybe I could have saved her."

"And maybe you would have gotten hurt." I came over and sat on the edge of her bed. Janet had covered it with a beautiful burgundy and deep blue quilt in a star pattern. I touched the fabric with my fingers. It was so soft and welcoming. Just like Janet. "I can tell you without any doubt that your mother would not have wanted you to be in danger, Cicely. Keeping you safe was more important to her than anything else." I stared into her green eyes. "You have nothing to feel guilty about, honey. You're a child. It was never your job to take care of your mother."

"Do you think she was scared?" she asked in a soft voice.

Emotion shot through me like electricity. What could I say? I had to tell her the truth. "Yes," I said finally, "but I believe the knowledge that you were safe next door gave her strength. That night, before she died, she was thinking of us, honey. How much she loved us. And how happy she was." I took her hand. "Hold on to that, Cicely. Okay?"

She seemed to accept this, and I breathed a sigh of relief and let go of her hand. "I need to ask you a question about your mom's Facebook friends. Do you know a woman named Julia?"

Cicely was quiet as she considered my question. "Yes," she said finally. "She was really nice. And kind of old. She had something wrong with one of her legs and wore a brace on it. Mom liked her a lot." She frowned at me. "Why are you asking about her?"

"I just want to make sure none of your mom's Facebook friends are involved with what happened to her."

Cicely's eyes grew wide. "She didn't have too many friends. A few from work and some she went to school with. None of them would hurt her."

"Cicely, is there anything else you can tell me about John Smith?"

"The man I told you about?"

"Yes. You said he called your mom a couple of times."

"Yes. I told you about him. I overheard Mom talking to him on the phone. About the flowers."

"That's right. Did you hear anything else they talked about? Besides the flowers, I mean?"

She shrugged. "He came to our house a couple of times."

I stared at her with my mouth open. "Cicely, why didn't you tell me this before?"

She shrugged. "You didn't ask."

My first reaction was to grab her and shake her as hard as I could. This was information we could have used earlier.

"What do you remember about him?" I asked, trying to keep my voice steady.

She frowned. "Well, he was very nice to me, but he seemed kind of . . . sad. When he came over, Mom made me go to my room. She always seemed a little upset after he left."

"Did you tell the police about John when they talked to you?"

She shook her head. "I didn't think about it, Aunt Sarah. I'm sorry."

Instantly, I felt ashamed for my momentary flash of irritation. "If you recall anything else about him, or what he and your mom talked about, will you tell me right away?"

She nodded. "I'll try. Sometimes I'm not sure if what I remember is important or not."

"I understand, honey. Just tell me everything you can. I'll figure out if it's important."

"Okay."

I stroked the side of her face. "I'd like Janet to send a message to your mom's Facebook friends. Can you help her?"

"Sure," she said.

"Why don't you take your laptop downstairs? And when you two are finished, Janet plans to make some chocolate chip cookies. Do you know anyone who might want to be her assistant?"

Cicely sighed. "I'm not five years old, Aunt Sarah."

I shrugged. "Okay. I'll tell her to forget the cookies."

She rewarded me with a small smile. "Don't do that. I'll help."

"Good. I'll come down and join you in a little bit. Save some cookies for me."

"I'll try."

She picked up her laptop and walked to the door of her room. Then she turned and looked back at me. "Aunt Sarah, do you think John Smith killed my mom?"

My breath caught in my throat. "I . . . I don't know, honey, but I'm going to make sure the police check him out. Just in case."

She nodded. "Good."

I watched as she left her room and went downstairs. Then I hurried back to my room and closed the door. I made my bed, opened my desk drawer, and took out all the papers I'd kept upstairs. Then I spread everything out on the bed and riffled through them until I found the one that mentioned a *J*. Once again I read Hannah's note. *J behind everything? Why? What is the connection to MLS?* I really didn't need to look at this again. I'd memorized everything. But looking at Hannah's notes helped me concentrate.

I grabbed Hannah's phone book and turned the pages until I found the entry for John Smith. Was he involved? He was actually in Hannah's house. But if she was afraid of him, why would she let him in? It didn't make sense.

I started putting the papers back into the envelope when the newspaper article about the other murder fell out. I'd only scanned it before, but this time I read it thoroughly. Why had Hannah saved it? Maybe Hannah and her reporter friend had noticed the similarities between our parents' murders and these killings. Reproaching myself for not paying more attention to the article the first time I found it, I slowly read through it, trying to understand why it was important.

A couple had been killed in their apartment about four months after Mom and Dad. The article said they'd been found stabbed to death. As I looked more closely at it, I realized that woman, Elise Summers, had worked at *The Kansas City Star,* the same place my mom had worked. I hadn't noticed that before. *The Star* was a big operation, but I found the coincidence a little odd. The husband, Martin Lewis Summers, was an accountant working at a firm in Kansas City. The article stated that no one had been apprehended in their deaths and police were convinced the couple was killed by a burglar looking for drugs or money. I went back to the computer and put in the name Martin Lewis Summers. Several old references to the case came up, but there was nothing saying the crime had ever been solved. I had just pulled up an old obituary when I realized that Martin Summers's initials were *MLS.* Just like the note my sister had made. *What is the connection to MLS?* That discovery surprised me, but the next thing I noticed shocked me even more. There was only one survivor named. A stepson.

John Smith.

CHAPTER TWENTY-TWO

I waited until after lunch to call Paul. He sounded rushed and promised to call me back when he could. Finally, a little after three o'clock, the phone rang. Janet answered it, and I told her I'd talk to Paul from the upstairs phone. After picking up the phone in my room, I waited until Janet hung up. Then I quickly ran through my findings.

"Wow. You really did make some progress," Paul said.

"So what do we do now?"

"Don't do anything. Let me think about this for a bit. Did you call Claire by any chance?"

"No. I planned to do that, but I got sidetracked with this new discovery."

"Why don't you call her and see what she knows. Specifically ask about John Smith. And mention the other names too. See if she can add anything that might be helpful."

"Paul, are you sure you shouldn't just turn this info in to the police?"

Paul hesitated. "Possibly, but I'd like to give them a little more evidence. Let's go as far as we can first. Then we'll contact them. Asking them to reopen a closed case won't be easy."

"Okay," I said. "I still haven't heard from Mike. Should I phone him?"

"I'm actually on my way to see him now. He's staying at the Fredericktown Lodge. I called my friend Tim, who works there, and he confirmed that Mike is a guest."

"You're not going to call him first?"

"No. I want to meet him face-to-face. I realize there's no real reason to think he's not on the level, but I want to be sure, Sarah."

"I understand. Just don't offend him. We need his help."

"Trust me, I'm not going to be confrontational. I just want to make up my own mind." He paused for a moment. "What is that clicking noise?"

"It's a problem on the line," I said. "It's been going on for quite a while."

Paul was silent for a moment. "When did it start?"

"I'm not sure. Janet already talked to the phone company about it. It should be cleared up soon."

"Okay," he said slowly.

"Is something wrong?"

"No. As long as Janet actually talked to someone from the telephone company."

I chuckled. "You don't think someone's listening in, do you?"

"Sorry. I guess I'm being paranoid. The more we look into Hannah's murder, the more concerns I have."

"Which makes it even harder for me to understand why the police in Kansas City don't take what I told them more seriously."

Paul sighed. "Unfortunately, it happens, Sarah. Big-city police departments get busy. Sometimes it's easier to close a case so you can move on to the next one."

"I hope it doesn't take much longer for us to get the evidence we need."

"I feel the same way, but the last thing I want is for them to dismiss us. We'd be back to square one." He grunted. "I've got to go. About Mike, don't worry. I'll be very careful."

"Okay," I said slowly. I trusted Paul, but sometimes people make mistakes. Even though I had faith in his law-enforcement instincts, he didn't have connections at the Kansas City Police Department. Mike did. I hadn't forgotten about Anson Bentley, but if the police were still calling Hannah's murder a burglary, it was a good chance he was in agreement with it.

"I'll call you back after I talk to Mike," Paul said. "In the meantime, why don't you see if you can get in contact with Claire?"

I told him I would and hung up. I hunted for the number in Hannah's phone book and dialed it. After the second ring, a woman answered the phone. "Kennedy, Worthington, Klemm, and Sparlin."

"May I speak to Claire Freeman?" I said.

"Yes, one moment."

A few seconds later, a different woman's voice came on the line. "This is Claire Freeman."

"Claire, this is Sarah Miller. Hannah's sister."

"Sarah. I'm so glad to hear from you. How are you? How is Cicely?"

After answering this question so often, my response had been whittled down to, "We're holding our own. Cicely is in school and doing well. We both miss Hannah."

"I miss her too, but I'm glad to hear you and Cicely are okay," she replied. "What can I do for you?"

"Claire, can you tell me anything about my sister that I might not know? I mean, was she afraid of anyone? Concerned about anything before her death? I'm looking into the possibility that her death wasn't the result of a burglary."

"The police already asked these questions," she said slowly. "You know that, right?"

"I'm sure they did."

"You think they may have missed something?"

"I don't know. Hannah's death is eerily similar to the way our parents died. It makes me wonder."

Claire was silent for a moment. "Can I call you back in a few minutes?" she said, her voice low and soft.

"Sure."

She didn't even say good-bye. The line just suddenly went dead. About six minutes later the phone rang, and I said, "Hello?"

"It's Claire. I'm calling you on my cell phone. I didn't want anyone to overhear me. It's not that they would care that I'm talking to you. It just feels . . . personal. I don't want Hannah's business turned into office gossip."

"Is something wrong?"

"I don't know. It's just that Hannah was acting strange for about a week before she was killed. I asked her several times if she was okay, but she wouldn't talk to me about it. And then the day she died, something really weird happened."

"Can you tell me what it was?"

"Yes. Someone sent her flowers and she freaked out. Her face went white and she looked like she was about to pass out. She told our boss, Mr. Kennedy, that she was sick and needed to go home. I asked her what was wrong, but she wouldn't tell me. I felt like she wanted to, but she was just too afraid. That was the last time I ever saw her. She was killed that night."

The hairs on the back of my neck stood up. "Claire, were the flowers white orchids?"

Another pause. "How did you know that? Does it mean something to you?"

I felt as if the air had been sucked out of my lungs. "Yes, it does. Did you tell the police about the flowers?"

"Yes. I told them twice."

"What do you mean . . . twice?"

She cleared her throat. I could tell she was nervous. "The first time was when the police came here not long after the murder. The second time was a couple of weeks later. A detective came by asking questions."

"Do you remember his name?"

"Yes, I do. He gave me his card in case I remembered anything else that might help him. I've still got it on my desk. Detective

Doug Sykes. Nice guy. Seemed very interested in the flowers."

"Can you tell me what kind of questions he asked you? Is there anything about your conversation that sticks out in your memory?"

"He asked a lot of the same things the police asked originally, but his questions were more detailed. He wanted to know what happened to the flowers. And he asked whether there was anyone new in Hannah's life."

"And was there?"

"Yes. I never saw his face, just his car. He picked her up for lunch a couple of times. She always seemed upset when she came back. I don't think she wanted anything to do with him."

"Did she ever mention his name?"

"No, I'm sorry."

"What kind of car was it?"

"I'm not sure, Sarah. Guess I'm not a car person. It was big and gray. Fancy. Like a Cadillac, but I don't think it was."

"Would anyone else have noticed this car?"

"I doubt it. He picked her up across the street. Never came in. Never got out. I only looked because I was curious."

"Claire, does the name John Smith mean

anything to you?"

"No, but Hannah didn't share her life outside of work. I wish I could tell you more."

"She called you a couple of times during the week she died. Can you tell me why?"

"Sure. One day she called in sick. She and Cicely both had the flu, and the other call came about an hour after she left work that last day. She apologized for running out, but she wouldn't tell me why she was so upset."

"Thanks, Claire. You've really helped quite a bit. If I have more questions, is it okay if I call you?"

"Of course. Anytime. Hannah was really a sweet woman. I know how excited she was about finding you again."

"She talked to you about me?"

"Yes. Even though she was a very private person, she told me how happy she was to have you in her life. We had lunch together a couple of weeks before she died. You were her hero, you know."

"Wh-what? Did you say 'hero'?"

"Yes. Hannah said she'd always wanted to be just like you. She not only loved you, Sarah, she admired you very much."

I mumbled my thanks and hung up the phone.

"Hannah said she'd always wanted to be just like you." Claire's voice echoed in my head. I'd spent most of my life wishing I were more like my sister, and she'd wanted to be more like me? I couldn't believe it. "I'm sorry, God," I said softly. "No more comparing. I'm done."

I felt as if a burden lifted from me, but I recognized it was up to me not to allow those kinds of thoughts to take root in my mind again. I'd programmed my thinking in the wrong way for so long, it could take a while for me to head in a more positive direction.

I forced myself to redirect my thoughts toward Hannah and the flowers she received. Wasn't this proof that her murder was planned? There was nothing random about it. Someone had sent those flowers the day she died. Why hadn't the police picked up on this? It seemed obvious to me. Did this have anything to do with what Detective Sykes wanted to tell me?

There were so many thoughts and questions dancing in my head, I felt it would explode. I'd just decided to take an aspirin for the headache that began to tickle my temples when the phone rang. It was Paul.

"I'm here with Mike," he said as soon as I said hello. "We're getting ready to head your way. We'll try to get there between six and seven. Sorry I can't nail down the time better. With the roads the way they are, we'll have to drive slower than normal. Is that okay?"

"Are you sure it's safe?"

"Mike and I are both used to snow and ice. We'll be fine."

I breathed a sigh of relief. "That sounds great. I have so much to tell you. I hit the jackpot today."

Paul put his hand over the receiver and said something. I could hear another voice in the background. It was obviously Mike. The men seemed to have hit it off, and I felt relieved.

"Great," Paul said suddenly. "We'll see you later."

I said good-bye and put the phone down. Checking the time, I discovered it was already after four o'clock. I wanted to get everything written down and organized so I wouldn't leave out anything important. Would Paul be as excited as I was about the flowers?

After running downstairs and telling Janet and Cicely that Mike and Paul were definitely coming for dinner, I went to work compiling all the information on paper. I finished at about 5:45 and spent the next thirty minutes trying to look presentable. I finally decided on a tan skirt with a white pullover. I pinned my hair up but let several tendrils fall around my face. It was like a messy bun, but the look was soft and feminine. I applied some foundation, blush, mascara, and light lipstick. I'd just started to put my makeup away when I heard Cicely say, "You need some eyeliner too."

She startled me, and I almost dropped my makeup bag. "You scared me," I said, followed by a little nervous laughter.

Cicely smiled at me. "You're not doing anything wrong, Aunt Sarah. You shouldn't feel funny about wearing makeup."

"I guess it seems . . . I don't know . . . vain somehow."

She walked over to me and took the bag from my hand. "Do you think my mom was vain?"

I shook my head. "No, sweetheart. Not at all. But your mom and I were different."

"You're not that different. Sometimes when you say or do something, it's just like Mom is standing right in front of me."

I felt my eyes fill with tears.

"Don't cry or I won't be able to get the liner on."

She opened the bag and looked through

it. "Look, you have a pencil. Why don't you use it?"

I smiled at her. "Do you know where I got this makeup?"

She shook her head.

"Your mom gave it to me for my birthday."

Cicely's eyes widened. "That's right. I remember now."

"I haven't used it much, but I think I'm ready now."

She nodded and told me to sit down. "Keep your eyes open and look up." I did as she requested and felt a little tickle under both eyes. "Now look down and don't move." I could feel the pencil gliding across my upper lids. "Don't move yet." She reached back into the bag and took out the mascara I'd used so sparingly. I started to protest, but she swiped my eyelashes several times before I had a chance to say anything. Then she put the liner and the mascara back in the bag. "Now look," she said with a big smile on her face.

"Oh my goodness!" I couldn't believe the woman I saw in the mirror was me. The liner made my eyes look so much larger.

"Where did you learn to do that?"

Cicely smiled. "I watched Mom for years. Sometimes for fun, she'd put makeup on me. Just to teach me how to do it when I was older."

"You did a great job, Cicely. Thank you."

She reached out to touch my face lightly. "You're so pretty, Aunt Sarah. I hope I look like you when I'm your age."

I was so stunned, it took a moment for me to respond. "I'd think you'd want to look like your mother. Why would you want to look like me?"

She frowned at me as if she didn't understand. "I look more like your daughter than Mom's. She even said that. She liked my red hair because I reminded her of you. She loved you a lot."

I tried to push back the emotions that flooded me, but I wasn't successful. *"Hannah said she'd always wanted to be just like you."*

"I didn't mean to upset you, Aunt Sarah," Cicely said, her expression full of concern.

"It's okay, honey. Knowing your mom felt that way means a lot to me."

She didn't respond, but I could tell by the look on her face that she was pleased. After she left I checked out my image in the mirror again. I looked good, and I felt good too.

"The world won't end if I wear a little makeup," I whispered to my reflection. Why had I avoided it for so long? Maybe I wasn't a model, and perhaps I'd never be as striking as Hannah, but suddenly it didn't matter.

I was on my way downstairs when I heard the doorbell. By the time I got downstairs, Janet had opened the front door, and Paul and Mike were standing in the living room.

"Sorry about the snow," Paul said apologetically, staring down at his boots.

"Not a problem," Janet said with a smile. "I put a mat down. Just wipe your feet and give me your coats. I'll hang them up in the laundry room so they can dry out."

Paul's eyes widened when he saw me, and he smiled. "You look very nice."

I returned his smile. "Thank you. How were the roads?"

"We didn't have much trouble getting here. Mike's SUV drives better than mine. Even with snow chains."

"I'm glad you made it," I said.

Cicely came down the stairs behind me, and Paul greeted her. Since she'd stayed in her room when Mike was here the last time, I introduced them.

"Very nice to meet you, Cicely," Mike said. "I'm so sorry about your mom."

"Thank you," she said softly. Tears filled her eyes and ran down her cheeks. She dabbed at her cheeks with her hand and turned away. It was obvious she was still very emotional after reading Hannah's Facebook message.

I could tell by the look on Mike's face that Cicely's reaction had touched him.

"Dinner's ready," Janet said. "I made some coffee to help warm you up."

"That's exactly what I need right now," Mike said with a smile. "Thank you."

We followed her into the dining room. She'd already set the table and put out several side dishes of food, along with a large carafe of coffee. She went into the kitchen and came out a few seconds later carrying a huge bowl of beef stew.

"I should have helped you," I said. "I'm sorry."

"Don't be silly," she said with a smile. "You were busy. Besides, you know I love cooking for people. I'm so happy to have a full table."

"It's good of you to ask me over," Mike said.

He seemed a little different tonight. Quieter. More introspective. I wondered why.

After Janet said the blessing, we started eating. Eventually the conversation turned to families. Paul told a funny story about his childhood, so I felt it gave me an opening to ask Mike about himself.

"You've never mentioned a family, Mike," I said. "Are you married?"

He shook his head. "Not anymore. My wife divorced me about five years ago."

"I'm sorry."

He shrugged. "It happens. I'm not happy about it, but I've come to terms with the situation."

"What about children?" Janet asked.

He nodded. "A daughter. Just about Cicely's age." He flashed a quick smile at my niece, who shyly returned his smile.

"What's her name?" Cicely asked.

"Kaitlin."

"A beautiful name," I said. "Does she live near you?"

He shook his head. "No. Kaitlin and her mother live in Tennessee. I don't get to see her much. This year I'm going for Christmas. I'll get to spend a few days with her, and I'm really looking forward to it."

It was clear that Mike missed his daughter. Seeing the big man's vulnerable side made him seem more human. Paul appeared relaxed around him. I had to wonder if he was ready to share everything we'd discovered with Mike. Time would tell.

We finished dinner and Janet announced she'd made a cheesecake for dessert. "Cicely and I will take our dessert upstairs," she said. "You all can carry yours into the living room or stay here at the dining room table. What would work best?"

I looked at Paul.

"Could we stay at the table?" he asked. "That way we have more room to work."

I nodded. "Sure, that's fine."

"Come on, Cicely," Janet said. "Why don't you help me serve the cheesecake, and then you and I will go upstairs. I need a Scrabble rematch. You beat me pretty badly this afternoon."

Cicely smiled. "That would be awesome."

I winked at Janet. I was certain she'd allowed Cicely to win. She was great at Scrabble.

After the three of us got cheesecake and fresh coffee, Janet and Cicely said their good-nights and went upstairs. Sure enough, Paul asked me to get all my papers, along with any notes I needed. I went up and gathered everything I'd put together in a folder and went back downstairs. Paul and Mike were talking in hushed tones when I came into the room.

"I was telling Mike about the phone and your discovery concerning John Smith," Paul said as I sat down. "This is the best lead we've had."

"Did you check out the numbers I gave you?" I asked.

Paul nodded. "The number for *JR* isn't working. It was a burner phone. No way to trace it."

"What's a burner phone?" I asked.

"It's a prepaid phone," Mike said. "A cheap, disposable phone that can be purchased in any store. Since it's not connected to any particular phone service, there's no way to track it."

"Some drug dealers use them," Paul said.

I frowned. "Why would Hannah have the number of a drug dealer?"

Paul shook his head. "Burner phones are used for all kinds of reasons, Sarah. Sometimes it's just because the user can't afford another kind of phone."

"And what about the number for John Smith?"

"That number was a landline," Paul said. "And it belonged to a John Smith. But he's moved, and there was nothing indicating he has a new number."

"You let me take care of that," Mike said. "As a PI I have resources you don't have, Paul."

"I'm sure that's true," Paul replied. "And I probably don't want to know about most of them."

Mike laughed. "You'd be correct about that."

"So after Hannah is killed, this John Smith moves? That's rather suspicious, isn't it?"

Mike nodded. "Very suspicious. That's why we need to find him. It's too bad he was Martin Summers's only survivor. We probably could have found him through his family."

Paul looked at me. "Did you call Claire Freeman?"

"Yes, I did. And it was very interesting." Paul's mouth dropped open when I told him about the flowers. "That's not all," I said. "Some guy Claire hadn't seen before started showing up at work to see Hannah a few days before she died. Unfortunately Claire never saw his face."

Paul drummed his fingers on the table as he thought. "So we know that Hannah was upset about something. The man who showed up at work was probably connected to whatever was going on. But she really panicked when she got the flowers. That's when she decided to leave."

"She got the flowers during the day, and she was killed that night," I said. "The same day she wrote me the letter. Doesn't this ruin the theory that Hannah was killed by a burglar looking for drugs or money? Whoever sent the flowers was obviously targeting her. He planned to kill her."

"It looks that way to me," Paul said. "I'm still confused why the police didn't ask the same questions."

"Maybe they did," Mike said. "But in their minds the flowers don't have to be from the killer. Hannah could have gotten the flowers from anyone, and a stranger still could have killed her."

"That's ridiculous," I fumed. "It seems clear to me." I was disappointed in Mike's reaction. I thought the flowers were the smoking gun we'd been looking for.

"One thing I don't understand," Paul said, frowning. "You told me Cicely didn't see any flowers at the house the night her mother died."

I nodded. "That's right."

"But they had to be there."

"Wait a minute," I said slowly. "I think I might be able to explain that. When I was inside Hannah's house, I found a white orchid lying on the floor in her bedroom. What if she had the flowers in her room?"

"But if she hated them so much, why wouldn't she just throw them away?" Paul asked. "Why keep them at all? And why put them in her bedroom?"

"Maybe she kept the flowers because she

358

wanted to find out where they came from," Mike said suddenly. "If I were Hannah, I'd contact the florist and see who bought them." He looked at me. "I read Hannah's file. There wasn't anything that identified the florist. You didn't see anything in Hannah's room that might give us a clue about that, did you?"

I shook my head. "I'll call Claire again and ask her about the company that delivered them." I sighed. "Sorry. I was just so excited about what she told me, I didn't think of it."

"You've done a great job," Paul said soothingly. "Now we need to find out how all these clues go together."

I pulled the newspaper articles out from the stack of papers on the table. "Here's the article about the murders of Martin Lewis Summers and his wife, Elise. Obviously, Hannah saw similarities between these murders and our parents' murders and contacted Mr. Smith. I think he might be the man who showed up at Claire's office. We know he called Hannah several times. And we also know that Cicely met him. His stepmother worked at the same newspaper where my mom worked, but it's a big place. Mom was a secretary, and according to the obituary, Elise Summers was a reporter, just like the woman who gave Hannah the file. They didn't work in the same department, so I'm not sure how they were linked. Mr. and Mrs. Summers were killed in almost the same way my parents were. Stabbed. It was called a burglary too. But in their case their kids were already grown and out of the house, so they were alone when they were attacked."

"Well, I think I have all the information I need for now," Mike said, standing up. "My job is to look for John Smith." He pointed at me. "You find out from Claire what flower shop sent the flowers."

"Isn't it possible the police already know this?" Paul asked.

Mike nodded. "Sure. But remember, they've basically closed this case. I'm afraid they never took Sarah's initial claim about the flowers seriously."

"Doug did," I said.

Mike shrugged. "He wasn't totally convinced either, Sarah. But he thought the coincidence should be investigated."

I felt a rush of anger. "Excuse me, but someone sent them to her. She had them. That's an important clue. Someone was sending a message. Someone was planning a murder."

"Slow down," Mike said. "I realize that.

I'm just trying to show you how the police think."

"I'm sorry, Mike. It's just that sometimes it seems that no matter what we learn, it doesn't get us any closer to the truth."

"Let's hope that's going to turn around," Paul said. "I'm not willing to give up."

"Nor am I," Mike said. "We'll just keep going until we find out what really happened. Okay?"

I nodded. "Mike, do you know a Captain Bentley with the Kansas City Police Department?"

"I know who he is, but I never had much contact with him. He and I started on the force about the same time, I think. Almost twenty-five years ago."

"He was really nice to me while I was in Kansas City. Said if Cicely and I needed anything we should contact him. What about bringing him in on what we're doing?"

Mike shook his head. "Absolutely not. Anson Bentley bleeds blue. If he thought anyone was working on his case behind his back, he'd be all over us. Besides, he might be the one who closed your sister's case. We can't be sure."

I nodded. The veins on Mike's neck stood out. Hearing Captain Bentley's name had certainly caused a reaction.

Paul told me that he'd call me tomorrow and they left, leaving me feeling oddly unsettled. Why had Mike reacted so violently when I brought up Captain Bentley? I packed up all the pages on the table and took them upstairs.

As I lay in bed that night, I could almost hear Hannah's voice warning me to be careful.

CHAPTER TWENTY-THREE

The next two days passed by quickly. The new storm had dumped almost a foot of snow, but a couple of days with temperatures above freezing helped to clear the roads. I was especially busy at school, which helped to keep my mind off Hannah's death. By the weekend, I was ready for some time off. There was no school on Monday because William and some other men from the Mennonite church needed that day to replace the furnace. Even though the work would start today, they'd asked to have until Monday evening to finish their task. I didn't mind the day off because I needed time to prepare for the tests I would be giving before the winter break.

Janet enjoyed cooking large breakfasts on Saturdays, so I woke up to the aroma of bacon sizzling in a pan and Janet's special pancakes cooking on the grill. She liked to cook bacon and then crumble it up and put it in her pancake batter. Although I was certain it wasn't the healthiest of breakfast dishes, it was absolutely delicious. I dressed in jeans and a comfortable sweatshirt, put my hair in a ponytail, and went downstairs to the kitchen. After eating more than I should, I was helping Janet with the dishes when I heard a knock on the front door.

"Are you expecting anyone?" Janet asked.

"No. I have dinner with Mike and Paul tomorrow night, but nothing's planned for today."

I wiped my wet hands on my apron and went to the front door. Murphy was already there, sitting in front of the door, staring at it.

"Move, Murphy," I said, pushing him away gently with my foot. When I opened the door, I was shocked to see Captain Anson Bentley standing there.

"Hi, Sarah," he said with a smile. "I hope I'm not intruding. I was in this area and remembered you lived in Sanctuary. Thought I'd stop by and check on you."

I was glad to see him, but Mike's warning echoed in my mind. *"Anson Bentley bleeds blue. If he thought anyone was working on his case behind his back, he'd be all over us."*

"Please come in," I said. My hand went to my hair, and I looked down at my dirty apron. "I'm sorry. I must look a mess. I wasn't expecting company."

He smiled, and I was surprised once again by how attractive he was. He was so charismatic I couldn't help feeling drawn to him.

"I think you look lovely. Besides, Saturday was created for relaxing. If you're busy, I could come by another time."

"Absolutely not. Please come in." I held the door open, and he accepted my invitation.

At that moment Janet came into the living room with Cicely on her heels. They both looked at Captain Bentley in surprise.

I introduced him to Janet. "And you remember Captain Bentley, don't you, Cicely? You met him outside your house in Kansas City?"

She gave him a shy smile. "Yes, I do. Hello."

He returned her smile. "Hello, Cicely. I just stopped by to see how you and your aunt are doing. How are you getting along?"

"Fine, thank you."

"Captain, would you like some breakfast?" Janet asked. "I was just getting ready to put some pancakes on the griddle for Cicely. It wouldn't be any trouble to fix some for you."

"That sounds wonderful, but unfortunately I already ate breakfast. Cold cereal and juice. The aroma coming from your kitchen tells me I made an unfortunate choice."

Janet laughed. "Well, at least I can get you some coffee, can't I?"

"I would really appreciate that. Thank you."

She held her hand out and came over to me. "Give me your apron. I'll finish the dishes. You and Captain Bentley make yourselves comfortable."

I quickly took off my apron and handed it to her. "Thanks, Janet."

"Please," he said. "Everyone, just call me Anson. I'm not here officially." He flashed another warm smile.

"That's an unusual name," Janet said. "I don't think I've heard it before."

"It's a family name. The same as my father's. I also have two uncles with the middle name Anson. And a great-grandfather with the first name Anson. Different middle names though."

"A great family tradition. You must all be very close."

"As much as any family, I guess. My dad died a few years ago, so I'm honored to carry his name. He was an amazing man and a top-notch detective. I've spent my career trying to be like him."

"I'm sure he'd be proud of you," Janet said.

Janet and Cicely said good-bye and headed back to the kitchen. I asked Anson to sit down.

"Thank you," he said as he lowered himself onto the couch. "I won't keep you. I just wanted to bring you up-to-date on your sister's case and make sure you and Cicely are okay."

"Have you learned anything new?" I asked.

Anson's eyes narrowed. "Yes. In fact, I'm becoming convinced there is more to your sister's murder than just a break-in and burglary."

I felt my pulse quicken. "What do you mean? I heard Steven Hanks was blamed for Hannah's death and the case had been closed."

He looked toward the kitchen. "Look, I'm not sure this is the time or place to get into details. I'm going to be in the area for a couple of days. Is there a way we could meet somewhere for dinner? I'm busy today, but I'm free tomorrow night."

"I . . . I'm not sure. Could you excuse me just a minute while I make a quick call?"

He nodded. "Certainly. But don't change

any plans on my account."

I stood up. "I really want to hear what you have to say. It's just —"

"Sarah, I know that a local deputy sheriff is helping you investigate this case. He called someone at the department and asked questions. I'm not upset about it. In fact, I applaud him. I also know that Mike Templeton is in town." He hesitated a moment before saying, "Mike has a lot of experience with the Kansas City Police Department. But" — he stared down at his hands — "I feel I need to warn you to . . . be careful."

"Of Mike? Why do you say that?"

"I don't want to worry you unnecessarily. Mike's retirement wasn't completely his idea. There were some problems."

"I don't understand," I said.

Anson frowned. "I'm not comfortable saying anything more. Just be on your guard. I feel responsible for you and your niece."

"Captain —"

"Anson, please."

"Anson, the only reason we've been pursuing Hannah's murder is because we want your department to look in the right place. Not only to find the killer but also to find out the real reason she was murdered. If Steven Hanks killed Hannah, and I don't

368

think he did, someone else was behind it. Someone who was also involved with my parents' deaths."

"I understand why you're concerned, Sarah. I want you to know that I'm working hard behind the scenes to find the truth."

I breathed a sigh of relief. "That's all I want, Anson. I'm not trying to get in your way. Really."

He leaned forward and took my hand. "I know that. It's our fault you felt you had to do this much. I talked to Doug before he died, and I have his file. I'm ready to do whatever it takes to solve this crime."

"Th-thank you," I said, trying to stay calm. "Let me call my friend Paul. I'm sure he'll be thrilled to hear this. We're meeting tomorrow night for dinner, and I'd love to have you join us."

"I'd like that."

I jogged up the stairs. Anson seemed sincere. Since he was directly connected to the police department and had a job with authority behind it, having him on our side was fantastic news. I went to my room and called Paul. He answered his phone right away. I told him about Anson and repeated what he'd said about helping us.

"Boy, I don't know, Sarah," he said slowly. "Mike seemed pretty opposed to telling this guy anything."

"Anson said Mike didn't just retire from the police department because he was injured. He said there were other problems."

"What kind of problems?"

"I don't know. I didn't feel right asking. As far as Mike's claim that you could get in trouble, it isn't true. Anson isn't upset by your involvement. In fact, he's apologetic for not getting to the bottom of this sooner."

"So what do you want to do? If we bring Bentley in, we may lose Mike."

"We have the ear of a captain in the Kansas City Police Department, Paul. Isn't that what we've been working toward all along?"

Paul was silent as he considered what I'd said. "Why don't you tell him to meet us for dinner? I'll deal with Mike."

"I'm glad you said that, because I already asked him."

Paul's sigh floated through the phone. "I hope this is the right decision. If it's not . . ."

"We shouldn't be so suspicious. Anson has been supportive from the start. And he took the time to come to my house. Why would he do that if he was out to get us?"

"I agree. It's just that Mike's instincts seem pretty good."

"If he really cares about solving Hannah's

murder, he'll stick with us."

"All right. It's your call. I think I should call Mike and tell him though."

"Are you sure?" I asked. "Maybe it would be better to just let him find out at dinner. It's not his business who we bring into this."

"I don't want to blindside him. I've got to give him a heads-up."

"Go ahead if you feel better about it."

"I'll pick you up about six-thirty."

"See you then."

I put the phone down and took a deep breath. Was I doing the right thing? It seemed right to me. Having Anson Bentley on our side was a great victory. One that we couldn't ignore.

I headed downstairs and found Anson right where I'd left him. I sat down on the couch. "Paul and I are meeting Mike tomorrow night at the steak house in Fredericktown. Paul said you're more than welcome to join us."

"Great. I'd like to hear what you've dug up. As I said, after looking at your sister's murder more closely, I have some questions." He looked toward the kitchen. "Will your niece be joining us?"

I shook my head. "No. I'm not comfortable talking about Hannah's murder in front of her. I'll fill her in when I have something solid to tell her."

"Good. It would be very difficult to talk freely with her there." He took a sip of his coffee and then put it back on the saucer. "So how is she doing really?"

I sighed. "Things are much better now. For a while I was very worried. She was angry. It's understandable, but anger can lead to poor choices." I told him about Cicely's impromptu visit to the mine. "It's very unstable, and there's a deep, uncovered shaft inside. She could have been seriously hurt."

"There are a lot of abandoned mines in this area," he said with a frown. "I thought the state was working to provide protection."

"It's a project in process. Most of them have been secured. Unfortunately, we're out in the boonies. At one time the town was mostly Conservative Mennonite, and they didn't welcome government intervention in their affairs. I think the state decided to leave us to our own devices. Since we don't really have any city government, there's no one to monitor the situation."

His eyebrows shot up. "You don't have any kind of city council to oversee things? How does that work?"

I smiled. "We have a mayor. He represents

us in state matters. Of course, the Mennonites don't recognize him as their mayor but they do as a friend, and they let him know what they're concerned about. In a casual way, of course."

"When I get home I'll see if I can pull some strings. Lots of mines have been reclaimed all over the state. Maybe I can help to speed the process along."

"That would be wonderful. Something needs to happen before someone gets hurt."

I was struck again by his rugged good looks. He reminded me of someone, but for the life of me, I couldn't figure out who it was. Probably an actor on television. If I watched TV more often, I'd probably be able to make the connection.

He took another sip of coffee. "I'm really glad Cicely's doing better."

I sighed. "I am too."

"But catching the person who killed her mother would certainly help, wouldn't it?"

"I hope so. Sometimes I wonder."

He cocked his head to the side and looked at me questioningly. "What do you mean?"

"Honestly, all she really wants is her mother. I believe someday she'll be glad the killer was brought to justice. But right now, all she can feel is Hannah's absence."

He nodded. "I understand. I really do.

Sometimes victims are completely caught up in seeing the guilty party punished. But when it happens, they still have to face the sorrow of their loss. There's nothing we can do to fix that. But I'll do everything I can to at least give her — and you — some closure. Okay?"

"Thank you."

Anson stood up. "I've got to get going, but I'll meet you tomorrow night. What time and where?"

"About seven o'clock?" I told him the name of the restaurant and how to get there.

"I'm sure I can find it. Fredericktown is so small, if I get lost, I'm confident I can find someone who can direct me to the steak house."

I smiled. "Especially since it's the only steak house in town. Believe it or not, their steaks are fantastic. Even someone from the big city will appreciate them."

He chuckled. "I'm sure I will. Thanks again for inviting me."

I walked him to the front door, said good-bye, and watched him drive away.

"Seems like a nice man." I turned to find Janet behind me, wiping her hands on her apron.

"Yes, he is," I agreed. "Just goes to show that the police do care." I sighed. "Hannah was always so frustrated with them. She started trying to get someone to look into our parents' murders when she was only nineteen, but no one would listen to her. Too bad she never connected with Anson."

"How old do you think he is?" Janet asked.

I shook my head. "I don't know. Mike said something about knowing him for over twenty years. I guess that makes Anson somewhere in his late forties or early fifties."

Janet shrugged. "Some people just look younger than they are. Unfortunately, that's never been my problem."

I frowned at her. "That's not true, Janet. You look great for eighty."

Her eyebrows shot up and she laughed. "Very funny. See if I ever make you another bite to eat."

It was my turn to giggle. "You look great, and you know it. I think you're just fishing for compliments."

She sighed dramatically. "Only because I have to. No one else gives them to me."

"Oh goodness. You *are* mistreated." I grinned at her. "I've noticed that Mr. Banks from Barnes brings his dog, Bowie, to the clinic every chance he gets. If Bowie sneezes, Mr. Banks makes an appointment. He's definitely got eyes for you."

"Oh, *pshaw.*" Janet turned pink. "That man doesn't even know I'm alive."

Hiram Banks was the president of a small bank in Barnes. Knowing a man named Banks who worked for a bank was a source of amusement, but he was actually a very nice man. An attractive widower who really did seem interested in Janet. I expected him to ask her for a date one of these days, and I prayed she'd accept. After her very unhappy marriage, I knew she was gun-shy, but Janet had a lot of love to give. She and Hiram would make a great couple.

"So what did Anson have to say?" she asked.

"He wants to help us, Janet."

She smiled. "That's wonderful." She came over and gave me a hug. "This is just what you've been working for. I'm so proud of you."

"I'm thrilled, really."

Janet stepped back and looked at me closely. "You don't look that thrilled. Is something wrong?"

I shook my head. "No, it's great. I hope that tomorrow night Paul and I will be able to hand everything over to Anson and go on with our lives. But Paul's not sure we have enough to give them."

"That's not all you're worried about, is it?"

I looked at her with surprise. "What do you mean?"

"You're worried that after Anson Bentley takes over, you and Paul won't have anything in common."

I looked at her with surprise. "How do you do that? Read my mind?"

Janet smiled. "It comes from knowing you, honey. Sarah, that man is crazy about you. Yes, your relationship will be different. It will be better. Now you'll have time to get to know each other without the specter of death hanging over you. If it's meant to be, your relationship will blossom."

"I know you're right." I met her gaze. "I think I'm in love with him, Janet."

"I know," she said softly. "And loving someone means putting your heart in their hands. It's scary."

I nodded. "Well, after tomorrow we'll see what Paul and I have left." I headed toward the stairs. "I just hope it's enough."

Chapter Twenty-Four

Sunday seemed to crawl by. Although Jonathon preached a wonderful sermon about trusting God, my mind kept wandering. I was happy to see Cicely paying close attention. The past two weeks she'd stopped arguing about going to church and actually seemed to look forward to it.

After church, we went home and had lunch. Cicely asked to go with Janet on Monday and help at the clinic, but I reminded her she needed to study for tests scheduled the rest of the week. A few weeks ago she would have pitched a fit when I said no to her, but outside of a little minor whining, she accepted my decision without much resistance.

Paul picked me up at six-thirty, and we headed toward Fredericktown. He was quiet as we drove away from Sanctuary.

"Did you talk to Mike about Anson?" I asked, breaking the silence.

"Yes, and he wasn't happy."

I shook my head. "I don't get it. Isn't this what we should all want? Why isn't Mike relieved that Anson is taking over? We can't solve these crimes ourselves. Nor can we prosecute anyone. This is the best thing we could have hoped for."

"Of course it is." He looked over at me, a frown on his face. "I don't know what to think about Mike's reaction. It's as if he doesn't trust Anson."

"Anson seems to feel the same way about Mike," I said. "Surely they're not in some kind of competition for who can solve the case first."

"That doesn't make sense. Hannah's murder is far from solved."

"You know, Anson could still decide Steven Hanks was totally responsible. And he hasn't reopened my mom and dad's case yet. It's still up to us to convince him to take our claims seriously."

"You're right." He pointed at the tote bag I'd brought with me. "I take it that's our evidence?"

I nodded. "Everything I could think of, along with my own notes." I smiled at him. "Well, they're not really notes now. I rewrote them so they'd make sense."

"It's a little hard to accept that it's none

of my business anymore. Except when it comes to you."

"I'm a little worried about that," I said slowly, turning to look at him. You know, we've never even had a normal conversation."

He was silent for a moment. "Okay, how about this? When we go on our date, we won't be allowed to talk about the past. Instead, we'll concentrate on getting to really know each other. Talk about our hopes and dreams. You know, all the stuff couples talk about."

I smiled at him. "Our hopes and dreams? That doesn't sound like you."

"I'm trying to sound sensitive. Don't judge."

I laughed. "Okay, you've got a deal."

I stared out the window at the passing scenery. There was still some snow on the ground, even though the streets were clear. I loved snow and always hated to see it melt away. A sudden memory from my childhood popped into my mind. Without realizing it I sighed.

"Something on your mind?" Paul asked.

"I just remembered something — a time when Hannah and I made snow angels. Her death has dredged up things I'd forgotten. To be honest, a lot of the past is a blank. It makes sense that I can't remember much from the murders. But why is it so hard to remember the good things? Cicely's going through the same thing."

"Because when it hurts too much, the mind protects itself."

I studied him. "Is it that way with you? About your brother, I mean?"

He nodded. "Yes. It's almost as if we had no past before the accident. Just little bits and pieces that jump into my head sometimes. Or in my dreams."

"After the truth comes out, I hope Cicely and I will be able to face the past more easily."

He smiled. "You will."

"Is that a promise?"

"Yes. It's a promise."

We rode in silence the rest of the way, both of us lost in our own thoughts. When we pulled into the parking lot at the steak house, Paul pointed to Mike's SUV.

"Mike's here."

"And that's Anson's car right next to him," I said.

"A silver Lexus," Paul said. "Nice car. I guess being a captain on the Kansas City Police Department pays pretty well."

"Are you jealous?"

Paul grinned. "Hey, don't knock my 2006

Chevy pickup. It's pretty classy."

"Yes, it is. And I'm not knocking it."

He turned off the engine, got out, and opened my door. Then he took my arm. There were a few slick spots in the parking lot, so I walked carefully, holding on to him until we reached the entrance. Once inside, we spotted Mike and Anson sitting at a table across the room. Anson smiled broadly and waved us over. Mike looked tense. Was he angry with us? Although I liked Mike, I was determined to do the best thing for Hannah. If that meant we had to trade Mike for Anson, so be it. Besides, if Anson Bentley had reasons to distrust Mike, it stood to reason we should be cautious.

"Hello," Anson said as we reached the table. He stood up and held out a chair for me. I slid into the seat next to him, and Paul sat down at the other side of the table, between Mike and Anson.

"Hi," I replied. "Thank you again for meeting with us." I smiled at Mike. "Hello, Mike."

He nodded but didn't say anything. Were we in for an uncomfortable evening? I shot a quick look at Paul, and he rolled his eyes. Obviously he was wondering the same thing.

Just then the waitress came up to the table. After giving her our drink orders, I studied Mike, who hadn't said a word except to the waitress. He wouldn't meet my eyes, and his jaw was working overtime. I opened the menu the waitress had given us and perused the choices.

"Their steaks are great," Paul said.

In the end, we all ordered steaks, but I went with a small filet, while the men ordered rib eyes. My stomach was doing flip-flops, and I wasn't sure I could even get that much down. Would tonight bring us the results I'd been praying for?

After some small talk, Mike finally joined in the conversation. I could tell he wasn't completely relaxed, but I forced myself to concentrate on Anson. Gaining his help was more important than massaging Mike's ego.

"Let's talk about your sister's case," Anson said finally. "I've reviewed the notes Detective Sykes made before he died, looked through your sister's case file as well as your parents' file. Doug's concerns have become mine. First of all, there are the flowers. Frankly, in and of themselves, they're not enough for us to rule Hannah's death as anything beyond a murder that occurred during the commission of a crime. But in looking at your parents' murders and reading Doug's notes, I see your sister received white orchids at work the day she was killed.

According to Doug, her coworker said she was very upset and left work immediately. That tells me those flowers meant something."

"Yes," I said. "They had to have been sent as a threat. By the person who killed her." I cleared my throat. "It proves the murder was premeditated. Steven Hanks was a drug addict, looking for a way to support his habit. From what I've heard, he wasn't the kind of person who could have planned a murder. Besides, why would he? He didn't know Hannah. And he certainly was too young to be involved in my parents' killings."

Anson nodded slowly. "You're right, Sarah. I'm willing to look at someone other than Hanks. By the way, I tracked down the flower shop. It wasn't easy. The flowers were ordered by a man who came into the shop and paid cash. He gave them the name Matt Brown. I suspect it's an alias."

"Could they give a description?"

Anson shook his head. "All anyone could remember was that the guy had a wool cap pulled down low and kept his collar high. They didn't think anything about it because it was cold that day. They were really busy getting ready for a wedding, so no one paid much attention to him. I suspect he picked that shop because everything was so hectic and there were no security cameras. He knew what he was doing."

"That's not much to go on," Paul said with a frown.

"I realize that," Anson said. "But it certainly made me sit up and take notice. Why would he work so hard to hide his identity?"

Anson looked at Mike. "What do you think, Mike?" he asked.

Mike flushed. "To be honest, the flowers are . . . interesting. But by themselves they won't lead us anywhere. I think we need to forget about the flowers and try to find some real evidence."

"But they were ordered the day before Hannah was killed, Mike," I said. "If nothing else it proves her death wasn't the result of a robbery gone wrong. Can't you see that?"

Mike finally looked at me. "Yes. I know why you think that's important, Sarah," he said, obviously frustrated. "But all that tells us is that Steven Hanks might not be the mastermind behind the murder. But he could have been hired by someone else."

"Who would hire a drug addict?" I asked. "It's too dangerous. I don't think he had anything to do with it."

"You might be right, but my point is that

flowers are not direct evidence. And until we have something that clearly connects someone to Hannah's murder, we have nothing that will move this investigation forward."

Anson nodded. "I think Mike's right. White orchids mean something to this killer, but we have no idea why. We need more."

"I believe Hannah took them home so she could figure out where they came from," I said. "Ever since Hannah was nineteen she'd been trying to solve our parents' murders. I guarantee you she took that flower delivery very seriously."

Anson nodded. "I'm certain she did. Let's put the flowers aside for now. Can you tell me what other evidence you have?"

Paul and I took turns bringing up the other suspicious clues we'd uncovered, from Hannah's house burning down, to the man showing up at her workplace, and the murders that happened soon after our parents' that seemed so similar. I told him about the names and numbers in her phone book and the corresponding calls on her phone.

"We haven't been able to find this John Smith," I said, "but this other crime was important to my sister. Somehow I think it ties into our parents' murders."

When we finished, Anson was quiet for a while. Finally he said, "That's very impressive."

"I brought copies of everything," I said, picking up the tote bag and handing it to him.

"I can take this back with me?"

"Yes. Maybe you can find John Smith. And figure out if he's the *J* Hannah refers to. Also, there's a *JR* in her phone book with a star by his name. The number doesn't work. He might be important, but we're not sure."

"I'll go through all this very carefully," Anson said. "You have my word."

Just then the waitress brought our food. A few minutes after we started eating, Anson brought the conversation back to our previous discussion.

"So, Mike," he said, looking at the detective. "You agree with everything Sarah and Paul have said?"

Mike nodded. "I've gone over all of their information. I think whoever killed Sarah and Hannah's parents may have also killed Hannah. I just can't find a motive. Maybe you'll do better."

I let out a deep sigh of relief. Mike seemed to be warming up, but I could still see tension in his face.

"I'd like you to work with me on this if you would, Mike," Anson said. "You too, Paul. I'm not ignoring you, but Mike lives and works in Kansas City. That makes it easier for him to get involved."

"I totally understand," Paul said. "Sarah and I are grateful for your help. All we ever wanted was for the police in Kansas City to look at this crime again, recognizing that there could be more behind it than what it originally appeared to be."

"Then you've achieved your goal," Anson said with a smile. "I'll contact you in a few days, after I've had a chance to go through all of it and confer with my associates."

"Thank you so much, Anson," I said gratefully. "You're an answer to prayer."

He smiled. "I don't know that I've ever been called *that* before, but thank you." He glanced at his watch. "I'm sorry to keep you so late. You have school tomorrow, don't you, Sarah?"

I shook my head. "Actually, I don't. Ongoing furnace problems and freezing temperatures have created a day off while the furnace is repaired."

Anson smiled. "I'm sure Cicely is happy about that."

"Not really. She wanted to go to the veterinarian clinic tomorrow and help Janet.

I told her she needed to stay home and study instead."

"I've never known a young person to enjoy studying."

I chuckled. "The funny thing is, she really does like to study. She's very smart. And she loves history. I don't think academics were stressed much at her school in Kansas City. Now that she's attending a school with children who enjoy learning, she's beginning to blossom academically."

"The sign of a good teacher," Anson said, lifting his coffee cup as if toasting me.

"Thank you. I hope so. I love teaching. There's nothing else I'd rather do."

We talked a little more and then called it a night. I wanted to talk to Mike, but Anson asked Mike to walk him back to his car.

"So what do you think?" I said to Paul as we strolled across the parking lot.

"Well, I think it went as well as we could expect. I really wanted a chance to talk to Mike though."

"Me too."

"I'll give him a call later tonight."

"Good idea. I don't want him to think we don't appreciate everything he's done for us."

Paul held the door of the truck open, and I climbed inside. Then I waited for him to come around the other side and get in. He immediately started the engine and turned on the heater, but instead of leaving, he just sat there.

"Something wrong?" I asked.

"Just thinking."

He seemed to be watching Mike and Anson. They appeared to be having a very animated conversation. What was that about?

"Wish I knew what they were saying," he said. "I don't want Anson to make trouble for Mike."

"But why would he do that? He told Mike he was appreciative of the work he's done and wants his continued help with the case."

"I know." He chewed on his bottom lip for a moment. "I thought he'd be happy that Anson took our concerns seriously."

"And he should be," I said. "I have no idea why he's upset, but it isn't our job to read his mind, Paul. We're trying to figure out who killed my family. Mike's ego isn't the most important thing here. He should know that."

Paul nodded. "You're right. I guess I respect him for coming to Sanctuary to help us without asking for anything. I mean, as a favor for a friend. But that was his choice, I guess. We can't make that the priority."

"So now what?"

"So now we wait. We've done everything we can do, Sarah. We let Anson go back to Kansas City with all the information we've gathered. Then we pray he can reopen the case and figure out what really happened." He looked over at me, his face illuminated by the light coming from his dash. "I'm sorry I couldn't bring you all the answers you wanted."

"Oh, Paul. Without you, none of this would have happened. You've been there for me all the way. Besides, your expertise helped to make sense of so many things. If it wasn't for you, I would have given up."

He laughed lightly. "I don't believe that for a minute. You're a lot like Hannah. She kept looking for answers, and you did too. When the truth finally comes out, it will be a testament to both of you."

"If only it hadn't gotten her killed."

"I'm just thankful you're safe, Sarah. There were many times I wanted to beg you to stop."

"I never felt I was in real danger. Besides God's protection, I had two very strong allies. A town full of people who watch over each other . . . and you. Hannah didn't have those advantages. That's what made it easier for someone to hurt her."

"I'm sure you're right. I have to say that I'm incredibly relieved we can finally walk away from this now."

"I hope we didn't just make Anson a target."

"Don't even go there," Paul said curtly. "That's his job. Besides, he knows what he's doing. He'll be fine."

"I would have said the same about Doug Sykes."

Paul reached over and put his hand on my arm. "Please don't start worrying about Anson. It's time for you to let this go and start living your life again." He smiled. "I'd like to be a part of that, Sarah."

"I'd like that too."

Even though I wanted to feel as if our journey for justice was almost over, I still felt a twinge of anxiety. I couldn't tell if it was concern for Anson's safety or something else still hiding in the shadows.

CHAPTER TWENTY-FIVE

I woke up Monday morning to frigid temperatures. First I heard Janet moving around and then the whoosh of the furnace as it came on. Not wanting to brave the cold house, I decided to stay in bed while the furnace did its job. Even though I respected my Conservative Mennonite neighbors, I was grateful I didn't have to rely on potbellied stoves or fireplaces for warmth. I was doubly grateful that after today, the school would be warm again too. A big blessing. William and the other men had pulled the old furnace out on Saturday and would install the new one today.

I got up around seven-thirty, said goodbye to Janet as she headed for the clinic, and lingered over coffee and rolls until almost nine. In the light of day, my apprehension about Anson's safety had lessened some. Last night in bed, I'd prayed for him, asking God to protect him and help him to find the truth. Now I was ready to do what Paul had suggested. Just let go of the past and live my life.

I'd just decided to get dressed when Cicely came into the kitchen looking sleepy. "Anything for breakfast?" she asked.

"Janet made pecan rolls before she left. Want me to heat one up?"

"Awesome." She nodded and plopped down in a chair at the table. Her hair hung over her face, but I could make out a smile as she said, "And hot chocolate?"

I laughed. "I think I can manage that." First I poured myself a sorely needed cup of coffee. After a few sips, I started heating up milk on the stove, then popped one of Janet's giant homemade pecan rolls in the microwave. As it heated, the smell of warm pecans filled the kitchen. When it was ready, I took it out and gave it to Cicely. She began eating the roll while I finished making her hot chocolate.

"How did you sleep?" I asked.

"Lying down."

It took me a minute to figure out what she meant, but when I did, I laughed. "Very funny."

Cicely pushed the hair out of her face. "That was my mom's joke. I guess it's mine now."

I sat down next to her. "I like it when you share parts of her with me. I missed so many years. Being with you . . . it's like getting some of that time back."

She nodded. "I like that, Aunt Sarah." Without a warning, she suddenly wrapped her arms around me in a hug. "I love you," she said softly.

I hugged her back while I tried not to cry. "Oh, honey, thank you. I love you too." When she let me go, I saw her eyes were wet. "We're going to make it, Cicely. I just know we are."

"I'm starting to believe that too, Aunt Sarah."

I got up and poured her hot chocolate. She finished her breakfast quietly, but I felt we'd crossed a critical point. My heart sang as I silently thanked God for His goodness. Cicely and I were becoming a real family, and concern about Hannah's murder had been passed into very capable hands. I felt a real sense of hope.

"Get dressed," I said when Cicely finished eating. "And start studying. When you're done, we'll work in a game of Scrabble."

She frowned. "I like Scrabble," she said, "but could we play something else? I'm getting a little tired of it."

"Sure? What would you like to play?"

"How about UNO?" she said.

"I've never played it, but I'm game."

"Mom packed our UNO cards with my clothes," Cicely said. "It will be fun to play it again."

"Sounds great," I said with a smile. "And if you need help studying, let me know. I'd be happy to help you."

"Awesome. Thanks, Aunt Sarah." She got up from her chair. "You know, I really like school now."

"I'm glad," I said. "Learning is so important." I smiled at her. "I've never asked you what you want to be when you grow up. I guess we've been so busy trying to get through *now,* there hasn't been much time to talk about the future."

A strange look came over her face. "For a while I thought I wanted to be a lawyer. Mom used to tell me that if she'd had the chance to go to college, she would have studied law. Working at a law office was as far as she got. But then I started thinking about being a veterinarian."

I smiled at her. "A veterinarian like Janet? That's wonderful."

She looked down at the floor. "But now I think I might like to be something else instead."

Typical of someone her age. She'd probably change her mind a dozen times by the time she really had to choose. "So now what do you want to be?"

Cicely was silent for a moment. When she gazed at me, she looked as serious as a ten-year-old could be. "Now I think I'd like to be a teacher. I never realized how much teachers can help kids. I think it's awesome." With that she turned and left the kitchen.

I sat in my chair, stunned by her comment. Wiping tears from my face once again, I had to laugh at myself. "You're going to drown yourself, Sarah," I said softly. I finished my coffee and was cleaning up when someone knocked on the front door. I opened it and found Wynter Evans standing there.

"How nice to see you," I said, holding the door open.

"I'm sorry, Sarah. I don't have time to stay and visit. Reuben and I are on our way to Fredericktown to get a marriage license. We've decided we don't want to wait any longer. We intend to hold the ceremony three weeks from today."

"Oh, Wynter! How wonderful!"

I hugged her, and we both giggled.

"I hope I'm invited to the wedding."

"Of course you are. We wouldn't get married without you, Janet, and Cicely."

"We'd be honored to attend."

She smiled. "Thank you." She handed me a large envelope she held in her hand. "Zac sent this."

I took it from her. "What is it?"

"It's a copy of the report from your parents' murders. I remembered it was something you'd really wanted and mentioned it to him. Zac's friend at the police department was able to find an old hard copy in the file room." She smiled. "I hope it helps."

"Thanks so much, Wynter. I really appreciate it."

"Let's have lunch this Saturday. You can bring me up-to-date on what's going on."

"That sounds great." I leaned to the right and saw Reuben sitting in his truck. I waved at him, and he waved back.

"Gotta go." She gave me another quick hug and then hurried back to the truck. I waved again as they drove away. I was thrilled to find out they were finally getting married. Wynter and Reuben had been through a lot, yet their love stayed strong. It gave me hope for Paul and me.

I hadn't told her that I already had a copy of the report because I didn't want her to think her help wasn't appreciated. I carried the envelope with me upstairs. After going into my room I tossed it on the bed and changed out of my pajamas. After putting on jeans and a sweatshirt, I brushed my hair and quickly braided it. Then I went to my bookshelf and pulled out a novel I'd been wanting to read. My plan was to go downstairs and curl up on the couch with Murphy for a while before spending a couple of hours this afternoon preparing the tests for this week. I was just getting ready to leave the room when the phone rang. It was Paul.

"Just calling to check on you," he said. "I've got a really busy day, otherwise I'd come by and take you to lunch."

"That's fine. I was just getting ready to settle down with a good book."

"Sounds nice. So how about a date Friday night?" he said. "There's a new movie in Farmington I think you'd like. We can go to dinner afterward."

"I'd love it, Paul. Yes, let's do it."

"Great. I'll pick you up around four-thirty."

"Sounds wonderful. Have you heard anything from Mike?"

"I tried to call him this morning, but the operator at the motel said he'd checked out." Paul sighed. "I think he's gone, Sarah."

"Oh. I thought you were going to call him

last night."

"I did, but he never answered his phone. I'll try his cell later today. If he's already on the road, I don't want to distract him. It's snowing near Kansas City."

"Okay. When you talk to him, please tell him how much we appreciate him. Wish I knew why he's so upset."

"Don't worry about it. I'll get to the bottom of it."

"Thanks, Paul. Guess I'd better let you go. Hope you have a good day."

"You too, Sarah. Talk to you soon."

I stared at the envelope lying on my bed and decided to throw it away. The darkness it contained was something I didn't want in my life anymore. After picking it up I started to toss it into the trash can, but at the last second I changed my mind. What if it was different from the original report? Shouldn't I at least make sure it was an exact copy?

I tore the envelope open and quickly scanned the pages. It did seem to be a duplicate of what I'd already seen. I was almost finished reading when I noticed something that stunned me. I read it over three times, trying to make certain my eyes weren't deceiving me. Sure enough, it said exactly what I thought it did. But how could this be? This information wasn't in the other report.

The doorbell rang, pulling me out of the fog that seemed to surround me. In a daze, I went downstairs, holding the report in my hand. When I opened the door, I found Mike standing on the porch, looking grim.

"I need to talk to you, Sarah. Right now."

He didn't wait to be asked inside. Instead he pushed his way past me.

"What are you doing here, Mike?"

"There's something I've got to tell you, Sarah." He looked around. "Where is Cicely?"

"Upstairs."

"Can we sit down?" he asked, his eyes wide.

I held the report out to him, my hands shaking. "I just read a report from my parents' murders. Do you know what it says?"

Mike stared at me, his expression unreadable. "If it's a copy of the original report before some of the information was scrubbed, I imagine it lists the investigating officers: Mike Templeton and Anson Bentley." He reached inside his coat and pulled out a gun. "You'd better sit down and listen to me, Sarah. If you don't, you and Cicely may not live through the day."

CHAPTER TWENTY-SIX

I sank down onto the couch, and Mike sat next to me. Although he lowered the gun, he kept it in his hand. There were beads of sweat on his forehead, and his eyes were wild.

"We don't have much time. You've got to let me explain, and then you need to get out of here. I'll find someplace safe for you and Cicely."

"What are you talking about?" I asked, my voice high with anxiety. "Are you going to kill me?"

"No, of course not. This gun is for your protection."

"Well, I don't feel protected. Put it down. What if Cicely sees it?"

"If she comes downstairs, act normal. I'm just here for a friendly visit. Send her back to her room for whatever reason you can come up with." He hid the gun under his jacket.

All I could do was nod at him.

Mike took a deep breath. "Listen carefully and don't ask questions. We may not have much time. This all started back when Anson and I were rookie cops. Not all cops are on the up-and-up, Sarah. I was Anson's partner. First he started taking drugs from the evidence room, telling me to sign off on lesser amounts than what we really confiscated from the drug dealers we arrested. Then Anson moved on to making arrangements with the dealers. They gave us a lot of money to look the other way when it suited them. He even planted evidence that led the department to arrest other people instead of those who were really guilty. By the time it got that far, I wanted out."

His sigh was so raw I shivered.

"I can't explain how things got so out of control. It happened little by little. Bit by bit. When I told Anson I wanted out, he refused to let me go. Threatened to ruin my life." He snorted. "I should have turned him in. My life was destroyed anyway. I was afraid, felt so guilty, that I was impossible to get along with. My wife left me and took my daughter."

"But . . . what does this have to do with me?"

"Anson sent me here to find out what you

403

know. How close you were to the truth. I tried to get you to quit pushing for answers, warned you to stay away from Anson. I was trying to protect you."

"From what?" I asked, trying to keep my voice from shaking. "I don't understand."

He took a deep breath. "Anson and your mom dated before she met your father. They became engaged. She was everything he wanted in a wife. He was . . . obsessed with her. But after Maggie was introduced to your father, she realized she'd made a mistake with Anson and broke it off. He was furious. He was used to getting everything he wanted, but he couldn't have Maggie. Years passed, but Anson never got over your mother. I don't know if he's capable of love, but if he has the capacity, he loved Maggie. Anson and your father knew each other. They crossed paths quite a bit. Your dad was a very smart man. Firefighters see things on the job. Meth labs blow up, drugs are uncovered. I'm not sure exactly how he found out what Anson was up to, but Ben told Anson he was going to turn him in. If only he'd just done it instead of warning him ahead of time. When we went to your house that night, Anson promised it was just to warn your dad to keep quiet." Mike's eyes sought mine. "I swear to you, Sarah. I had no idea what was going to happen."

I couldn't tear my gaze away from his. "Are you . . . are you telling me . . ."

He nodded. "Anson Bentley killed your parents before I could stop him. If I'd known, I would have done something."

A realization hit me almost like I'd been slapped. "It was you. You were the one who found us hiding under the stairs."

He nodded. His dark skin looked almost gray. "Thank God Anson assumed you weren't home. I couldn't take the risk that he'd kill you too. He's a sociopath. No feelings for anyone. No compassion at all. Anyone who gets in his way . . ." He took a deep breath. "After he killed your parents he went to his car and got a bouquet of flowers. White orchids. Your mother's favorite flowers. He'd started sending them to her after they broke up, just trying to let her know he still loved her."

"But Hannah and I don't remember any white orchids."

"That's because she threw them away," Mike said. "Told him to quit sending them. That made Anson livid. And that's why he spread white orchids around her body."

"But why didn't my dad make him stop?"

"Your mother never told Ben about Anson. She got rid of the flowers before he

405

saw them. She was afraid of Anson, Sarah. Afraid of what he might do. She thought she could handle him on her own." He shook his head. "Anson Bentley is responsible for a lot of deaths. Including a friend of your mother's. Although your dad didn't tell your mom everything he knew, he said enough about what was going on with drugs and fraud in the police department to worry Maggie. She told a reporter, a friend of hers, that she suspected there was corruption in the department. She had no idea Anson was so deeply involved, because your dad didn't mention him by name."

"But why? That doesn't make sense."

Mike sighed. "Your father was a good man. He'd given Anson a chance to come clean on his own, thinking it was the right thing to do. He had no idea how dangerous Anson was. The reporter your mom talked to decided to do some investigating for a series of articles. Anson found out. I have no idea how. He killed her before she could write the story. He murdered her husband too."

"Martin and Elise Summers?"

"Yes. It was staged to look like a robbery. Just like your mom and dad's murders. Just like Hannah's. Anson figured that if it worked the first time, it would work again.

406

Of course it helps that he's able to manipulate crime scenes. After your parents died, he worked things around until the case was closed. After he killed the reporter and her husband, he removed our names from both crime scene reports. That way, in the future, no one would ever connect us to it." He pointed at the papers in my hand. "Obviously he missed at least one original hard copy. I'm surprised it slipped past him. He and the men working for him control all kinds of cases that come through the department. And now that he's got more authority, it's even easier. No one wants to go up against him, because they're afraid of him. He's the one who closed your sister's case, Sarah. And I'm about as sure as I can be he's behind Steven Hanks's death. It's easier to blame a murder on someone who can't defend themselves."

I shivered involuntarily. "How does John Smith play into this?"

"As you know, John Smith is the Summers's stepson. Hannah discovered the connection and called him. John met with her, and somehow they found out Anson had been assigned to both cases. Hannah went to Anson, asking for answers. She had no idea he'd actually killed your parents. She realized the truth too late. When Hannah died, John suspected it had to do with what they'd been talking about, so he moved and left no forwarding address. Anson's been looking for him."

"Hannah told Anson about John?"

"I have no idea. It's possible. Is there any chance you mentioned his name during a conversation on the phone?"

"I . . . I don't know. I think I did." I swung my gaze to the phone. "You bugged it?"

"It wasn't me. Anson sent someone else in to do that. He's still heavily involved in the drug trade, and he has people he can use to do his bidding. Drug dealers and dirty cops." He shook his head. "He had someone else kill Hannah. He had her laptop stolen and her house burned down so all the evidence would disappear. Anson can manage what happens at the department, but he couldn't control what your sister did. He had to stop her. He thought he'd accomplished that until he happened to run into you at your sister's house."

"And I told him I'd removed boxes of papers from her house."

Mike's hand moved a little, bringing his gun back into view. "Yes. From that moment, you became his new target. There's more," he said. "But I can't tell you everything now. We've got to get out of here.

Anson told me he was going back to Kansas City today, that he was going to leave you alone, but I don't believe him. I'm afraid he's going to make sure you don't cause any more problems."

"What do you mean?"

His voice was harsh. "I mean that you and Paul are in real danger."

"Where's Paul?"

He shrugged. "I have no idea, but right now you and Cicely are the most vulnerable. Let's get you to safety, and then we'll take care of Paul."

"Why would Anson want to hurt Cicely? She doesn't know anything."

"I can't be certain he would harm her. If Anson Bentley ever cared about anyone, it would be her. But to be honest, I don't think he'd even spare her if he felt he was at risk."

"I don't understand."

"When Hannah turned nineteen, she began searching for the men who killed your parents. She contacted the Kansas City Police Department. Anson was ready and willing to be there for her. To misdirect her. He's a handsome and dynamic man. Your sister was young and vulnerable."

Suddenly I realized why Anson Bentley looked familiar. It was his eyes. "He's

Cicely's father."

Mike nodded. "Hannah was in love, and Anson took advantage of her. I think he got some satisfaction from being with Maggie's child. If he couldn't have Maggie, he could have her daughter. After he felt he'd successfully led Hannah away from his involvement in your parents' murders, he broke off their relationship. It wasn't until recently that he found out about Cicely." He stood up. "We've got to get going, Sarah. I don't know where Anson is, but he suspects that I'm not willing to hide his crimes anymore. That not only puts me in danger, it puts you and Cicely into his cross hairs."

"So Anson had my sister killed to shut her up." Even as I said the words, I found them hard to believe.

Mike nodded.

"If Cicely had been home, would he have had her killed too?"

"I don't know the answer to that, Sarah."

I shook my head. "One thing I can't understand. Why didn't Hannah just go to the police?"

I knew the answer before Mike said, "Who could she trust? She knew there was corruption at the police department, but she had no idea how deep the cover-up went."

The gray car Claire had seen outside Hannah's workplace. "He was seen with her a few days before she died."

"Until the very end, I don't think she knew the extent of his involvement." He sighed. "I tried to stop it. Tried to save her. I sent her those flowers as a warning, hoping she'd leave town. But it was too late. I went to Hannah's house that night, but she was already dead. I spread the flowers around, trying to leave a clue that would lead back to Anson. I prayed that someone would see the connection between your parents' murders and Hannah. And someone did. Doug Sykes."

Anger raged inside me. "You sent flowers, hoping they would lead back to Anson? Why didn't you turn him in? You could have saved her life. Now she's dead and so is Doug."

He looked away from me. "I'm a coward, Sarah. I was too afraid of Anson. Besides, like Hannah, I have no idea who Anson's got under his thumb in the department. I retired to get away from him, but it also cut off my contacts. If I'd picked the wrong person to confide in, Anson would have killed Hannah and me too. Once I realized Doug was clean, I decided to confide in him. Tell him everything. But before I could, Anson had him killed. That's when Anson contacted me. Told me to come here, to Sanctuary, and tell you Doug had asked me to follow up on the case."

"So you could report back to Anson?"

"Yes, but I didn't tell him anything that should have concerned him. I did everything I could to set his mind at ease so he'd leave you and Cicely alone. Unfortunately I didn't know the phone was tapped until a couple of days ago. That's what got Doug killed. I have no idea what triggered his call to you, but my guess is that when the investigation was shut down, Doug smelled a rat. I'm also not sure when Anson began to suspect me, but what he heard on the phone didn't line up with what I was telling him. Although he hasn't actually accused me of double-crossing him, it's obvious he knows he can't trust me anymore."

"So you tried to protect us?"

"Yes, Sarah. I'm not a complete monster. Look, I'll tell you anything else you want to know, but we've got to get out of here. After I get you to safety I'm going to the new chief of police and tell him everything. I've been told he's a real law-and-order guy who won't protect dirty cops. I don't care what happens to me anymore. I'm tired of this. Tired of the fallout from my cowardice. Now, go throw some things into a bag for you and Cicely, and don't take longer than five minutes. I'm afraid Anson —"

"You're afraid Anson what, Mike?"

Mike and I turned to see Anson Bentley standing in the doorway to the kitchen, holding a gun. And it was pointed right at me.

Mike stared at Anson, his face ashen. "Please. You don't need to do this."

Anson walked into the room. The compassionate expression I'd seen on his face before was gone. In its place was something so cold it almost took my breath away.

"Obviously, I do. Thanks to you, Mike."

"He's not the murderer, Anson," I said. "You're the one who killed my family."

"I didn't want to do it," he said in a monotone. "But your father was going to ruin my life. I couldn't allow that to happen. When Hannah contacted me, I tried my best to lead her in a different direction, but she wouldn't let it go." He shook his head. "I cared about her, Sarah. I know you probably don't believe me, but it's true. Unfortunately, when you get in over your head, all you can do is keep swimming."

"You can't kill me too," I said. "You'd never get away with it."

"You're probably right. But I know how

to make it look like an unfortunate accident."

"Someone will figure it out," I said. "This will come back on you."

"I don't think so. I've planned everything very carefully. After I got to your charming little town, I spent quite a bit of time coming up with a scenario I'm confident will work just fine. You gave me the idea. And no one will connect me to it. You see, I'm already on my way back to Kansas City. I have people willing to swear to it."

I didn't say anything. I was certain he was telling the truth. Right now all I could think about was Cicely.

"Why can't we just walk away?" Mike said. "There's no way Sarah can prove you had anything to do with Hannah's death."

"Sorry. I'm not taking advice from you anymore, Mike. I figured you were the one who sent those flowers. You were the only one who knew about them. That's why I sent you here and bugged the phones, so I could keep an eye on you."

"Doug Sykes saw the connection between you and the murders. There's some other smart detective who will see the same thing."

"Yes, Doug had suspicions. That's why he came to me for help. But now the investigation is closed. Having contacts in prison silenced the perfect suspect."

"But there's nothing to link him to Hannah's murder," I said. "How could you close the case without evidence?"

He gave me a small smile. "That's a good question, Sarah. You see, several things stolen from your sister's house conveniently showed up in a downtown pawn shop. The owner, who is a friend of mine, will swear Steven Hanks brought them in."

"You've thought of everything, haven't you, Anson?" I said.

He shrugged. "Yes, except I was hoping I was wrong about my friend Mike. But people let you down. It's a sad fact of life." He walked toward me, put his arm around my neck, and stuck his gun to my temple. "Put your gun on the table, Mike. Then take the phone off the hook. Go upstairs and get the girl. If you try anything funny, I'll shoot Sarah right here. You know me well enough to be confident I'll do it."

"You can't afford to —"

"If you don't do what I say, the police will find the gun in your hand — after you blow your brains out. No one will even know I was here."

I wanted to ask him about Cicely, but I couldn't get the words out. The possibilities were too dreadful to consider.

"Go get her, Mike," I said. "Staying together is our best defense."

Mike put his gun on the coffee table and stood up. I could tell he was trying to figure out if there was any way to subdue Anson. But with the gun so close to me, there wasn't anything he could do without risking my life. After taking the phone off the hook, he headed slowly upstairs. Tears fell down the sides of my cheeks, knowing what Cicely was getting ready to face. I called out to God for help, praying quietly.

"Stop it," Anson snapped. "Praying won't help you. There's no one listening."

"You're counting on that, Anson. But if you're wrong, you'll pay for everything you've done. You know that, don't you?"

"Never believed in God. Never will. Now shut up." Still holding on to me with one hand, he grabbed Mike's gun and put it in his pocket.

We sat quietly, waiting for Mike and Cicely to come downstairs. It only took a couple of minutes before I heard footsteps on the stairs. Cicely came into the room, her eyes wide, fear plastered on her face.

"What's going on, Aunt Sarah?" she asked, her voice shaking.

"Everything will be all right, honey," I

said. "For now, I want you to do what you're told. Do you understand?" Anger bubbled inside me. Cicely had been through so much. Now this.

She nodded slowly, staring at Anson.

Anson moved away from the couch but kept his gun trained on me. "Anyone makes a wrong move, and I will kill Sarah. I mean that. Do you understand?"

Cicely nodded, tears sliding down her face.

He walked away from me and grabbed Cicely. She cried out, and rage rose inside me.

"Leave the girl alone, Junior," Mike said. "You can hold the gun on me."

Anson shrugged. "Sorry. Cicely makes the best hostage."

"Junior?" I said, looking at Mike. "Why did you call him Junior?"

"That was my nickname when my dad was alive," Anson spat out. "I lived in his shadow every day of my life."

I looked over at Mike. *JR.* Not initials. Hannah was writing 'Junior.' " I looked back at Anson. "You're *J.*"

"Yes, I'm *J.*" He laughed. "Your sister used to call me Junior too. I don't think she ever used my real name. She thought I was just a chip off the old block, but I'm nothing like my father."

I was certain that was true, but I kept my mouth shut.

"You'll both do everything I say, or I'll kill this girl. Mike, empty your pockets and put your cell phone on the table. Then pull your pants up and show me your ankles."

Mike pulled a cell phone from his pants pocket and put it on the coffee table. He emptied his pockets, and then he pulled up his pant legs. "I didn't strap on my other pistol today," he said. "Obviously, that was a mistake."

Then Anson pointed his gun at me. "Pat him down. If you try to hide something from me, I'll shoot her."

I patted Mike down, but there wasn't anything else on him, and I told Anson that.

"What about you?" he said. "Anything on you? Cell phone?"

"No, I don't have a cell phone, and my pockets are empty." I pulled the pockets of my jeans inside out.

"Get your purse," he ordered.

I retrieved my purse from the closet and held it out to him, but he waved it away.

"Dump it out on the coffee table. I want to see what's in it."

I followed his instructions. Out tumbled my keys, my wallet, some breath mints, a small note pad, my brush, and a couple of pens.

"Is that it?" he barked.

I shook it one more time. The magnet I'd picked up outside Hannah's house fell out with a clunk. I'd forgotten it was even there. Unsure why I hadn't found it earlier, all I could do was stare at it. *I Am With You.* The reassurance gave me a sense of peace that didn't make much sense under the circumstances, but I began to believe we could make it through this alive.

"All right, put it back. We're all going for a ride. But first you're going to write a letter for me, Sarah." He pointed to the pad of paper and the pen we kept next to the phone. "Get a piece of paper, sit down, and write exactly what I tell you."

I got the paper and pen and sat down.

"Write this verbatim. Don't add anything. I'm going to check it, so no funny business."

I nodded and lifted the pen, ready to write. I snuck a look at Cicely, trying to find a way to reassure her that she would be okay. A line from one of the Psalms whispered to me: *"The righteous cry, and the Lord heareth, and delivereth them out of all their troubles." I'm crying to you for help, Lord,* I prayed silently. *Deliver us. I put my trust in you.*

"Janet," Anson dictated, "Cicely is gone. I'm afraid she's at the mine again. Mike is taking me to look for her. We'll be back soon."

I carefully wrote what he said. Would Janet really believe that Cicely had gone to the mine again? It was improbable but not impossible. It was certainly believable that Mike and I would drive over and look for her. Obviously, Anson's plan was for all of us to die in the mine, making it look like an accident. I snuck a look at Mike. It was clear he knew what was happening too. He gave me an almost imperceptible nod. Did he have a plan?

"Now sign it," Anson said.

"All right. It's done."

Anson came over to me, dragging Cicely with him. He looked over my shoulder at the note. "That looks okay. Hang up the phone, put the note on the coffee table, and let's go."

"We're going to the mine?" Cicely said. "Why?"

"Don't worry," I said, trying to sound calm. "Everything will be okay." I looked at Anson. "She needs her coat and so do I. It's freezing out there."

"Where are they?"

"In the closet by the front door."

He let go of Cicely and pushed her toward the closet. "Get your coat and your aunt's too." He looked over at Mike. "Drive your car around to the back of the house. If you decide to drive away, I'll kill them."

I glanced out the window, but Anson's car wasn't parked outside. I suspected he had someone set to pick him up at the mine after our "accident."

Mike picked up his keys from the table.

"Put your billfold back in your pocket," Anson said. "I don't want anything left behind that looks suspicious." He nodded at me. "Take your purse." He noticed the large envelope lying on the table. "What's that?" he asked.

There wasn't any use lying to him, since he could read it himself. Trying to keep him from getting angry and hurting Cicely, I told him the truth. "It's a copy of the report written when my parents were murdered. Before you had it changed. It names you as one of the officers on scene."

He glanced at Mike. "Hand it to me."

Mike put his billfold in his back pocket and picked up his keys. Then he carried the report over to where Anson stood.

"That's far enough," Anson barked. He slid over next to Cicely, who stood next to the closet holding our coats. "Put your coat on," he ordered her.

"Get going, Mike. Now." He poked Cicely with his gun.

With one last look at me, Mike walked out the back door. Anson took my coat from Cicely and handed it to me. It wasn't my warmest coat, but it didn't seem important at that moment, so I took it without saying anything. Then holding Cicely by the arm, he walked over to the fireplace and threw the envelope into the fire.

Then the three of us just stood there, waiting for Mike and watching my evidence burn away. Would Mike leave us here? Would he take a chance that Anson wouldn't kill us? I honestly didn't have the answer. If he ran for help, it was possible we'd all make it out of this alive. It was just as possible that in anger, Anson would kill Cicely and me, even though it would be harder to explain. I suspected that by now Anson believed he could get away with anything. He'd been doing it for a very long time.

There wasn't a sound in the room except my ragged breathing and Cicely's whimpers as we waited. I stuck my hands in my coat pockets and almost cried out when my fingers touched Cicely's cell phone. I'd forgotten I'd put it in the pocket of my coat when I took it away from her. I hadn't worn this particular coat since we went looking for Cicely and Jeremiah at the mine.

I almost collapsed with relief when I heard Mike's engine at the back of the house. Although I couldn't be sure he'd made the right decision, at least Cicely and I were still alive. A few seconds later, I heard Mike come in the back door. He walked into the living room and stared at Anson.

"Pat him down again," he ordered me. "And remember, I will search him myself once we get out of here. If I find anything that shouldn't be there, I'll kill the girl."

"I don't have any guns in the car, Anson," he said. "You know I don't believe in leaving loaded weapons in my vehicle."

Anson shrugged. "I do know that, but there's a first time for everything."

I patted Mike down again, almost hoping there would be a gun. But there wasn't. "No guns," I said, turning toward Anson. The look on Cicely's face made me want to cry, but I was determined to stay strong and try to help her remain calm.

"All right. Everyone out the door and into the car."

We filed out silently. Anson told me to get into the passenger's seat. Then he took Cicely and shoved her in the back. As he'd promised, he patted Mike down before ordering him to get into the driver's seat. Once Mike was belted in, Anson slid into the back with Cicely.

"Get down on the floor," he ordered.

I turned to see if she was okay and found him staring at me.

"As we drive out of town, the only people anyone will see is you and Mike. If you gesture to anyone, I will kill her immediately. Do you understand?"

"Yes."

"Drive to the mine, Mike. And don't try anything cute."

I couldn't tell what Mike was thinking, but I had to assume we were both on the same page. Waiting until we could find the right moment to turn this around was our only option. Anson was crouched down in the backseat next to Cicely, with his gun trained on her. In that position, I wasn't in his direct line of sight. Even so, I didn't dare turn on Cicely's phone. I needed to find a few seconds when Anson wouldn't hear any sounds it might make.

As we began to drive out of town, I spotted some men on the front porch of the school. With everything going on, I'd forgotten they were working on the furnace today. Jeremiah stood on the porch, watching Mike's SUV approach. An idea popped into my head and even though it frightened me, I decided I had to try it.

"I forgot to fasten my seat belt," I said. I wrapped my right hand around the belt but left my thumb sticking up. I could only do it once and prayed Jeremiah would see it. I reached over with my left hand and pointed three fingers down. I looked over to see Jeremiah staring right at me. I clicked the belt as I watched him in the side mirror as we drove away. Had he understood me? Did he realize what I was trying to say? The chances were very slim, but I had to do something. Anson didn't say anything, so I was confident he either hadn't noticed my sign, or he'd been oblivious to what it meant.

I continued to stare in the mirror as Sanctuary disappeared from sight.

CHAPTER TWENTY-SEVEN

"Get out of the car."

I'd hoped we wouldn't be the only people at the mine, but it was deserted. Anson ordered Mike to drive around to the side and park in a grove of trees. It made the SUV harder to see, but the way the road curved to the mine, unless someone turned down the mine road, there was no way to see our car from the main road anyway.

Anson ordered Mike and me to stay in the car while he and Cicely got out of the backseat. I took that opportunity to pull Cicely's phone out of my pocket. I turned it on the way Paul had shown me. I was grateful to see that it worked the same way his did. Then I quickly punched in Paul's number. Mike, who saw what I was doing, kept one eye on me while watching Anson. I pressed Send and then slid the phone back into my pocket. Thankfully, Anson hadn't heard the quiet beeps when I dialed the number.

Mike and I got out of the car when Anson told us to. Then Anson held out his hand for Mike's keys. It was clear he planned to drive the SUV back around near the mine entrance after he dealt with us. That way it would look as if Mike parked near the entrance before we all went inside.

Anson waved his gun toward the entrance. "Get in there," he ordered.

The boards had been torn away, though I was certain Reuben had nailed the entrance shut after we were here the last time. I wondered if Anson had done it earlier while trying to make sure the mine would accomplish what he wanted. Obviously, this was the "business" he had to take care of the day he'd arrived in Sanctuary. Once we were all inside, he took a flashlight from his coat and shone it in front of us so we could see to walk. He stayed behind Mike and me, still holding on to Cicely.

The mine was musty and dank. Something skittered in the dark. Anything could be living in the shadows. Raccoons, possums, snakes. There were probably all kinds of animals that called the empty mine home.

Cicely suddenly cried out, and I swung around to see what had happened.

"She just tripped on a rock. Keep going,"

Anson said gruffly.

We walked deeper into the mine, past the posts that should be supporting the ceiling. They were ancient and split. The rock overhead had already fallen in several places. It was obvious it wouldn't take much to bring it down. For the first time, I began to seriously wonder if we would make it out alive. Then I remembered the magnet. *I Am With You.* I took a deep breath and calmed myself. My mind drifted back to the conversation Paul and I had about listening to God's voice. *Help me to listen to you,* I prayed. *Tell me what to do.* Peace immediately flowed through me.

We finally reached the shaft. Someone had constructed a wooden fence around it, but just like everything else in the mine, it was falling apart.

"No one's going to believe we all fell down the shaft," Mike said. "It's ridiculous."

"I agree. But they will believe the girl fell down the shaft and you were trying to rescue her when the ceiling collapsed." He walked over to an old beam that was already crumbling. "After I disable you two, my friend and I will attach a cable to this beam, then fasten it to his bumper and pull. The ceiling should cave in nicely. We pull out our cable, and it will look like a tragic accident."

"So if we resist, what will you do, Anson?" he asked. "Shoot us? Won't that ruin your plan?"

"I'm not worried. Neither one of you will rush me, knowing the girl will surely die. You're hoping somehow you'll be saved at the last minute. People like you never give up."

He was right. Even though I knew Mike had been involved with my parents' death, I had no doubt he was trying to keep us safe. Just like he'd decided to save Hannah and me when we were children, I knew he'd fight until the very last second to protect Cicely and me now. And so would I.

Suddenly a soft, high-pitched sound echoed in the tunnel. Horrified, I stuck my hand in my coat pocket and tried to silence Cicely's phone.

"Give that to me," Anson yelled. "What is it?"

Fingers shaking, I lifted the phone out of my pocket. "I . . . I forgot it was there. It's Cicely's. I took it away from her —"

"Shut up!" he screamed, causing Cicely to jump.

Afraid that he might accidentally shoot her, I quickly brought him the phone. He forced Cicely to sit down on an old wooden box a few feet away and snatched the phone from my hand.

"It's on," he said in a low voice. "Who did you call?"

"I didn't call anyone."

He pointed the gun at Cicely and glared at me. "I said, who did you call?"

The fear on Cicely's face made me spit out, "I called Paul. He's been listening to you all this time. I'm sure he's on his way here right now."

The rage on Anson's face crumbled, and he laughed. "You called Paul?" He shook his head. "Sorry. I've already taken care of Paul. Your deputy friend responded to an accident this morning out on a country road. But unfortunately his car went off the side of the road, down an embankment, and burst into flames. He's dead."

"What?" My knees buckled, and I collapsed to the floor.

Anson looked closely at Cicely's phone. "No one's on the line, Sarah. It's almost out of power. That's why it beeped." With one smooth flick of his wrist, he tossed the phone down the shaft. It took a while before we heard it crash and shatter. Then he took his phone out of his pocket and spoke into it. He put it up to his ear and waited.

Someone obviously picked up, because he said, "You took care of that . . . problem, didn't you?" He nodded at the response. "Good. How long until you get here?" Another pause. "Okay, but make it fast." He disconnected and slid his phone back into his pocket. "I just confirmed that your boyfriend is no longer my concern."

At that moment, I wanted to kill Anson Bentley. I knew it wasn't right, but anger exploded inside me, making me tremble uncontrollably. I felt as if a part of me had just died, but then I looked over at Cicely. She needed me, and I didn't want to let her down. What could I do? Again, the same strange peace settled over me.

"Well, folks, my ride is on the way, so we need to get on with this."

"Wait a minute," Mike said. "At least you could let us say good-bye."

Anson sighed. "I guess it's only right, but make it fast. And remember, I'm the only one with a gun."

I got up slowly. "You might as well just shoot us, Anson, because I'm not going to allow you to throw my niece down that shaft. Surely the bullets in your gun will lead the authorities back to you. Then everything will come out."

"If it were my gun, that might work," he

said. "Unfortunately for you, it's not. In fact, it's registered to your sister. She got it in an attempt to protect herself. The night she was killed, a friend removed it. If I have to use it, it will look like you were the one who took the gun from your sister's house, Sarah." He sighed. "Overcome by grief, you shot your niece. Mike tried to intervene, and you killed him too. Then, full of remorse, you shot yourself." He glared at me. "Everything was supposed to end that night, you know. After killing Hannah, I found out you'd gone into the house and removed her papers. I couldn't take the chance you'd track her murder back to me, so my friend grabbed her computer, and we torched the house so that anything else that might lead back to me would be destroyed. If you'd just left things alone, we wouldn't be here now. Now I have to clean up everything. This is all your fault." He nodded at me. "After your untimely death, I'll send someone to your house to wipe your hard drive and remove any other evidence. All the evidence you've collected will disappear. Just like you."

I stared at Mike. What could we do? How would we get out of this? And then I saw it. A wink. So quick I almost missed it. What did he have up his sleeve?

"Let Cicely come over here and hug her aunt," Mike said. "Let us say good-bye. You promised."

Anson pulled Cicely to her feet and pushed her toward us. She ran to me, and I put my arms around her. I felt something between us and looked down. Cicely was holding a gun in her hand. Trying not to react, I took it from her and put it between the folds of my coat.

Mike walked up to us. "I'm sorry," he said. The tears in his eyes showed that whatever else he had planned, his apology was from the heart.

He hugged me, and I slipped him the gun. When he backed away, we all looked over at Anson. The next few seconds seemed as if they were in slow motion.

"Get down!" Mike yelled suddenly.

I grabbed Cicely and pulled her to the ground, covering her with my body. Two shots rang out. To my horror, Mike fell next to us, an ugly red stain spreading across his shirt. I waited for the next shot to come from Anson, but there was only silence. When I turned around I saw him lying on the ground, but he wasn't dead. He was struggling to sit up, his gun lying next to him. Without thinking I jumped to my feet and ran toward the weapon. But before I could reach it, Anson grabbed it and sat up. I stopped in my tracks and steeled myself for the bullet I knew was coming. Sure enough the sound of a gunshot echoed through the abandoned mine. But I didn't feel anything. I watched as a look of surprise spread over Anson's face and he fell backward. Not sure what had happened, I spun around and saw Paul standing a few yards away, his gun drawn. Behind him stood Jonathon, William, and Jeremiah.

Tears of relief flowed through me, and Cicely ran over and put her arms around me. I held her tight. "Mike's been shot," I said to Paul. He was lying so still, I was afraid he was dead. Paul ran over to check on him.

"He's alive, but we've got to get him to the hospital." He radioed the station and requested an ambulance. Then he put his hand on the wound and pushed down. "I need to apply pressure until the ambulance gets here. We don't want him to bleed out."

"Will he be okay?" I asked through my sobs as Cicely and I clung to each other.

Paul smiled. "Yes, I think we're all going to be just fine."

CHAPTER TWENTY-EIGHT

After two days of intensive questioning by officials from the Kansas City Police Department, Paul and I were finally free to go on with our lives. We decided we were past due for our first date, so the first Friday after we returned to Sanctuary we made reservations at a wonderful pasta restaurant in Farmington. As I waited for Paul to pick me up, Janet cornered me in the living room.

"Before you leave, I have a few questions," she said. "You haven't shared much about what happened in that mine. You don't have to tell me if you don't want to."

"I . . . I do, Janet. It was just so awful that it's hard to talk about. Anson Bentley was a terrible man, but I'm not rejoicing over his death. I thought I wanted revenge, but in the end, I only felt sad. What a terrible waste of a life." I shook my head. "The experience was so traumatic for all of us. Paul had never taken a life before, but he did it to save us. And no child should have to endure what Cicely went through."

"Oh, Sarah," Janet said, her voice catching. "*You* endured it. And who better to help her now? No one can guide her through this better than you."

I stopped to think about what Janet had just said. It was true. Experiencing my parents' murders meant I could understand Cicely's pain. It was a terrible thing to share, but maybe God could bring healing out of it.

"Thanks, Janet. I hadn't really thought about it that way. Ask me whatever you want to. I'll do my best to answer your questions."

"I understand you made a 'help' sign to Jeremiah when you drove past him. But how did he know you were going to the mine?"

"He didn't, really. But after I made the sign, I quickly flashed an *M.* I just prayed he'd get it. Not sure what I meant, he ran after the car and watched us turn right onto the road out of town. The mine is really the only thing that way except for your clinic and some farmhouses. That's when he decided the *M* had to be for *mine.*"

"Oh, honey. You took a real chance. What if Bentley had seen you?"

"Well, he didn't. But in the end, that

wasn't what saved us."

"Are you talking about the gun?" She frowned. "Where did it come from?"

"Mike had it in his ankle holster. He figured Anson would find it, so when he went upstairs, he shoved the holster under Cicely's mattress and gave her the gun. It never occurred to Anson to check a little girl for weapons." I smiled. "I wasn't referring to the gun, though. In the end, God used Paul to save us."

Janet smiled. "Bentley really underestimated Paul. He assumed he was an easy target for his gorilla, but Paul took control of the situation and arrested the man Bentley sent to kill him."

"Yes, and then Paul got a call from Evan Bakker. Not having a phone, William had gone to Evan and asked him to contact Paul after Jeremiah told his father he thought we were in trouble. Realizing there was no way out, Bentley's partner decided to spill the beans. When Anson called to make sure Paul had been taken care of, Paul answered the phone and pretended to be Anson's partner in crime. By that time, he was already on his way to the mine."

"So now the police will fully investigate your mom and dad's murders as well as Hannah's?"

I nodded. "Not sure how much investigating they'll need to do. They have all the answers now. Mike told them everything. The guy who was supposed to kill Paul is the same man who murdered Hannah. He's asking for a deal."

Janet shivered. "Will the authorities really make a deal with that scumbag?"

"I don't know. If they can get everything they need from Mike, they'll have no reason to work with him. He's a terrible person, Janet. A violent drug dealer. Hannah isn't the only person he's murdered for Anson Bentley."

Janet paused at the stove and turned around to study me. "You're glad Mike survived, aren't you?" she asked quietly.

"Yes, I am. His cowardice may have cost Hannah her life. I'll never be sure about that. But I can't hate him. He saved Hannah and me when we were children, and he tried to save Cicely and me, even putting his own life on the line."

"Too little too late, as far as I'm concerned," Janet huffed.

"I know. I truly believe he started out as a good man who got in over his head. I guess when that happens, it's like quicksand. Mike got in deeper and deeper, and before he knew it, he was drowning."

Janet snorted. "You make it sound as if you know what that's like. You've always been an honest, decent person."

I sighed. "We all have the ability to deceive ourselves, Janet. Maybe the deceit in my life didn't lead to violence, but I spent a lot of years elevating my own insecurity above my faith in God's plan for my life."

"Burying your talents in the ground. Just like the man in the Bible."

"Exactly."

"I think we all do that to some extent," Janet said. "We tell ourselves we're just being humble."

"Maybe, but I've come to the conclusion that true humility is believing what God says about you when everything inside you screams you're *not* who He says you are."

"And now you believe you're good enough."

"Good enough for God. And good enough for me."

"And what about Paul?"

I smiled. "He seems to think I'm good enough for him too. Hence our first date."

Janet sighed. "It's about time."

Cicely came into the kitchen. "When does Paul get here?"

She'd been traumatized by our narrow escape. Last night and the night before she'd slept in my room. I'd called Jonathon earlier in the day and asked him to visit with her. I felt having someone like Jonathon to talk to would help. He'd agreed but had insisted I come too. *"You both have emotions to work through,"* he'd said.

I had to admit he was right. Since the incident with Anson, Cicely had clung to me. Even though I'd begun to feel like a real mother, I didn't want her feelings for me to be based on one traumatic moment. We had a long way to go, but I finally felt confident that with some effort and a lot of honesty, we'd do just fine.

"Aunt Sarah," Cicely asked softly. "What will happen to Mike?"

"Why, honey?"

"I . . . I like him. I know that he did wrong things, but I hope he gets another chance."

"He's working with the police in Kansas City to catch some other really bad guys. Because he's trying to help them, he might not go to prison. Either he'll be put on probation, or he'll be put into something called witness protection."

"What's witness protection?"

"It means Mike would change his name and become someone else. The authorities would move him to a different city, and he'd have a new life. That way the bad guys he turns in can't send people to hurt him."

She considered this. "I think that sounds like a good idea. But what about his daughter?"

I looked at her in surprise. "How do you know he has a daughter?"

"He told me when he came upstairs and he asked me to take that gun. At first I said no because I was afraid of it. But he told me I reminded him of his daughter because I was so brave. That made me feel better."

"You really were courageous," I said. "I'm very proud of you, Cicely."

"I'm proud of you too, Aunt Sarah. I've never known anyone as brave as you — except my mom."

"She really was brave," Janet said. "If it wasn't for her, Anson Bentley would have continued to hurt people and ruin lives. Your mom just wouldn't give up. Wouldn't quit fighting for what was right."

Cicely nodded. "I know."

I hadn't told Cicely that Anson was her father, and I didn't intend to. At least for right now. It would be too hard for her to deal with.

"William stopped by while you were taking a nap," Janet said. "He wanted to see how you were doing."

"How nice of him," I said with a smile.

"And he wanted me to tell you that he's ready for Jeremiah to learn sign language. He wondered if you'd teach him and Trina too."

"That's wonderful. I'd be honored. We owe Jeremiah and William a lot."

"I wonder if William will let Jeremiah and me be friends," Cicely said.

"Let's take one step at a time," I said. "But it might help if you went to William and apologized for getting Jeremiah in trouble."

She nodded. "I will." Cicely took a deep breath. "Aunt Sarah?"

"Yes?"

"I know it might seem silly to ask about this now. Everything has been so weird . . ."

I put my hand over hers. "What, Cicely? You can ask me anything."

She frowned. "It's just . . . you know, it's December. . . ."

I caught Janet's wink and smiled. "Are you asking about Christmas?"

She cast her eyes down and nodded. "I know it's awful to bring it up."

"Oh, honey," I said. "It's not awful at all. It's perfectly normal, and I think we're all ready for some normal."

Someone knocked on the front door, and Murphy began to bark. "Why don't you open the door? I think Paul has something for you."

She got up and hurried to the living room. Janet and I followed. When Cicely swung the door open, she saw Paul standing on the front porch with a Christmas tree that was bigger than he was.

"Awesome!" Cicely said. She turned and ran over to me, throwing her arms around me. "Thank you, Aunt Sarah!"

Paul, who was trying to hold on to the tree, knocked on the outer glass door.

"I think you just closed the door on the guy with our Christmas tree," I said, laughing.

Her eyes got big and she rushed back to open the door.

Janet came up and put her arm around my waist. "We're going to be all right."

I nodded. "I think so too."

As we watched Paul and Cicely struggle to bring the huge tree into the house, I silently thanked God for never leaving me. A voice inside told me that the dark echoes of the past were finally fading, and a new chapter in my life was beginning. As if he knew what I was thinking, Paul looked over at me and smiled.

I smiled back. "Awesome," I whispered.

ACKNOWLEDGMENTS

Thanks to my Inner Circle for their support and encouragement:

Mary Gessner, Tammy Pendergast-Lagoski, Lynne Young, Zac Weikel, Michelle Durben, Michell Prince Morgan, Karla Hanns, Susan Fryman, Larry Timm, Bonnie Traher, Mary Shipman, Rhonda Nash-Hall, Cheryl Baranski, and JoJo Sutis. God bless you all for your support and prayers.

Thanks to the incredible Janet Dowell for allowing me to use her name for a character in *Deadly Echoes*. Your friendship is a constant blessing, and your smile makes my day.

As always, a shout-out to my friends and editors at Bethany House, Raela Schoenherr and Sharon Asmus. Thanks for everything, ladies! The journey has been wonderful.

ABOUT THE AUTHOR

Nancy Mehl is the author of twenty-one books and received the ACFW Mystery Book of the Year Award in 2009. She has a background in social work and is a member of ACFW and RWA. She writes from her home in Missouri, where she lives with her husband, Norman, and their puggle, Watson. Visit her Web site at www.nancymehl .com.